LOST LOVE

and

SHIPWRECKED

Madeline Pike Finds Hope in the New Land

Jessica Marie Dorman
Cathy Lynn Bryant

Published by
Innovo Publishing, LLC
www.innovopublishing.com
1-888-546-2111

Providing Full-Service Publishing Services for
Christian Authors, Artists & Organizations: Hardbacks, Paperbacks,
eBooks, Audiobooks, Music & Film

LOST LOVE AND SHIPWRECKED
Madeline Pike Finds Hope in the New Land

Library of Congress Control Number: 2012951373
ISBN 13: 978-1-61314-071-0

Cover Design & Interior Layout: Innovo Publishing, LLC

Printed in the United States of America
U.S. Printing History

First Edition: October 2012

Our characters include actual historical figures intermingled with fictional characters. Some of the events are actual historical events, such as the wreck of the *Angel Gabriel.*

Table of Contents

The Voyage and Shipwreck 7

On to Ipswich to Begin Life in the "New Land" 15

Awakening of Feelings/John Bailey, a Sad Story/
    Plans to Move 19

The Move and Making New Acquaintances 25

Emma the Mentor a Woman of Character 31

Seeing Old Friends/Antinomian Accusations 37

The "Oath"/Accusations Refuted 45

Adventures on Carr's Island/An Unexpected Meeting/
    The Misunderstanding 53

Revelations and New Accusations Regarding the Pirate
    "Dixie Bull" 63

A Frenzied Town/Affidavit Arrives from Salem 73

The Misunderstanding Abated 79

Maddie Takes a Stand/All Is Well with Christopher 87

A New Man in Town/Haven't I Seen You Before? 93

An Unexpected Blessing 99

The Confrontation/Madeline and Emma Travel to Ipswich 105

A Journey to England/A Secret Mission/
    Regretful Goodbyes 111

An Unexpected Loss/A Move to Salisbury 117

New Friends and Bad Company 123

Quilting Experts/Adjustments/ Anthony's Concern 131

Midwifery/Jane Discovers the Truth 137

The Joke/Susanna North a New Acquaintance......................... 147

Rumors and Lies.. 155

Birth Anomalies/Jarret's Wicked Scheme/

    Waiting for Proof.. 163

Arriving in England during a Time of Unrest/

    Mr. Carr's Wedding Plans...................................... 171

Jane's Nightmare/Reputations Destroyed/Reassurances 185

The Return Voyage/Decisions and Confessions/

    New Acquaintances.. 193

Jarret's Scheme/Confessions....................................... 199

Formal Accusation/Christopher's Return/

    The Arrival of Rebecca Bailey 209

Waiting for Christopher/Decision to Conceal a Secret............. 217

Christopher Brings Good News/Unspoken Feelings 223

Jane and Jarret Summoned to Appear/

    The Selectmen Reprimanded.............................. 233

A Blessing for the Bleasdells/A Private Audience/

    Mr. Bailey's Comfort.. 239

The Proposal/The Publishing of Banns/

    Expressions of Gratitude.. 247

Happy Endings 253

Chapter 1

The Voyage and Shipwreck

Madeline Pike grasped tightly to a piece of the wreckage to keep herself afloat amidst the hurricane winds and splashing waves. She could hear off in the distance the call of one of the other passengers that had been aboard the *Angel Gabriel*. Though she was grateful to hear another voice, it was difficult to make out to whom it belonged. Floating along in the storm for what seemed like hours, she had lost all sense of direction. Madeline knew that she had to find her way to the shore, soon, or she would be lost.

It had been twelve weeks since Madeline had felt the dry ground beneath her feet. Setting sail from King's Road, Bristol, England, for New England in the year 1635, the *Angel Gabriel* had carried Madeline and nearly thirty other passengers along on their journey. Madeline had heard numerous stories of how the tough old 240-ton ship had survived mighty storms, Spanish attacks, and other harrowing voyages. She and her husband, Oliver, were fully confident in the *Angel's* ability to convey them to the "new land." As part of the "Great Migration," they had only dreamt about the kind of freedoms they hoped to experience once they braved their way across the ocean to a new land.

As Madeline felt her last bit of strength waning, her mind drifted back to the home she had left behind in England. She thought of her beloved Oliver. "If only we had not taken this journey. Is this how it is all going to end? Oliver, oh Oliver, how I miss you," she cried.

Oliver was a kind and loving man of but eight and twenty. Many of the people in Madeline and Oliver's hometown had often remarked that they were the handsomest pair around. Madeline, a woman of the age of four and twenty, medium height with a slender build, was most admired for her shiny blonde locks, which she kept loosely tossed and pinned atop her head. Oliver was a tall, slender man with thick brown hair and a soft smile that endeared him to everyone. Madeline had been so happy in this their first year of marriage. Now, Oliver was lost to her forever.

It was the fourth week into their journey. Some of the children had come down with smallpox soon after setting sail. Oliver had spent many hours with the little ones holding their hands and telling them stories, attempting to ease their suffering. In the end, each of the children recovered; however, Oliver, weakened by exhaustion, was stricken and did not survive.

A familiar voice calling, "Maddie," brought her mind back to the reality of her situation. It was Christopher Osgood, a man she had come to know and admire during their twelve-week journey. Madeline had observed that Christopher was a kind and loving husband and father. To Madeline, he and his wife, Hannah, seemed to be the perfect match. They filled their hours aboard the ship affording the other parents many breaks as they occupied the children with games and Bible lessons. It was clear to all that they had a deep passion for children.

Christopher and Hannah's son, Zachary, a boy of age three, was a magnificent combination of his mother's beauty and his father's wavy brown hair and strong, square jaw. He and Henry Bleasdell, also age three, had the time of their lives running about the ship, oftentimes to the chagrin of the other passengers. Christopher and Hannah, however, did not mind very much, as Zachary had been extremely ill early in the voyage. He had been amongst the children who had come down with smallpox a few weeks into the journey. Christopher had admired Oliver Pike's compassion for the children during this time, which had served to put him at great risk. When Oliver fell sick and ultimately died, Christopher felt the loss supremely.

Madeline called out in desperation, "Christopher, I am here, I am here," hoping to be heard over the crashing waves and howling winds.

Before too long, she heard Christopher say in a reassuring voice, "Maddie, I am right here. It is going to be all right. Take my hand so that I can pull you over to me." Unaware that Christopher had also tried, unsuccessfully, to rescue his wife and son, she reached out and took hold of his hand.

"I could not decide in which direction to go," cried Maddie.

"It is all right, Maddie, I am here now," whispered Christopher softly.

Other than Oliver, no one has ever referred to me as Maddie, she thought, finding it to be strangely comforting.

With a sigh of relief, she settled in under Christopher's arm as he made his way through the waves in the direction of the land. To their great relief, it was not long before they could feel the ocean floor beneath their feet.

In sheer exhaustion, Christopher and Madeline fell onto the shore, neither stirring for hours. Startled awake by the sound of someone yelling, Madeline glanced over at Christopher. The memory of the last several hours came flooding back as a storm. Just then, a small child came running up to them. It was Henry Bleasdell looking no worse for the wear. Henry, a spunky little fellow, was loved by everyone; though aboard the ship, many were relieved when he was down for a nap. His energy seemed endless, which could be trying at times. Before long, Henry's parents, Mr. Ralph Bleasdell and his wife, Elizabeth, came searching for him. They chuckled when they found him snuggled down in between Madeline and Christopher.

"Henry, we have been looking for you. You should not have run off like that," said Elizabeth, who treasured her little man. As an older mother of forty-two, she doubted before Henry came along that she would ever be blessed with a child to raise, for she had already lost two children in their infancy.

For Ralph and Elizabeth Bleasdell, the wreck of the *Angel* was just another trial in what had been a rather traumatic journey. As part of the Puritan movement, the Bleasdells had suffered numerous hardships in England. Many who shared their beliefs had been fined or imprisoned. Consequently, the Bleasdells left England in secrecy not knowing until they were well away whether they would be caught. They desired a better life for themselves and for Henry where they could worship God according to the precepts of scripture rather than obligatory service to the edicts of the Church of England.

Madeline, relieved to see that the Bleasdells had made it ashore, was beginning to wonder who else had survived the terrible nightmare. Mr. and Mrs. Bleasdell recounted everyone they had seen that had made it safely to dry land. Madeline whispered, "thank you," to the Lord, seeing that most of the passengers had survived. Then a dreadful thought came to her; the Bleasdells had not yet mentioned Christopher's wife and son. She sheepishly peeped over at Christopher just as he was brushing away a tear.

Oh how terrible; it must be true. He has lost his family, she thought.

Just then, Christopher, rising to his feet, said softly, "I will return in a little while."

Madeline, Elizabeth, and Mr. Bleasdell watched him as he walked somberly away.

Mr. Bleasdell, a tall, rugged-looking man of middle age, rose up quickly to walk alongside Christopher. Placing his arm on his shoulder, he whispered, "We are all here for you. You are not alone."

By now, all of the survivors had gathered to discuss their situation. Nearly everyone had lost most of their belongings when the ship went down. Each one stacked up what they had salvaged into one pile. In the midst of it lay Mr. John Cogswell's tents. Somehow, the tents had survived the wreck and were now their best hope of a temporary shelter.

Mr. John Cogswell, an amiable middle-aged gentleman, was accompanied by his wife, Elizabeth, and eight of his children on the journey from England. Mr. Cogswell called out to his sons, John Jr., who was twelve and, William, who was sixteen. "John, William, start setting up the tents."

Thomas and Robert Burnham, Captain Robert Andrews' nephews, decided to lend a hand. Everyone, though still in shock over the events of the day, somehow managed to pull themselves together. The friendships that had begun in the twelve weeks at sea helped to bond them together during such a crisis. At this point, with all gathered around, Mr. Bleasdell lifted his voice to heaven and gave thanks for God's mighty hand of protection. He also recognized that there were a few who had lost their lives and prayed that God would grant their families comfort and peace.

John Tuttle, age seventeen, and William Furber, age twenty, took it upon themselves to dig through the pile to find something with which to fish. They called out, "We are going to catch some dinner. We shall be back before it grows dark." They finally returned just as the sun was going down, bellowing, "Success!" as they held up their catch of the day.

It was not long before a fire was crackling beneath the starlight and the smell of fish was drawing the weary survivors to dinner. After everyone had eaten, many of the passengers were conversing about their frightful day.

John Bailey, who was traveling with two of his children, John Jr. and Joanna, exclaimed, "My wife, the poor dear woman, desired for me to leave off from taking this voyage! I dare not give her an account of the terrible storm and the wreck that claimed all of our belongings. She may then be afeard to cross the ocean with our other children."

The passengers were beginning to realize that their lives in the "New Land" had just become more difficult. Many wondered how they would start over devoid of any of their belongings.

Madeline had been so distracted by all of the events of the day that she had nearly forgotten her own predicament. A wave of fear swept over her as she thought, *I am all alone in a new land without my husband.* She knew from experience the only thing she could do to calm herself would be to inquire of the Lord regarding her situation.

"Entrusting Him with the troubles that are too great to bear alone has always proven to be a wise decision, as many a trial has come to naught in His capable hands," she said. Madeline, unaware that she had been speaking aloud continued, "Of course this time the need is much greater." As she stood up to go and find a place to pray, she caught a glimpse of a little smile that had come upon Christopher's face. Embarrassed by the knowledge that she had been speaking loud enough for others to hear, she quickly made her departure.

Following her time of petitioning the Lord, Madeline felt a renewed sense of calm. She did not yet know the manner in which the help would come, but she felt assured that it would. Madeline rejoined the others just as Christopher was returning from gathering up some extra clothing from the salvage pile to set out to dry. Madeline's respect for him grew all the more as she observed his peaceful demeanor even after having lost his wife and son.

He is truly a man of great strength, she thought.

By now, just about everyone in the group had developed an attitude of acceptance over their circumstances. In spite of the wreck, a sense of awe was beginning to sweep over them as they realized that they had made it to the "new land."

Early the next morning, Mr. Cogswell and some of the younger men returned from the little settlement upon which they had stumbled when they were out exploring the area. Bubbling over with what appeared to be good news, his cheerful expression was contagious, as everyone seemed to be smiling while patiently waiting for him to speak.

He began by explaining, "While we were out having a look around we found a little settlement, which apparently is called Pemaquid. It seems that the area was granted as the Pemaquid Patent to merchants from Bristol, England. As some of you are aware, I have been given a land grant in Ipswich, part of the

Massachusetts Bay Colony. We have procured a ship to carry us there, the owner of which is Captain Gallup. As some of our things were sent on ahead by another ship, we are in a better position to offer assistance. Though it may not have been your original destination, anyone who wishes to may travel on with us."

Many in the group were happy to take advantage of the opportunity to go along with the Cogswells, including Mr. and Mrs. Bleasdell who were also pleased to accept his generous offer. They decided that Ipswich was a good location as any from which to investigate all opportunities in the surrounding towns.

At this point, Madeline, keenly aware of her situation, thought, *I must make a decision. Oliver would have known what to do, but now I am left alone to decide.* Fear was, once again, sweeping over her at the thought of having no means by which to support herself.

Elizabeth Bleasdell, realizing Madeline's dilemma, said, "Madeline, we would be most happy to have you reside with us upon our arrival to Ipswich. I could do with a bit of help with Henry."

Madeline, overflowing with gratitude, replied, "Oh thank you, Elizabeth, I believe I shall accept your generous offer."

After some tearful goodbyes with the few who did not venture on with the Cogswells, the rest of the survivors of the wreck of the *Angel Gabriel* traveled on to begin their lives in the new land. They each loaded onto the ship the few things that had been salvaged and were off on the next leg of their journey.

Chapter 2

On to Ipswich to Begin Life in the "New Land"

Before long, the travelers were disembarking from Captain Gallup's ship. Mr. Cogswell's family as well as his servants, William Furber and Samuel Haines, were planning to settle in Ipswich. Some of the others who were going to do the same were Captain Robert Andrews and his Burnham nephews John, Thomas, and Robert. The others intended to remain in Ipswich for as long as it took to prepare to travel on to other destinations.

The residents of Ipswich rallied around the survivors, lending a hand by giving generously of their food and clothing. They seemed more than willing to suffer a little hardship to be of assistance to their new neighbors. In addition, the town leaders allowed the Bleasdells to make use of a small home for a temporary shelter. The previous family had not survived their first winter, leaving the home abandoned. Madeline and the Bleasdells had no way of knowing, at the time, what a blessing the meager home would become, as it would be a couple of years before they could move on to a new place.

Christopher Osgood procured work with some of the local fishermen. One of which, a man by the name of Nathaniel Bellamy, with empathy for him offered him a place to stay. Nathaniel, a rugged young man, had lost his family to illness and had since been living alone. Christopher's mind was consumed with a yearning to continue his dream of furthering the gospel, especially among the children. He was sure that Hannah would have desired for him to carry on. He remembered how eager they had been to teach without the restrictions of the Church of England.

Still, how can I go on without Hannah? he thought.

Madeline busied herself with Henry Bleasdell for hours each day. She had grown to love the curly-headed little boy. She was greatly amused by his indomitability and his quirky smile that always popped up on his pudgy little face whenever he got the best of her. Elizabeth was grateful for the help, especially throughout the weeks that Mr. Bleasdell was away.

During their time in Ipswich, Mr. Bleasdell made frequent trips to Agamenticus and Colechester. At first, the purpose for the trips was to obtain additional work to help his family. However, as time went on, he became very fond of the towns, especially Colechester. He was beginning to believe that Colechester might be the place in which he and his family should settle; however, he found himself a resident of Agamenticus for a time, assisting them in establishing the town. During this time, Elizabeth, Maddie, and Henry remained in Ipswich, for Mr. Bleasdell had not planned to be there long.

During Madeline's first few months in Ipswich, she intentionally kept herself exceptionally busy. She knew that if she allowed herself time to reflect on the life she had planned with Oliver, she might become overwhelmed by sadness. However, on one particular day, Madeline found that she had time on her hands in spite of her efforts to the contrary; thus, she decided to go exploring.

Recalling that the townsfolk had warned them of straying too far alone, as there were wolves and at times some of the Indians could be hostile, she determined that down by the water would be a safe destination. She knew that it had always been bustling with people. As she could see that she was rapidly approaching the water, she grew excited, for, in England, she had loved gazing out over the water and skipping stones across its surface.

Madeline was so enjoying the day, she scarcely noticed it had almost passed until the sparkle of the sunset reflecting on the water caught her eye. She was so captivated by the shimmering beauty of it that she began, as she often did, to converse with herself. "How beautiful. I could never tire of God's magnificent creation."

All at once, she heard a voice coming from behind her, saying, "I wholeheartedly agree."

Her heart skipped a beat as she whirled around and found Christopher Osgood standing there.

"I ah . . . I did not see you standing there," she stammered.

"I am often overcome myself by the splendor of a sunset," replied Christopher, attempting to make Madeline feel at ease.

Madeline's mind was racing over the embarrassment of having been caught, once again, talking to herself, as well as the excitement at seeing Christopher. She began to question why she was reacting this way. *After all, we are just good friends*, she thought. Feeling the need to escape the awkwardness of the situation, she said, "Well, I better be running along while there is enough light by which to make my way home. Goodbye Christopher, it was good to see you."

With that, she was off with Christopher scarcely able to get out a "goodbye," before she was too far away to hear him.

As Madeline was dashing home, she replayed in her mind the entire scene with Christopher. Why had she felt so ill at ease? How stupid she must have seemed to run off so quickly. *What must he think of me?* she wondered.

All at once, her thoughts began to shift to when she might see him again. She began to wonder why it had been so many months since she had last seen him. *He does not make much of an effort to come to call on me . . . I mean us*, she thought, clearly frustrated.

However, after a few moments of reflection, she began to feel a sense of guilt. *After all, it has not been that long since Oliver passed and Christopher is still mourning the loss of Hannah.* She was determined not to allow such thoughts to enter her mind again.

Later that night, Christopher recalled how Maddie had seemed ill at ease with him down by the water. He wondered if it had simply been that she was aware that he had overheard her talking to herself. He wished she had not rushed off so quickly, for he had missed spending time with her in the way that he had on their voyage. "She was such a bright light for everyone on board the ship with her compassionate words and bright smile," he heard himself say aloud. "What am I doing? Now I am talking to myself. Maddie would laugh if she knew."

Much to Elizabeth and Henry's delight, Mr. Bleasdell finally returned with good news from Colechester. "Elizabeth, the town has made a promise to give us a land grant. It includes a parcel of land in town for a home and another just past the center of town to farm. Moreover, after some weeks in prayer regarding God's will for us, I am of the opinion that it is His desire that we should remove to Colechester as soon as it can be arranged. I know that it cannot happen overnight, but by this time next year, I hope to be all settled in our own home on our own land," he said, with excitement in his voice. "As I continue to have obligations in Agamenticus, I shall be off early tomorrow to conclude my business there."

Chapter 3

Awakening of Feelings/John Bailey, a Sad Story/Plans to Move

Upon his return from Agamenticus, Mr. Bleasdell met up with Christopher in town one day. "Christopher, I have news."

"What news?" Christopher asked with a quizzical look on his face.

"Christopher, I have plans to move my family to Colechester," replied Mr. Bleasdell. "However, as things are not yet arranged, it shall not happen right away. You see, the town has made us the promise of a land grant. Moreover, it is my belief that as a property owner I shall have further opportunity to provide for my family."

"I had thought you were to remove to Agamenticus or rather to Bristol as it is now called," replied Christopher, as he was mulling over the news.

"Yes, I have property there as well, but I believe Colechester offers more opportunity. Mr. Robert Knight shall purchase my holdings in Bristol, formerly Agamenticus, as soon as he is able."

"Shall ah . . . er, I mean to say, will all of you be going?" Christopher asked, with a discomfited expression.

"If you mean to inquire as to whether or not Madeline will be moving with us, the answer is yes," Mr. Bleasdell replied with a smile. "You ought to consider doing the same."

"Oh, I do not know. After all, I am established here in Ipswich," remarked Christopher. "However, it will sadden me to part company with you. I cannot conceive of my life here without all of you. You are much the same as family to me."

"I shall say no more on the subject under the condition that you at least consider the possibility," replied Mr. Bleasdell. "But, in the meantime, we should like to see more of you."

"To be sure," replied Christopher.

The following evening after Christopher had completed his work for the day, he stopped by to call on the Bleasdells.

"Good evening, Christopher, it is wonderful to see you," said Elizabeth, leading him by the hand. "Henry and Madeline are out for a little walk at the moment, but we expect them back very soon. Will you stay and dine with us this evening?"

"I really cannot stay long, but I thank you just the same," responded Christopher, as he was taking a seat.

"We have not seen enough of you these days, dear boy. Even on worship day you are out the door before we are able to greet you," remarked Elizabeth.

"I have been so busy, I scarcely have time to eat and sleep," replied Christopher.

Mr. Bleasdell, Elizabeth, and Christopher conversed for nearly an hour before Henry came bounding into the room with Madeline trailing behind.

"There is the little man," said Christopher, with a smile.

Henry squealed with excitement as he jumped into Christopher's lap.

"Maddie, it is good to see you," said Christopher, glancing in her direction.

It was not long before everyone in the room noticed something peculiar regarding Madeline. Henry, while they were out for their stroll, had taken up the idea that Madeline seemed a good candidate for a mud fight. Maddie, mortified at seeing

Christopher sitting there, scampered quickly from the room. Grasping the situation, Christopher, Elizabeth, and Mr. Bleasdell started to chuckle.

"I must see to Madeline," whispered Elizabeth, with a little grin.

"I should take my leave," said Christopher, with an understanding nod.

"Very well, but come again soon," replied Mr. Bleasdell, as he walked Christopher out.

The following week, Mr. Bleasdell was met by his friend John Bailey, from the *Angel Gabriel*, who inquired after his knowledge of Colechester. Mr. Bailey had become legally entangled while residing in Ipswich. Though he had been released from the charges, his reputation had been irreparably damaged. Consequently, he earnestly desired to settle in a new location where he would have the benefit of anonymity and might make a new start.

Mr. Bleasdell, with compassion for Mr. Bailey, offered to recommend him to the selectmen of Colechester. As he was aware of Mr. Bailey's situation in Ipswich, as well as the details regarding his lonely life without his beloved who would not venture to cross the ocean, it was his desire to offer him assistance.

Mr. Bailey traveled with Mr. Bleasdell on his subsequent visit to Colechester. Upon their arrival, Mr. Bleasdell sought to introduce him to the selectmen in hopes of recommending him for a land grant. He was warmly received by the town and his hopes for an offer of property were realized, resulting in great joy for Mr. Bailey. Mr. Bleasdell was pleased as well with the turn of events for Mr. Bailey.

Upon their return to Ipswich, Mr. Bailey was not long in arranging for his move. He left for Colechester soon after with plans to meet up with Mr. Bleasdell on his next visit. The Bleasdells were very pleased that Mr. Bailey, once again, would be their neighbor when they moved to Colechester. Elizabeth determined that when they were settled she would not delay in seeking him out, for she had long wished to be of some comfort to the poor man.

A few months had passed before Christopher visited again with the Bleasdells and Madeline. Madeline came running inside when she spied him coming up the road.

"Elizabeth," she said nervously, "Christopher is almost here."

"Well, all right," said Elizabeth. "Go and greet him."

"Oh, Elizabeth, I cannot," grimaced Madeline. "I do not wish for him to know that I saw him approaching."

Elizabeth laughed as she opened the door to greet Christopher. "Good day to you, Christopher," she said, still grinning. "It is so nice of you to call on us."

"I'm sorry that I have been so long away. I have not had time for anything other than work these days," disclosed Christopher.

"Mr. Bleasdell had kept us informed regarding your work demands," remarked Elizabeth.

"Good day to you, Maddie," said Christopher, with a smile.

"And to you, Christopher," said Maddie nervously. "I imagine that I appear a little less soiled than when we last met," she said, with a giggle.

Christopher was glad to see that she had regained her sense of humor.

"Where is the little man?" asked Christopher.

"He is down for his nap," replied Elizabeth. "I should not have been surprised if Madeline had required a nap as well. Henry has her going from sunup to sundown."

"I do not mind as he is, to me, the dearest boy," replied Madeline.

Christopher filled Madeline and the Bleasdells in on all that had been going on since his last visit. They were happy that he had come to call in spite of the little time he had available for visiting.

"I am sorry to have missed seeing Henry," said Christopher, "but I cannot stay any longer. I must take my leave, as tomorrow shall be another long day of work."

"Do come again, soon," replied Elizabeth.

Later that night, once Christopher had gone, Madeline remarked to Elizabeth about the agreeable nature of his visit and how nice it had been to see him. "I am going to retire to my bed now," said Madeline, with contentment in her voice.

I fear that there shall very soon be two broken hearts, thought Elizabeth. *I am not sure that they comprehend how fast the day of our move is approaching.*

Chapter 4

The Move and Making New Acquaintances

The weeks flew by and moving day was upon them. As the time had come for Madeline to say her farewells, a sense of sorrow swept over her. She did not want to admit it to herself, but she knew the reason for this feeling. Her heart was heavy as she walked somberly with the Bleasdells into town.

Elizabeth was beginning to detect that Madeline was not her usual cheery self so she casually strolled up to her and asked, "Are you ill, my dear? You do not seem quite yourself today."

Madeline did not wish to reveal her thoughts to Elizabeth, so she said, "I am all right, perhaps just a little weary."

Though Elizabeth was unconvinced that her young friend was being truthful, she decided not to press her for more information.

All and sundry came out to say their farewells to Madeline and the Bleasdells. There were many hugs and tears as well as invitations to return at any time. Madeline, with a desire to be discreet, had been subtly glancing around to see if a tall, wavy brown-haired figure was anywhere in sight. After a while, she began to feel ashamed of herself for fretting over Christopher and whether he would be there to say goodbye.

While walking back to the little house, the Bleasdells remarked on how they had come to love all of the people in town. "We are going to miss them terribly," said Elizabeth sadly.

"Indeed we are," replied Mr. Bleasdell. "Nevertheless, I am excited about once again becoming a property owner. As such, I shall have influence in this new land. I believe that God has great plans for all of us who have traveled here. It is my desire to do my part to encourage the people to follow after His will."

Madeline was extremely quiet as they strolled along. She had quickly glanced back a few times hoping to go unnoticed, especially by Elizabeth. She muttered, "Elizabeth might suspect that it is Christopher I am searching for. What would she think if she knew how I long to see him before we set off for Colechester?"

Elizabeth, hearing Madeline's voice, said, "Did you say something, dear?"

Realizing she had spoken aloud, Madeline gave a hasty reply, "No just talking to myself again." She and Elizabeth had often joked about the frequent conversations that Madeline had with herself aboard the *Angel*.

With the help of their former captain, Robert Andrews, the Bleasdells had procured free passage aboard a shallop heading for Colechester. The captain of the shallop, Theodore Barnes, had heard about the *Angel Gabriel's* misfortune and wanted to be of assistance to the travelers. Mr. and Mrs. Bleasdell, with hearts full of gratitude, gave thanks to God that, once again, He had made provision for them; then they loaded up what little they had and were off to Colechester.

Madeline inquired of Mr. Bleasdell, "What is the distance to Colechester?"

Mr. Bleasdell replied, "Over land, it is not further than thirteen or fourteen miles."

Madeline had not realized that Colechester and Ipswich were so close. "Christopher I . . . ah . . . I meant to say Ipswich will be nearer to us than I thought!" exclaimed Madeline, with an obvious joyful tone to which Mr. Bleasdell and Elizabeth smiled.

Meanwhile, back at Ipswich, Christopher came scurrying into town to inquire after Mr. and Mrs. Bleasdell and Maddie. He had been detained by a rather chatty fisherman and could not get away. It was not long before he discovered that he had failed to make it there in time. After learning that they had already set off, Christopher felt a deep sense of sadness. Though he attempted to deny his feelings, he was, at that moment, acutely aware of his ever-increasing affections for Maddie.

Once the passengers had sailed out around Plum Island, it was not long before they reached their destination. With the assistance of some of the gentlemen in town on his previous trips, Mr. Bleasdell had been building a modest home for his family, which he was eager to show them. Making their way to the location of their new home, Elizabeth and Maddie felt a sense of great anticipation. Once they arrived, they stood gazing at their new home with a contented feeling washing over them knowing they were at the place they might finally put down roots.

"God has truly blessed us," remarked Mr. Bleasdell.

Some of the neighbors came to call on the family upon observing their arrival into town. They expressed their delight in having new neighbors and offered to have them come and dine with them once everyone was settled in. After their new acquaintances had departed, Madeline and Elizabeth remarked on how affable the new neighbors seemed to be.

"I can truly conceive of a life here where making new friends appears to come quite easily," commented Elizabeth.

Elizabeth and Mr. Bleasdell were busy arranging their things in the new home while Madeline entertained Henry.

An idea came to Madeline that she believed would please Henry. "Let's take a stroll through town and have a look around."

Henry's eyes lit up with excitement, for he was more than willing to join Miss Madeline on her adventure. Madeline whispered to Elizabeth, "I am going to take Henry on a walk. We will return in a little while," to which Elizabeth gave a smile and a nod.

Mr. Bleasdell remarked, "Having her here with us has been a Godsend."

"Yes, and I believe that it has been good for Madeline to be with us, although this move has been hard for her. Though she will not admit it, there is no doubt but that she shall miss Christopher exceedingly."

Henry began to point out the little saltbox-style houses that were stretched out around the circular road leading through town. Next, they came to a little meetinghouse. Madeline explained to Henry as they were passing by, "They make use of the meetinghouse for town business as well as to hold church services. I have been informed that it is the custom to meet there on the Sabbath for worship and on Thursday nights for lectures. Henry, now that your father is a landowner, he will be able to attend town meetings."

"What do they do at the meetings?" asked Henry.

"They make a lot of the decisions for the town. Someday, when you are all grown up you too may attend the meetings," replied Madeline, with a smile.

On the far end of the road stood the new church, which was presently under construction. Madeline was overflowing with excitement owing to the realization that many of the people occupying the homes had made similar harrowing journeys to a new homeland in order to serve God in freedom.

Oh, how I wish that Oliver had lived to experience all of this, she thought. Madeline was abruptly shaken out of her daydream by Henry's little hand pulling on her dress. "All right, Henry," she said, with a smile, "we will continue on."

Down the road a bit further, Madeline noticed a garrison house that she knew to be the place in which the residents barricade themselves in the event of an Indian attack. *However, I think I shall keep that bit of information to myself. I do not think Henry would sleep well tonight if he were made aware of it*, thought Madeline.

Madeline recalled a sad turn of events that Mr. Bleasdell had told her about concerning a plague earlier in the century that had killed many of the members of Pentucket tribe. She then thought about a very kind member of the Abenaki tribe that she had become acquainted with on their journey to Colechester. She remembered being quite impressed with his friendly manner with the captain and the other passengers; and that following that experience, she had learned not to fear Indians altogether, though she knew she needed to be cautious.

While Henry and Madeline were having an enjoyable time conversing about the town, some ladies approached. After introducing themselves, they expressed a desire to include the new members of the town in some upcoming activities.

Madeline ecstatic, exclaimed excitedly, "I was so hoping to make the acquaintance of some of the ladies in town! I cannot think of a better way in which to accomplish it."

The most outspoken of the group, Mrs. Bridget Dudly, a stout, fine-looking, young woman, replied, "Good, we shall collect you this time tomorrow for a time of quilting instruction at Emma Foster's."

Madeline, responding in the affirmative, in great anticipation took her leave.

Emma Foster, a kind and handsome woman of forty-three, owing to her talents in quilt making had been teaching some of the younger ladies in town. This afforded her the opportunity to forge a mentoring style of friendship with many of the young wives and mothers. Being a woman of great character, she endeavored to also instruct in the art of service to others rather than allowing the time to be spent increasing the population of busybodies. Therefore, she did not tolerate a lot of gossip amongst the ladies who frequented her home.

Madeline and Henry scurried on back to the Bleasdell homestead. Once there, Henry began to talk on and on, excitedly, as he described everything that he had seen. "We saw little houses, and . . . um . . . a meeting hut or a house."

Elizabeth said with a giggle, "Slow down Henry, you are getting ahead of yourself."

Just then, one of the men from town came sauntering up. "Good day to you, Mr. Bleasdell, thought I would come by to make the acquaintance of my new neighbors. Will you not introduce me to these lovely ladies and this cute little lad?"

"Very well, Jarret," said Mr. Bleasdell, with a grumble. "This is my wife, Mrs. Elizabeth Bleasdell," he said, gesturing toward her, "and our friend, Mrs. Madeline Pike. My son's name is Henry."

"Delighted to your acquaintance," said Jarret. "Please allow me to introduce myself; I am Jarret Ormsby. Is your husband about, Mrs. Pike? I would be pleased to make his acquaintance as well."

"I lost my husband on our journey over from England," replied Madeline somberly.

"I am very sorry for you," said Jarret disingenuously, as he was delighted that Madeline was unattached.

I wish I had warned Elizabeth and Madeline about Jarret. He is a bit free with the ladies, thought Mr. Bleasdell.

Madeline and Elizabeth decided to take Henry away for a little while to leave the two gentlemen alone to talk.

Before too long, Madeline overheard Jarret saying, "I will take my leave. Good day to you, Mr. Bleasdell." With that, he was on his way.

Madeline asked Elizabeth, "Did you take note of Mr. Bleasdell's countenance upon Jarret's arrival?"

"He did seem a little bothered," replied Elizabeth, "which is a bit out of character for Mr. Bleasdell, as he is always so kind to everyone. It is not like him to be so dismissive. However, knowing him like I do, there must be a good reason."

Chapter 5

Emma the Mentor a Woman of Character

The following day, Madeline put Henry down for a nap before setting off for an afternoon of quilting. She considered the fact that she did not have anything with which to work. However, she decided she might enjoy getting acquainted with more of the ladies in the town regardless of whether she could join in with the quilting.

Just then, Bridget Dudly came strolling up beside Madeline. "Good day, Madeline, I am so happy that you have decided to come today. It is going to be a wonderful day."

"Thank you," said Madeline. "I have been so looking forward to it."

As Bridget and Madeline were passing by the little meetinghouse, they heard someone call out, "Good day, Maddie." Jarret Ormsby, having spied them as they were coming up the road, made haste to catch up.

"And how are you ladies today?" he asked.

The ladies turned to see who had called out to them. They soon discovered that it was Jarret Ormsby. Madeline—after hearing her pet name "Maddie" being uttered by a virtual stranger—felt a shiver run up her spine. She instantly thought about Oliver and Christopher. "They are the only people who have ever affectionately called me 'Maddie.' Moreover, I scarcely know him; what right has he to be so familiar?" she muttered.

Bridget was becoming uneasy, as well, by all of the attention Jarret was lavishing on them. "After all, I am married woman," she later remarked to Madeline.

Bridget and Madeline made a quick escape as they approached Emma's house.

"Goodbye, Jarret," they said in unison, as they disappeared behind a closed door.

Once inside, Madeline and Bridget were affectionately greeted by their host. Emma had a way of making everyone feel comfortable in her lovely little home. The various colorful quilts she had strategically placed hither and thither added softness and warmth to the room.

All of the ladies had finally arrived, prompting Emma to begin. "It is my custom to introduce anyone new to the group and the group to anyone new." Each one in turn spoke out their name and a brief synopsis of themselves, such as I am the wife of so and so, or the mother to such and such.

It was not long before Madeline had learned something about each of her new acquaintances. *It may have taken me months on my own to learn this much about each of these ladies,* she thought.

The hours passed quickly, and it was soon time to leave. All of the others said their goodbyes and were on their way. However, Emma held Madeline back for a moment saying, "If you will remain, I should like to speak with you."

As Bridget, the last one to leave, was getting ready to set off, she asked, "Madeline, would you like for me to walk you part of the way home?"

Madeline replied, "I thank you but no, I am going to stay a few moments and speak with Emma." With that, Bridget was gone and Madeline was left alone with Emma.

Emma said, "Have a seat over here by me, Madeline. I wish to tell you a little bit about myself that there was no need of divulging to the whole group. Looking intently into Madeline's eyes, she began, "When I first arrived from England a few years ago I was married to a wonderful man by the name of Samuel Fletcher. He died of an illness our first winter here. I do not have to tell you how devastated I was. If it had not been for my trust in the Lord, I think that I should have gone mad with fear. I was left all alone not knowing what to do. Like you, I had acquired some wonderful friends on my journey that took me in for a couple of years."

She must have been informed of my circumstances, thought Madeline.

Emma continued, "There were a few gentlemen during that time, some of whom paid me a great deal of attention. One in particular kept pursuing me until I had almost given in to his persistent attempts to marry me. If it had not been for a friend who cared enough to be honest with me regarding his duplicitous nature, I might be miserably married to him today. Once I heeded her warning, it was not long before I became acquainted with Morris. He is as kind and loving a man as I have ever known. He loves my daughter, Jane, for to him she is not unlike his own child."

"Oh, I was unaware that you have a daughter," said Madeline.

"Yes, she is now almost twenty and married to a young man by the name of Nathan Dickson. When they left Colechester, they moved to Salem. However, just recently they removed to Ipswich. So you see, my dear, God's provision is never too late, as He provided a husband and father just when we needed him the most."

Madeline sat quietly fighting back the tears as she hung on every word of Emma's story. "Emma, you too have had a great loss. I wish you could have known my Oliver," she said, through the tears that, despite her attempts to stop them, were now flowing freely.

However, she was beginning to wonder, *Why is she sharing this with me? I understand the similarities with Samuel and Oliver, but why tell me about the scallywag she almost married?*

Emma, sensing that she had not conveyed the message within her story, decided to speak plainly so there would not be any misunderstanding. "Madeline, as I saw you and Bridget arrive here today, I observed Jarret Ormsby shadowing you. I am not one to express ill feelings about another person, but I feel that I must leave you with one warning." Then, in a stern tone, she said, "Suffice it to say, where Jarret Ormsby is concerned, be ever so cautious!"

Madeline was beginning to believe that her instincts about Jarret might have been right. "I am obliged to you, Emma," she said, as she got up to leave. "It means a lot to me that you care enough to give a warning. I will heed your advice; though, before I take my leave, I must say that I am glad to know that you have found, in Morris, another man to love."

***

Back at home with Mr. and Mrs. Bleasdell, Madeline recounted the events of her day; however, she left off telling them about her conversation with Emma, as she believed it to be a private matter.

Little Henry was fast asleep for the night, when Elizabeth and Madeline began preparing food for Mr. Bleasdell and Captain Barnes' trip the following day. They were planning to travel to Ipswich to collect a supply of victuals for Colechester.

The next morning, Henry was up with the dawn. "No extra winks for us today," said Elizabeth, as she proceeded to feed Henry his breakfast.

Before long, Mr. Bleasdell was off to Ipswich, leaving Madeline, Elizabeth, and Henry with instructions to "beware of wolves," as he had seen a pack of them just a few feet away from their land.

Henry said, "Why do we have to beware of wolves, Mamma?"

"Henry, though they may resemble a dog, they are, in fact, wild animals that may bring great harm to you. You must stay away from them, if you happen to see one," replied Elizabeth.

"All right," replied Henry.

"Madeline," whispered Elizabeth. "You and Henry need to take care when you are out and about."

Later that afternoon, Mr. Morris Foster and Emma came to call on Madeline and Elizabeth. Madeline was filled with excitement upon seeing Emma. "Elizabeth, may I introduce you to Emma? And this must be Mr. Foster."

"So nice to make your acquaintance," said Elizabeth, ushering them in. "Please take a seat over here by the fire."

"Elizabeth, my purpose in coming is to invite you to our next quilting gathering. The ladies so wish to make your acquaintance, and I could do with a companion at the event nearer to my own age," chuckled Emma. "Do not misunderstand me, Madeline; I am very fond of you and all of the other young ladies."

Madeline and Elizabeth just smiled and gave each other an understanding nod as Emma continued, "Henry is always welcome to come too," assured Emma, as she and Morris rose to leave. "We must be going, as we had not planned to stay long. It was lovely to have met you."

"I left Mr. Bleasdell in town the other day with the understanding that I would see to your needs whilst he is away," said Mr. Foster. "Thus, if a need arises, please send for me."

"That is very kind of you, Mr. Foster," said Elizabeth. "Thank you both for coming."

Once they had gone, Madeline and Elizabeth spoke with delight regarding the Fosters.

"Madeline, Emma seems like such a lovely person. I am pleased to have met her. From what you have told me about her, I suspect we are very similar and might become quite good friends."

"Yes, you are very much alike. I believe you shall form a strong friendship," replied Madeline in all sincerity.

Elizabeth gave Madeline's hand a squeeze and the two friends sat down on either side of little Henry, each feeling content that God's plan had brought them to this place.

Chapter 6

Seeing Old Friends/Antinomian Accusations

Upon his arrival to Ipswich, Mr. Bleasdell was met with warm greetings by some of his old friends, many of whom had questions as to the reason for his visit. He explained that he had returned with the captain of the shallop that had carried him and his family to Colechester in order to assist him with a shipment that had arrived there.

Once the transfer of goods from one vessel to the other had taken place, the captain released Mr. Bleasdell from any further obligations for the rest of day.

"Mr. Bleasdell, you have been a great help. I shall see you early tomorrow for our return trip."

"Good enough, until the morning then," called out Mr. Bleasdell, as he headed down the road.

Once in town, Mr. Bleasdell went in search of Christopher. He happened upon his old friend and captain, Robert Andrews.

"What are you doing back around these parts?" asked Robert.

"I returned on Captain Barnes' shallop to help him with a load of supplies for Colechester. It is good to see you, Robert. What have you been filling your time with these days?"

"I was granted a license to open a tavern," replied Robert. "You may know, my nephews are still with me. In addition to working with me, they are becoming quite the experts at shipbuilding."

"I am glad to know that all is well with you," said Mr. Bleasdell. "Would you happen to know where I might find Christopher Osgood?"

"He may be at his home. I happened to see him a while ago walking in that direction," Mr. Andrews replied.

"I hope to see you again before I set off for home tomorrow," said Mr. Bleasdell.

"To be sure," replied Robert, with a wave goodbye as Mr. Bleasdell was leaving.

To Mr. Bleasdell's surprise, Christopher came ambling out the door just as he was approaching.

"Christopher, it is so good to see you," said Mr. Bleasdell excitedly.

"Mr. Bleasdell, when did you arrive? I cannot tell you how good it is to see you. I have missed you all exceedingly. How is Miss Madd . . . er, ah I mean everyone?" asked Christopher, without taking a breath or giving Mr. Bleasdell a chance to answer his previous question.

Not much ever slipped by Mr. Bleasdell, as he quickly took note of Christopher's stammering and embarrassed expression. With a smile on his face, he commenced with encouraging Christopher to come to Colechester. "Christopher, why remain in Ipswich when there is so much opportunity in Colechester? There are still available land grants as well as prospects for work if you know where to look. In fact, I had just heard about something the other day you might find to be of interest."

"Indeed, do go on," replied Christopher, with great curiosity.

"There is an island in the Merrimac, directly across from Colechester, that has recently been granted to Mr. George Carr. It is his intention to start a ferry service between Colechester, Carr's Island, and Newbury. Therefore, he is in need of some men to assist him in this endeavor," stated Mr. Bleasdell.

"Is it your opinion that Mr. Carr would look favorably upon me for the task?" asked Christopher.

"I feel certain that he would," replied Mr. Bleasdell. "He could not hope to employ a finer man."

"That is high praise," said Christopher, with a smile.

"In addition to the splendid opportunity that such a move would proffer, you would be closer to us, for Carr's Island is an easy distance from the town of Colechester. In fact, it is only a few minutes out."

"That would truly be wonderful, as things have not been the same here without all of you," replied Christopher.

"Christopher, you have been greatly missed by all of us," expressed Mr. Bleasdell.

"Mr. Bleasdell, I first ought to inquire after the Lord's will and direction in this matter before I make any decisions."

"You are right, Christopher," answered Mr. Bleasdell.

Following a time of prayer, the two friends conversed for hours before retiring for the night.

***

Mr. Bleasdell rolled out of bed early the next morning. Rubbing his tired eyes, he whispered to Christopher, "I must take my leave. Captain Barnes will be wondering what has become of me. Thank you for allowing me the use of your quarters."

"You are always welcome," replied Christopher, as he rose to say goodbye. "I shall continue to seek the Lord's will for me with regard to a move. Perhaps you will see me again very soon," he said, joyful at the thought of it.

Back on board the shallop, Mr. Bleasdell discussed with Captain Barnes his conversation with Christopher and his hopes that he might come to Colechester. "He is very much alone without any real friends or family to speak of in Ipswich. What kind of a life is that for such a fine young man?" asked Mr. Bleasdell.

"It is clear that you care a great deal about him," replied Captain Barnes

After conveying his thoughts on Christopher to the captain, Mr. Bleasdell decided to leave it in God's hands. *If He wills it*, he thought, *it will happen.*

Back in Colechester, the town selectmen were gearing up for a meeting while Mr. Bleasdell was away. As the construction of the church was finally nearing completion, the property owners who had taken the "Oath of a Freeman," were ready to officially establish the First Congregational Church. The selectmen were church members first and town selectmen second, as matters of the church always ranked above any other business.

Excitement was in the air as the meeting commenced with Reverend Nicolas Worcester presenting the opening speech. The reverend was a slender middle-aged man with a commanding presence. Everyone at the meeting listened intently as he spoke about the future of the church, the town, and the "new land." His words impressed on them a deep sense of the importance of establishing the right atmosphere for the town to grow spiritually:

> Our town ought to be one in which there is a genuine worship of God! However, as I have observed, there are many who hold to the erroneous belief that salvation comes by our works. The scriptures declare something quite different, for it is clearly stated: "It is by grace that ye are saved, through faith and that not of yourselves: it is the gift of God; not of works, lest any man should boast." The scriptures also declare: "For whosoever shall call upon the name of the Lord shall be saved," and that, "faith without works is dead." In the aforementioned passages, we observe the order in which we are to do good works. Upon having received salvation as the free gift of God, we must observe that works should follow if it is a genuine faith. Thus, our good works ought to be a response to our salvation rather than a means by which we gain

salvation. Therefore, we are no longer to judge whether or not a person shall receive entry into our church based on an established list of prerequisite works. Someone new to the faith may not, yet, have fulfilled any good works. Ought they to be kept out until arbitrary decisions are made by the elders as to whether or not enough good works have transpired to prove an authentic faith? How are they to learn and grow in their faith unless they are received into the congregation to be mentored?

The speech was met, mostly, with approval. Nevertheless, a few objectors led by Jarret Ormsby were seen huddled outside at the end of the meeting. Their primary complaint was that, in their perception, the reverend had displayed "antinomian" sentiment.

Mr. Bleasdell returned home the day after the meeting of the selectmen. It was not long before the rumors began to blow in his direction as Jarret Ormsby cornered him in town one day. "Mr. Bleasdell, I fear that Reverend Nicolas Worcester may be of the same faction as one Anne Hutchinson, as he is surely teaching antinomianism, which, as you know, is frowned on by the Colony."

"What evidence is there on which to base your accusations?" asked Mr. Bleasdell angrily.

"Well, ah . . . er, well, if you had been there to listen to his speech, you too would have been convinced," asserted Jarret.

"I have not the time for this, Jarret," grimaced Mr. Bleasdell. "What is more, it is not your usual practice to concern yourself with such matters. What is the reason for your sudden interest in what Reverend Worcester is teaching?"

Jarret mumbled on about it being his duty to bring this to the attention of the town. However, after coming to the realization that Mr. Bleasdell took no interest in the conversation, he excused himself and hurried off.

A little while later, Mr. Bleasdell, as he was on his way to call on George Carr, met up with Morris Foster.

"Good day to you, Mr. Bleasdell, and did you have a successful trip?" inquired Mr. Foster.

"It was fine until such time as I returned home only to be bombarded by someone with complaints regarding what took place in the meeting last night!" exclaimed Mr. Bleasdell.

"Yes, I am aware that there was some dissention over the meeting. Some people have nothing better to do than to stir up trouble," grimaced Mr. Foster.

"You are right about that, but I am a little concerned that this person might try to make a mountain out of this particular molehill," replied Mr. Bleasdell.

"If you truly desire to have a voice in such matters, it is essential that you take your 'oath' as soon as possible. Once you have done so, it will be acceptable for you to become a selectman. We are in need of sensible people like you at the meetings. What has been the reason for your delay?" asked Mr. Foster.

"Time has not allowed for it as yet," replied Mr. Bleasdell. "But it is my desire to do so very soon. Mr. Foster, I must speak with Mr. Carr so I shall take my leave."

"All right, Mr. Bleasdell. When last I saw him he was over at the church."

"Thank you, Mr. Foster."

Upon his arrival, Mr. Bleasdell was pleased to find Mr. Carr in the back of the church conversing with Reverend Worcester.

"Good afternoon, Reverend Worcester and Mr. Carr. It shall not be long now, Reverend, before we will hear the new church bell calling all to come to worship. You must be very eager to hold service in the new building rather than the little meeting house," said Mr. Bleasdell.

"Yes, I am so looking forward to it," answered Reverend Worcester.

"I am sorry to interrupt the two of you, but I am in need of a brief consult with Mr. Carr. However, if this is an inopportune time, I shall speak with him later," said Mr. Bleasdell.

"No, no, now is fine. We were just finishing up with our business," answered Reverend Worcester. "I shall take my leave. Good day, Mr. Bleasdell, Mr. Carr."

Mr. Bleasdell and Mr. Carr had been friendly acquaintances ever since their first meeting. Mr. Bleasdell began by explaining to Mr. Carr many things pertaining to Christopher's life and experiences. He expressed a hope that he might have use for him in the ferry service. He concluded the conversation by telling him, "He is an exceptionally honest and industrious young man."

"Mr. Bleasdell, it appears that I would do well to become acquainted with this Christopher Osgood. Furthermore, I may, indeed, have use for him on the island," replied Mr. Carr, fully confident in Mr. Bleasdell's recommendation.

"There is another matter I should like to discuss with you regarding the Freeman's Oath. Will you consider fulfilling this obligation during the next quarterly court session? Once completed, any barriers for me in recommending you for the board of selectmen shall be removed. I have long held the opinion that it would be a good thing for the town if you were to hold a seat on the board," expressed Mr. Carr.

"I am honored by your wish to recommend me," maintained Mr. Bleasdell. "I had intended to take it long before now. Thus, I shall attend the next quarterly session at Ipswich to fulfill my obligation."

"Perhaps I shall accompany you to Ipswich for the purpose of meeting with Christopher Osgood," suggested Mr. Carr.

"That is an excellent proposal, but I have kept you too long," replied Mr. Bleasdell. "We shall soon confirm our plans to travel to Ipswich."

"Agreed, and thank you for recommending Christopher to me," replied Mr. Carr.

Mr. Bleasdell was met by Mr. Foster, once again, as he was returning home. "Mr. Foster, I believe there is a conspiracy between you and Mr. Carr to get me on the board of selectmen," he said with a chuckle.

"Who me?" laughed Morris. "I shall own to it. I suggested you as a candidate for selectmen. I believe that this town deserves a good start with dependable men leading it. You, Mr. Bleasdell, are one of those very men of whom I speak. Though I have held only a short acquaintance with you, I am convinced that you are also a man of excellent character. What is more, my wife and I are visited regularly by a little songbird who is always singing the praises of Mr. Ralph Bleasdell and his good wife, Elizabeth."

"Madeline is a great friend and rather like a daughter to us, but at times, a little too generous with her compliments," he replied. "I can only hope to live up to such a reputation."

Chapter 7

The "Oath"/Accusations Refuted

The Ipswich County Court was holding its quarterly session as Mr. Bleasdell and Mr. Carr were arriving. It was not long before Mr. Bleasdell had taken his "Oath of a Freeman," and they were making their way out of the court. The other business that they had in mind to attend to was for Mr. Carr and Christopher Osgood to become acquainted.

Christopher was uninformed of their arrival in town and was taken quite by surprise upon seeing Mr. Bleasdell standing at his door. "Mr. Bleasdell, what are you doing here?" asked Christopher, with great excitement while grasping Mr. Bleasdell's shoulders and shaking him half out of his boots.

"Christopher, I have good news!" he exclaimed as he shuffled Mr. Carr up to shake hands. "This is Mr. George Carr of Carr's Island."

"I am pleased to finally make your acquaintance. This gentleman has nothing but the highest praise for you," said Mr. Carr as he motioned to Mr. Bleasdell. "I am developing a ferry service between Newbury, Carr's Island, and Colechester, and I am still in need of additional men to assist me in this vast undertaking. We have also begun building vessels to convey the town's staves to the West Indies. Have you any interest in coming to Colechester to work?"

"Indeed I do!" exclaimed Christopher, with excitement. "I have been in prayer about it from the time when Mr. Bleasdell had occasion on his last visit to share with me the possibility of working for you. I should like for you and Mr. Bleasdell to lodge here tonight. Perhaps we can discuss it further. Come in and make yourself at home."

***

As the three men were saying their goodbyes the following morning, Mr. Carr said, "Come as soon as you have everything settled. I have accommodations for you upon your arrival to the island."

"Very well. I am much obliged," replied Christopher, assuring Mr. Carr that he would see him within a fortnight.

With that, Mr. Bleasdell and Mr. Carr set off for home. They traveled by way of the ocean around Plum Island on in to Colechester.

Once there, Mr. Carr remarked, "Mr. Bleasdell, as soon as I can get the ferry up and running, there will be a more direct route to travel between Ipswich and Colechester."

Mr. Bleasdell smiled and nodded in agreement.

***

Elizabeth and Mr. Bleasdell embraced each other the moment he arrived while Henry stood between them bellowing, "What about me!" to which his father and mother gave a loud chuckle.

Mr. Bleasdell scooped him up, squeezed him tight, and asked, "Did you miss me, little man? I have not been gone very long. I am sure that you and Madeline have been far too busy with your own adventures to think of me."

Madeline, not wanting to appear too anxious, waited a while before inquiring, "Did you call on Christopher while you were in Ipswich?"

Mr. Bleasdell, desiring to use discretion, gave a halfhearted response, "Certainly. I would not visit Ipswich without stopping in to see Christopher."

Hoping for more information, Madeline ventured another question. "And was he in good health?"

Mr. Bleasdell answered, "Oh, just fine, just fine."

It was at this point in the conversation that Elizabeth sensed Madeline's frustration at the lack of information she gleaned from Mr. Bleasdell. "Mr. Bleasdell," said Elizabeth, in a stern voice but playful expression on her face, "tell Madeline all that you have learned regarding Christopher."

Madeline, though happy she might finally learn more, was a little embarrassed that she had been so obvious.

Desiring a way out of answering any more questions, Mr. Bleasdell decided he would do well to excuse himself and go out of doors before he divulged too much. "Well, that is about all I know, dear," he stated as he got up to leave.

***

A few days had passed when Mr. Foster came by to inform Mr. Bleasdell of his confirmation, by general consent, to the board of selectmen.

"This is an awesome responsibility. May God grant me the wisdom to know His will as I exercise my duties. I am obliged to you for coming by to inform me of the decision."

"Well, I have other news, the nature of which is serious," said Mr. Foster, with a grim look on his face. "I dislike having to inform you of this so soon after your confirmation, but it cannot be avoided. Just as you feared, Jarret Ormsby and a few others have brought accusations against Reverend Worcester. They are charging him with embracing antinomian beliefs and are requesting that we discharge him from his duties."

"Heaven help us!" exclaimed Mr. Bleasdell as he sat down on a log. "I was afraid of this."

"I must say that you displayed great insight regarding this situation. I am aware that this is extremely short notice, but the meeting regarding this situation is tonight," said Mr. Foster.

"I shall be in attendance," assured Mr. Bleasdell.

The meeting was about to begin when Jarret demanded that he be allowed to speak. After the moderator, Mr. Carr, acknowledged him, he commenced with his accusations:

> We are all aware of the banishment and excommunication of one Anne Hutchinson for her antinomian views. I am of the opinion that Reverend Worcester shares her beliefs. Are we going to allow such heretical notions to permeate our town just as the General Court has granted us incorporated status? To do so would jeopardize our standing in the Colony. If anyone has any doubt that what I have said is true, we need no further proof than that of his own words put forth in his speech at the last meeting of the selectmen. As you may recall, he spoke of doing away with the works by which we adhere to the moral law.

As Jarret concluded his discourse, the moderator inquired, "Is there anyone who would speak in defense of Reverend Nicolas Worcester?"

Mr. Morris Foster stood up to speak; after which, the moderator instructed him to come to the podium. He argued:

> Jarret would have us believe that upon hearing Reverend Worcester's speech, one may only come away with a single conclusion. Let me say that I emphatically disagree with Jarret Ormsby's analysis of the aforementioned speech. In as much as Reverend Worcester made no mention of a moral law, he could not have been

aligning himself with the view that we are not required by God to observe a moral law. More accurately, it should be concluded that he was simply putting forth the biblical view of salvation and that it is not acquired by good works. It was his desire that we understand that good works should be a testament to our salvation, not a means by which it may be achieved. Furthermore, it is my opinion that Jarret Ormsby may have had a vindictive motive for bringing this charge. I happened upon a confrontation between Jarret and Reverend Worcester, quite by accident, in which Jarret was receiving a verbal chastisement for displaying improper behavior toward the ladies of our town. After which, Jarret has chosen to be absent from our Sunday services. I do not make a practice of making such a thing public, but the character of our beloved reverend is being called in to question. For this reason, I believe that all matters pertinent to the situation should be divulged at this time.

A strange silence fell over the room as Mr. Foster concluded with his assessment of the situation.

"Thank you, Mr. Foster. Is there anyone else who would speak?" asked the moderator.

The meeting continued for another hour with both sides of the argument having representation. Mr. Carr, at last, called the meeting to a vote. After which, the tally came out in favor of Reverend Nicolas Worcester.

Upon hearing the results of the vote, Jarret stomped out of the meetinghouse in disgrace, as his secret chastisement had been exposed, and he had failed at his attempt to be rid of Reverend Worcester.

Mr. Bleasdell, Mr. Foster, and Mr. Carr remained a while as the others exited the meeting.

"Mr. Foster, I am obliged to you for speaking up. I believe that what you expressed turned the tide in the reverend's favor," said Mr. Carr.

"I simply communicated what I know to be true. However, I regret having to expose Jarret in such a public way," he replied, in an apologetic tone.

"Having been absent from the meeting in question, I could make no defense so I quietly entreated the Lord on Reverend Worcester's behalf," informed Mr. Bleasdell.

"As moderator, it is my duty to deliver the good news to Reverend Worcester. I would welcome the company if either of you should desire to come along," said Mr. Carr.

"I thank you but I must decline, as I am expected at home," replied Mr. Bleasdell, with Mr. Foster nodding in agreement.

"Very well," replied Mr. Carr. "However, there is another matter I wish to discuss with you regarding a trip to Salem, but I shall wait for a more convenient time."

***

Early the next morning, Jarret spied Madeline proceeding toward Emma's house. Desiring not to draw attention to himself, he waited around the side of his house for her departure from the Foster's home.

While he waited, he thought, *I need to make known to her that she has become the object of my affections before she is made aware of what was disclosed in last night's meeting regarding my chastisement. If at a later point in time it becomes known to her, I will simply claim it to be a vicious rumor.*

By and by, he observed Madeline strolling past his home; thus, he quickly made his way in her direction. "Good day to you, Miss Maddie, and how are you this fine day?"

She answered, "I am fine, Jarret Ormsby, but I cannot speak with you now as I have long been expected at home."

"As you wish. I shall wait until tomorrow to come calling," replied Jarret.

"Well, ah . . . I have to work with Henry on his studies tomorrow. It would not be a good day to call," Madeline called over her shoulder as she made a hasty escape.

Furious that he had been evaded, Jarret thought, *I shall not continue to be put off.*

Chapter 8

Adventures on Carr's Island/An Unexpected Meeting/The Misunderstanding

Mrs. Bridget Dudly and Madeline met early one morning for a day of adventure and exploring on Carr's Island. "Madeline, are you ready to be off?" inquired Bridget excitedly as she entered the door to the Bleasdell's home.

"Elizabeth, are you sure that you can do without me today?" asked Madeline, with a twinge of guilt in her voice.

"Madeline, you and Bridget go and have a good time. You deserve a day to yourselves," said Elizabeth, with an encouraging smile.

"Very well," replied Madeline as she and Bridget departed.

"Be careful," called Elizabeth after her.

Bridget, scarcely able to contain her excitement, explained to Madeline that her husband, John, had arranged for them to take a canoe across to the island. "His friend, Charles Banister, negotiated a good trade with an Indian in which he acquired a canoe. Mr. Carr is regularly carried out by Charles to and from the island. Are you aware that Mr. Carr is going to start a ferry service for the residents of Colechester and the surrounding towns?"

"No, I have not heard of it until now," replied Madeline joyfully. "But that will be wonderful. It will be much easier to travel across the river and then over land to Ipswich."

"Ipswich, why Ipswich of all places?" asked Bridget, with a quizzical look on her face.

"Oh, I was just observing that travel, to anywhere, will be much easier," said Madeline unconvincingly.

Noticing Madeline's change in demeanor, Bridget was curious as to why she should desire to travel to Ipswich.

Changing the subject, Madeline remarked, "Bridget, you should try and remember that our town is now called Salisbury."

"Oh, I know, Madeline. I am simply not as yet accustomed to the change. Why did they have to go and change the name anyway? What was wrong with Colechester, may I ask?"

Charles was patiently waiting as the two young friends reached the Merrimac. "Good day, ladies. Are you prepared to be conveyed to Carr's Island?"

"Indeed we are," replied Bridget with glee.

Charles gently assisted the young ladies into the canoe, and they were off to the island. Bridget conversed with Charles about the island as Madeline look fixedly off in the distance as though she were miles away. As it was a short distance, it seemed no sooner had they stepped into the canoe that it was time to disembark onto the island. With a wave to Charles, and a promise to be back for the return trip before sunset, the friends were off on their expedition.

***

Meanwhile, at the Bleasdell homestead, Elizabeth was beginning to wonder why Mr. Bleasdell seemed so giddy. *He does not seem a bit concerned with what the girls might encounter on that island*, she thought. However, just as she was about to ask him about it, he decided to let her in on his little secret.

"Elizabeth, I have news. Mr. Carr is starting a ferry service. On my last trip to Ipswich, I had the occasion to introduce Mr. Carr to Christopher. Upon my recommendation and his own observations of Christopher's merit, Mr. Carr has asked Christopher to come and work for him. Is that not good news?" inquired Mr. Bleasdell, grinning from ear to ear.

"I knew you were up to something," squealed Elizabeth with delight. "Do you suppose that Christopher is already out on the island?"

"I cannot say, but I have been informed that there are plenty of men working out there to watch out over our two young friends."

"Now I understand why you appeared so unconcerned," she said, with a smile.

"Elizabeth," said Mr. Bleasdell, "I have another bit of news. Mr. Carr has briefly spoken to me of a trip to Salem. I believe it is his intention that Mr. Foster and I accompany him."

"When is the trip to take place?"

"I do not, yet, have any of the particulars. However, I am reasonably sure that there shall be sufficient time to prepare for my departure."

"I hope you will not be gone for long," replied Elizabeth.

"With all that Mr. Carr is involved with here in town, he shall not wish to be away for too long," replied Mr. Bleasdell.

"I do hope that Madeline enjoys her day with Bridget, for with you off on another trip, I cannot say when she might have another opportunity to take a day for herself," said Elizabeth.

***

With fall vastly underway, Carr's Island appeared clothed with the radiant colors of red, yellow, orange, and green. Enraptured by the cascading leaves that were all around her, Madeline began spinning round and round.

Bridget crept slowly over to Madeline, and whispered, "Be still; I hear something coming from behind us." The two ladies stood grasping each other's hand unsure of what to do. Just then, Jarret Ormsby came strolling out of the woods.

"Well, bless my soul, my two favorite ladies. Good afternoon, Maddie, Bridget. What are you doing out here all alone?"

"We are not alone. Can you not see that there are two of us," retorted Madeline. "You are the one who has come alone."

"Oh, I see," said Jarret, chuckling at her response.

"And what may I ask are you doing out here? You are aware, are you not, that this is Mr. Carr's island?" inquired Madeline.

"I am indeed, and may I inquire after your reason for trespassing on Mr. Carr's island," replied Jarret.

"Mr. Bleasdell requested permission on our behalf," declared Madeline.

"In any case, Jarret, you may return to whatever it was that you were doing," muttered Bridget, anxious to be done with the conversation.

"I ought to stay and be your protector," quipped Jarret. "There may well be Indians or wild animals about."

"No need," replied Madeline, as they turned to leave.

Bridget and Madeline strolled on ahead hoping to be out of the sight of Jarret.

"I have never been able to muster a good opinion of that man from the moment that I became acquainted with him," remarked Madeline. "He is simply too presumptuous where women are concerned."

For a second time, the young ladies could hear someone approaching. "It must be Jarret again," said Bridget, with disgust.

"We would do well to be out of sight until we know for sure," whispered Madeline.

Stepping behind a large tree, the two friends quietly waited. At last, two men came sauntering past completely unaware of the ladies' presence. Madeline and Bridget did not make a move until the men were out of sight.

"There surely are a lot more people out here than I had expected to see today," said Bridget, as she stepped out from behind the tree.

"Indeed there are," replied Madeline.

Strolling along further down the trail, Madeline and Bridget came upon a modest saltbox style home, which they supposed belonged to Mr. Carr. They were quite surprised to find that there were several men roaming about the grounds.

A couple of the men happened to notice Madeline and Bridget as they were approaching. "How do you do, ladies? I am Cornelius Tucker. We had been informed there might be some visitors today. Are you enjoying the island?" asked the young gentleman.

"We are!" the pair exclaimed in unison.

"What are you all doing out here on the island?" asked Madeline.

"Mr. Carr has employed us to help him with the implementation of a ferry service," Cornelius replied.

"Oh, Bridget just informed of the ferry. However, I did not realize it would require so many men," replied Madeline.

"Yes, well, we are also working with him to build ships for exportation to the West Indies."

"Well, we better be on our way. It was nice to have met you, Cornelius."

"And you," he replied as he turned to go.

Madeline and Bridget wandered around the grounds for hours, thoroughly enjoying the day, before proceeding down the trail toward the spot on the river where they were to meet Charles.

"Bridget, let us go down to the edge of the water and skip a few stones before we leave the island," suggested Madeline.

"Madeline, whatever do you mean?"

"Just follow my example. Look for flat rocks such as this one," she said as she demonstrated a skip.

Before long, Bridget was as skilled at skipping stones as Madeline.

"Bridget," said Madeline, "you are as good a friend as I have ever known."

"Thank you, Madeline. My feelings are similar," said Bridget, with a smile. "This has been simply a wonderful day."

"It is time to make our way to where we shall meet Charles Banister," said Madeline, with a sigh.

"I wish this day would never end," remarked Bridget.

Just as they were starting back, the two men who had passed by earlier were heading their way.

There is something strangely familiar about the tall one, thought Madeline. "Bridget," said Madeline, "it is too late to hide this time, as the men are fast approaching. Besides, I am sure they are only Mr. Carr's men."

The closer they came the more Madeline was beginning to think that she recognized one of them. "But it could not be," she reasoned aloud. "He is in Ipswich."

"Who is in Ipswich," inquired Bridget.

As Mr. Carr and Christopher came into full view, Madeline blurted out loudly, "Christopher, is that you?"

Christopher, realizing that it was Maddie, came running toward her. "Maddie, what are you doing here?" he asked, while grasping her by the hand.

"I . . . oh excuse me," said Maddie. "Christopher Osgood, this is my good friend Mrs. Bridget Dudly."

"Good afternoon, ladies," said Mr. Carr. "I am delighted that you were able to come out for a visit. Have you been enjoying the day?"

"We have," chuckled Bridget, realizing that she and Mr. Carr were the only two involved in the conversation.

"Oh, I am sorry, Mr. Carr," said Christopher at last. "This is my good friend, Madeline Pike. We came over on the *Angel* together. We have not seen each other since she moved here with the Bleasdells."

"I am pleased to make your acquaintance, though I am sure I must have seen you about town," replied Mr. Carr.

After observing the group from a distance, Jarret strolled up and insinuated himself into the conversation. "Well then, this is quite the gathering," he said, with a scowl after taking notice of Maddie and Christopher's familiarity with each other. "It's obvious that the two of you are acquainted with each other by the way you are holding each other's hand."

Realizing the uneasiness of the situation, Mr. Carr spoke up. "What brings you out to my island, Jarret?"

"Simply having a look around," replied Jarret, as he inched his way closer to Maddie.

Christopher, sizing up the situation, let go of Maddie's hand and moved back beside Mr. Carr; at which time, it became evident to the ladies that Christopher had misunderstood and now believed that there must be something between Maddie and Jarret.

"We must be going now," said Christopher, glancing over at Maddie and Jarret. "It was great to see you again, Maddie. Please give my regards to the Bleasdells," he said somberly.

Maddie was too befuddled to respond.

"Enjoy the rest of the day," said Mr. Carr, as he and Christopher went on their way.

Bridget glanced over at Maddie, uncertain of what to say.

Jarret felt victorious with the knowledge that he had run off Christopher as a suitor for Maddie. "Well, come on, ladies," said Jarret, "I shall accompany you back to the canoe."

"No thank you," snapped Madeline, in a dejected voice. "We can make it back on our own."

"It really is not a problem, as I am heading in that direction," demanded Jarret.

This time, Bridget spoke up. "We are fine on our own. Goodbye Jarret."

After coming to the realization that he was not getting anywhere by insisting that he accompany the ladies, Jarret took his leave.

Madeline and Bridget, for the moment, were finally rid of Jarret. Bridget decided to take this opportunity to inquire about Christopher. However, before she could get a word out, Madeline began to weep.

"I knew there was something between the two of you, but Jarret ruined it, did he not?" inquired Bridget. "He was obviously attempting to paint a picture for Christopher that there was something between you."

"Oh, Bridget, I have to tell someone," sobbed Madeline. "I have known Christopher ever since our voyage over from England. I lost my husband at sea about four weeks into our journey. When we finally reached Pemaquid, the ship broke up in a terrible hurricane."

"Yes, I am aware of all of that," Bridget replied gently.

"Christopher lost his wife and son in that shipwreck. After failing to save his family, he was the one who rescued me. After that, I lived with the Bleasdells in Ipswich before moving here. I never even had the opportunity to say goodbye to him the day we left."

"So this is the reason for your excitement about the ferry and your mention of the distance to Ipswich," replied Bridget.

"Yes, Bridget. I have endeavored for some time not to allow myself to have feelings for him, but to no avail."

"Why must you deny your feelings?" demanded Bridget. "You are no longer married, and from what you have said neither is he."

"I just cannot. It would not be right," replied Madeline.

"Though I never knew your husband, I suspect that he would have desired for you to be happy. Furthermore, it is too late for any attempt at stifling your feelings, as it is apparent that he shares them. Oh, I could just kick that Jarret," said Bridget, angrily. "And another thing, how did Jarret know about the canoe and that it would be waiting for us precisely at this time?"

"That is an excellent question," said Madeline angrily.

"I am going to ask Charles about it when we see him," said Bridget.

On the return trip, Bridget inquired of Charles as to whether or not he had seen Jarret Ormsby lately. "We had a chance meeting with him on the island today," she explained.

"Yes, of course you did," replied Charles. "He was in town the day John and I were setting up your trips to and from Carr's Island. He stated at that time that it was his wish for me to make a second trip in which I would convey him there as well. He was willing to pay for the service so I was obliged to say yes. In fact, he is waiting there now for me to fetch him."

Things were finally beginning to make sense to Madeline and Bridget. "Jarret is a most underhanded sort of man," proclaimed Bridget. "Do not worry, Madeline, we will find a way to let Christopher know that there is nothing whatsoever between you and Jarret."

Chapter 9

Revelations and New Accusations Regarding the Pirate "Dixie Bull"

Elizabeth and Mr. Bleasdell could not help but notice that Madeline seemed very troubled when she and Bridget returned home from the island.

"Madeline, is there anything amiss with you?" asked Elizabeth.

"Jarret!" exclaimed Bridget, answering for her. "I must take my leave now, but I shall be back tomorrow."

Mr. Bleasdell observed that Madeline had been crying. "If that Jarret has done anything to upset you, I am going to—. Just then, Mr. Bleasdell noticed that Henry was listening intently.

Madeline spoke up, "Mr. Bleasdell, when Henry retires for the night, I shall make known to you and Elizabeth the story in its entirety."

After putting Henry to bed, Elizabeth hurried over to where Madeline and Mr. Bleasdell were reclining. "We are desirous to hear your account of the day's events."

"Bridget made us aware of the fact that it has to do with the despicable Jarret Ormsby," growled Mr. Bleasdell.

"You are right on that account," Madeline mumbled in a somber voice. "The story begins with Christopher, whom I had the unexpected occasion to be in the company of today."

Mr. Bleasdell and Elizabeth were surprised by her downcast manner regarding Christopher. They had always known her to be joyful at the mention of his name.

"What has this to do with Christopher?" inquired Mr. Bleasdell.

"As I have already mentioned, Bridget and I were surprised to discover Christopher on the island today. He was so stunned to see me that while we were speaking, he had innocently taken hold of my hand. Jarret happened along as we were conversing; at which point, he felt compelled to comment that Christopher had hold of my hand. As he was speaking, he positioned himself beside me," explained Madeline as she began to sob again. "It was obvious, by the way Christopher quickly let go of my hand and moved away from me, that he had the mistaken impression that Jarret and I are courting."

"Which I am confident is precisely what Jarret intended," declared Mr. Bleasdell.

"I share your opinion, but even knowing how he is, I did not have time to react," cried Madeline. "Everything just happened so quickly."

"Madeline, there is no need to be so concerned. I shall speak to Christopher and make the truth known just as soon as I return from Salem," assured Mr. Bleasdell, with a smile.

"You will? Oh thank you," cried Madeline. "But as there is no understanding between us with regard to any future together, you must not let on that I made such a fuss. No doubt, you and Elizabeth are aware of my feelings for him after my dreadful display."

"We believed it to be so for a long time," replied Elizabeth.

"Though I have struggled in vain to veil my affections for him, I would not have them declared to Christopher," said Madeline.

"It is not for us to make such a declaration regarding something so personal to you," replied Elizabeth.

"When I speak to Christopher, regarding Jarret, I shall be careful not to disclose anything," assured Mr. Bleasdell.

"Did you know that Christopher was coming to Salisbury?" inquired Madeline.

"Yes, though the timing of which was uncertain; however, I had planned to inform you once I was confident that he was coming," replied Mr. Bleasdell. "The truth of the matter is that Mr. Carr and I met with him on our last trip to Ipswich. I had inquired of Mr. Carr whether or not he was in need of additional men for his ferry service. After telling him about Christopher, he desired to meet with him with the intention of asking him to come and work for him. Christopher seemed so forlorn the times I saw him after we had left Ipswich; it was my belief that he would welcome such an offer. After all, for him we are the nearest thing to a family. He has even said as much."

"I am pleased that you asked him to come," replied Madeline.

***

The next day, Mr. Carr, Mr. Foster, and Mr. Bleasdell met together to discuss their trip to Salem.

"What is this all about," inquired Mr. Bleasdell.

"Besides the two of you, only myself, the clerk, and one other person were present to hear what I am about to tell you. It is beyond comprehension!" exclaimed Mr. Carr.

"Let me assure you that whatever you tell us shall be held in the strictest confidence," said Mr. Bleasdell.

"Jarret Ormsby has made another of his accusations; however, this time he has levied it against Christopher Osgood."

"What possible accusation could he make against him?" asked Mr. Bleasdell angrily.

"It would be laughable if it were not for the possibility of the serious repercussions against Christopher," replied Mr. Carr. With a heavy sigh, he began his account of the accusations. "Jarret has made the claim that Christopher Osgood is one 'Dixie Bull,' the pirate."

"What?" snapped Mr. Bleasdell.

"Hold on now. I shall explain all," replied Mr. Carr. "Let me continue. When asked for the basis of this claim, he asserted that Christopher came from Pemaquid, which he claims is a known conquest of Dixie Bull's. He went on to say that there are no accounts of him anywhere subsequent to the Pemaquid incident."

"This is absurd," said Mr. Foster crossly.

"Indeed it is, but there is more. He further contends that the infamous pirate's description corresponds with that of Christopher. Jarret believes he can stand uncontested on this owing to the fact that not many have ever been acquainted with Dixie Bull."

"You cannot be in earnest. This is just too ridiculous. I cannot believe that anyone would lend credence to such an assertion!" exclaimed Mr. Bleasdell.

"Jarret has acquired various allies in this town. Some of whom are of consequence that we would do well not to underestimate," warned Mr. Carr.

"I was not aware of his friendship with any of the men in the town. However, he may very well have beguiled some of the ladies with his charm," replied Mr. Bleasdell.

"Indeed, and some of them have influential husbands who are easily swayed by their wives' opinions," replied Mr. Carr.

"Nevertheless, I am well acquainted with Christopher and his family considering that we came over together from England. Therefore, I can very well offer testimony that he is not Dixie Bull," insisted Mr. Bleasdell.

"I have already declared as much to Jarret, but he would have none of it. He accused you of having a bias where Christopher is concerned, given that you are friends. Therefore, he deems your testimony to be unreliable," replied Mr. Carr.

"You have yet to inform us of what this all has to do with traveling to Salem," said Mr. Foster.

"I am coming to that part," replied Mr. Carr. "My original plans for travel to Salem, in which I had thought to include the two of you, were for town business. However, I have set all of that aside for now to take care of this matter. I have been informed by the clerk that there is a man in Salem, one Thomas Corbitt, who survived the attack of Dixie Bull on Pemaquid. Moreover, he has seen him face to face; thus, he is familiar with his description. Perhaps if we might obtain an affidavit, signed by Thomas Corbitt, in which he gives the pirate's description, Christopher might well be exonerated."

"Has Christopher been made aware of the accusations that have been levied against him?" asked Mr. Bleasdell.

"I desire, if possible, to handle this matter ourselves and not involve Christopher. He need not be anxious of the outcome as long as he remains uninformed," replied Mr. Carr.

"I am in full agreement with your decision, as Christopher has already suffered much with the loss of his family," replied Mr. Bleasdell. "Mr. Carr, I believe that I know Jarret's reason for doing such a dreadful thing to Christopher."

"After observing all that took place on the island the day that Jarret met up with Christopher, Madeline, Bridget, and me, it has become rather obvious to me as well. He has designs on Madeline and desires to have Christopher out of the way," replied Mr. Carr.

"Where Jarret is concerned, we are all going to have to be on guard. The sooner we quietly lay this matter to rest the better!" exclaimed Mr. Foster. "We must not reveal to anyone, other than our families, our plans to meet with Thomas Corbitt, or Jarret may learn of it."

"Mr. Foster, I share your opinion. Therefore, I have asked the other selectmen who are acquainted with the situation not to make it known until we return," explained Mr. Carr. "So, if there is no objection, it is my desire that we set off for Salem tomorrow morning."

Mr. Bleasdell returned home to explain everything that had taken place to Elizabeth and Madeline.

"We must not speak of this to anyone," warned Mr. Bleasdell.

"To be sure, we shall keep silent," responded Elizabeth, with Madeline in agreement.

Early the next morning, the three men set off for the town of Salem, while Madeline and Elizabeth were left behind to beseech the Lord for a successful trip. Once again, Mr. Bleasdell was aboard Captain Barnes' shallop. Before too long, they disembarked in Salem, as it was a reasonably short jaunt from Salisbury.

"Mr. Carr, how will you find Thomas Corbitt?" asked Mr. Foster.

"I have been informed that he may be working at the glass works factory. Captain Barnes is familiar with the place and has graciously offered to direct us," replied Mr. Carr.

Captain Barnes chimed in, "It is just down the road a piece. I shall be happy to conduct you to him in the morning."

The men settled in at the local ordinary for the night. Early the next morning, after a restless night for one and all, they set off to meet up with Captain Barnes.

"Good morning," said Captain Barnes. "Are we ready to search out Thomas Corbitt?"

"Lead the way," replied Mr. Foster.

"It is an easy distance," informed Captain Barnes.

Within a short time, the glass factory was in view and the men began discussing what they were going to say to Mr. Corbitt.

"Mr. Carr, as you are the one with the firsthand information concerning the accusation, you ought to be the one to speak first to Mr. Corbitt," explained Mr. Bleasdell.

"Perhaps you are right," replied Mr. Carr. "However, you may need to follow up, as you have held the longest acquaintance with Christopher and can verify the time of his arrival from England."

"To be sure, Mr. Carr," replied Mr. Bleasdell.

As the three men approached the door to the factory, it opened from the inside. "Good morning. I am the foreman here," said an elderly man with a cheerful disposition. "What can I do for you?"

"We wish to speak with a man by the name of Thomas Corbitt," replied Mr. Carr. "We do not wish to disturb you, but we have an urgent matter to discuss with him."

"I shall send someone straight away to fetch him," replied the foreman.

"I hope we find him to be sympathetic to Christopher's plight," said Mr. Foster, in a skeptical tone. "He may not wish to become involved."

Just then, Thomas Corbitt, with a look of concern, came into the room where they were waiting. "What has happened?" he asked with alarm. "Has there been an injury?"

"No, no. I am sorry to have distressed you," replied Mr. Carr, apologetically. "It is a matter of urgency, but only to us. Let me explain, ah, but first let me introduce myself and my companions. I am Mr. George Carr; this is Mr. Ralph Bleasdell, and Mr. Morris Foster," he said, gesturing to the others. "We have come from Salisbury after having been informed that you were once a resident of Pemaquid."

"Indeed I was," replied Thomas, "but what is this regarding?"

"Let me start at the beginning," said Mr. Carr, with a heavy sigh. "We have a man in our town who is a bit of a troublemaker. When it suits him, he has on occasion made accusations against members of our town."

Mr. Bleasdell interrupted, "The accusations are by no means ordinary; in fact, they are very outlandish in nature. My apologies, Mr. Carr, but I felt the need to prepare him for what you are about to disclose."

By now, Thomas was wide eyed with anticipation. "All right, but what has this to do with me and Pemaquid?"

"Thomas," replied Mr. Carr, "the man in question has levied an accusation against a very fine young man. He is alleging that the pirate, Dixie Bull, and Christopher Osgood are one and the same."

"What? Is this true? He has accused another man of being Dixie Bull?" asked Thomas in utter shock. "Is he able to substantiate such a claim?"

"The entire basis for Jarret Ormsby's allegation is that Christopher Osgood came from Pemaquid, and he alleges that he fits the pirate's description," replied Mr. Carr. "He did indeed come from Pemaquid; however, that his description corresponds with that of the pirate is yet to be determined."

"Before we continue, I must tell you about Christopher so that there will be no doubt in your mind as to the ridiculous nature of this accusation," asserted Mr. Bleasdell. "Most importantly, Christopher did not even arrive at Pemaquid until 1635 on the *Angel Gabriel*. I believe the attack took place in '32, did it not?"

"Indeed the year was 1632, and I am aware of the *Angel Gabriel*," said Thomas. "I was residing there at the time of that terrible shipwreck."

"Yes, and Christopher lost his wife and son in the wreck," explained Mr. Bleasdell. "I know this because I was a passenger on that voyage as well. They were such a wonderful young couple. At that point, he was only six and twenty, she but four and twenty, and their boy was scarcely three."

"There is one thing I must inquire after; did you speak the name 'Jarret Ormsby' as having been the accuser?" asked Thomas.

"Yes, that is his name," replied Mr. Carr.

"Before we continue, I must share some information with you regarding Jarret Ormsby," said Thomas.

"Are you acquainted with him?" asked Mr. Bleasdell.

"Indeed, he was living in this very town not long ago. I would not sully another man's reputation for the world, but in this case, I feel that I must. There was a young woman in this town who had been charged, a few of years back, with adultery. There had been talk of Jarret along with some other men who had often been seen in her company. It is only my opinion, but I believe that Jarret learned of the pending charges and fled the town, abandoning her to face the charges alone. That may well be when he showed up in your town," confided Thomas Corbitt.

"Alas, that surely sounds like Jarret," replied Mr. Foster.

Thomas continued, "What I thought not to disclose but now feel that I must is that the young woman was my niece. She was a sweet girl, married to an older gentleman, when she was seduced by some iniquitous men. It continues to be beyond my comprehension that she was found guilty whilst Jarret Ormsby and the others suffered no ill effects. She died of an illness soon after the trial. I believe it was simply too much for her to bear. I have told you all of this so that you may use this information, if necessary, in the defense of your friend."

"That is an astonishing story. Are you quite sure of the name of the man?" asked Mr. Foster.

"I am quite sure, as it is not a common name; I believe that they are one and the same. As you might well imagine, I have a great desire to put a stop to him as well. Therefore, what may I do to be of assistance?" asked Thomas, in a sincere voice.

"We were hoping, in view of the fact that you have come face to face with the pirate, you might sign an affidavit in which you provide a full description of him," replied Mr. Carr.

"Do you have something with which to document what I have to say?" asked Thomas.

"We are prepared to do so," replied Mr. Carr. "Mr. Foster will take down the account of your dealings with the pirate."

"To begin with," began Thomas, "I had the unhappy occasion to set eyes on one, Dixie Bull, at the time of his barbarous attack on Pemaquid in the year 1632. He sailed into the harbor and fired upon the settlement, causing much confusion and devastation. After which, he commenced with sacking the town, dispossessing us of our furs and victuals, and leaving us essentially destitute."

Thomas sighed as he recounted the troubling events, "We worked hard to restore our fortunes and rebuild our town. However, around the time of the wreck of which you speak, the French and English were disputing over the rights to the territory. I felt that as I had stayed following the infamous attack, this additional insult to the peace of the town left me and many others to seek out opportunity elsewhere. It was then that I came to Salem."

As they listened intently, Thomas continued, "As for the description of the pirate, you mentioned that Christopher is a young man, now but one and thirty. By all accounts, that is the chief discrepancy between the two, as the pirate is by this time considerably older. In addition, he was about medium in height with dark hair strewn with gray about the temples."

Upon completion of the affidavit in which the details regarding the pirate were set down, Thomas Corbitt signed it with the following declaration: "This is an exact account of my dealings with the pirate, Dixie Bull, signed Thomas Corbitt."

"We are indebted to you for your willingness to disclose such personal matters in the defense of our friend," replied Mr. Carr. "Please accept our condolences on the loss of your beloved niece."

"I believe that you have given enough information to vindicate Christopher, as you have made it clear that he is not only too young, he is too tall and the color of his hair is not the same," replied Mr. Bleasdell.

"I am happy to be of assistance," replied Thomas, with a smile. "From what you have told me about Christopher Osgood, I reason that he has had more than his share of suffering. Therefore, if you have need of any further proof, I would be pleased to appear in person."

"Thank you, but I hope it does not become necessary," replied Mr. Bleasdell. "With gratitude, we shall take leave of you now, as we must hasten our return to Salisbury."

"Well then, I shall say farewell and God be with you," replied Thomas as he turned to go.

As the three men returned to the shallop, they decided not to divulge the information with regard to Jarret and Thomas Corbitt's niece unless it became necessary.

"By your countenance, it is plain that you must have met with success," said Captain Barnes.

"Thomas was exceedingly accommodating in passing on to us the information that will be required if we are to lay this whole matter to rest," replied Mr. Carr.

"Let us set forward with all speed. There is no telling what kind of mischief Jarret may well be getting into!" exclaimed Mr. Foster.

Chapter 10

A Frenzied Town/Affidavit Arrives from Salem

Upon returning to town, Mr. Carr, Mr. Bleasdell, and Mr. Foster were deeply disturbed to find the whole town in an uproar, as Jarret had made his accusations known.

"It is essential that I find Christopher as soon as possible!" exclaimed Mr. Bleasdell. "There can be no doubt but that he has been informed of the accusations against him."

"Indeed, you must make haste. In the meantime, Mr. Foster and I shall call for a meeting of the selectmen to be held as soon as possible," replied Mr. Carr. "This nasty business has the potential of having grave consequences if it is not soon set right. I shall take leave of you now."

Mr. Bleasdell was pleased to find Charles Banister by the water's edge, for he had need of him to be conveyed to Carr's Island.

"Charles, it is essential that I be taken across to the island as quickly as possible!" exclaimed Mr. Bleasdell.

"Has this anything to do with the ludicrous rumors surrounding Christopher Osgood?" inquired Charles.

"Yes," replied Mr. Bleasdell, "and with the rumors spreading so far and wide, I have no doubt but that Christopher has been made aware of the accusations against him. It is, therefore, imperative that Christopher see the affidavit, of which I am in possession, wherein his innocence has been declared by an eyewitness who has come face to face with the dreadful pirate."

"That is sure to settle the matter," replied Charles. "Let us make haste for the island."

Upon their arrival to the island, Charles offered to help in the search for Christopher.

"Your assistance is most welcome," responded Mr. Bleasdell, in appreciation.

After a short time, the two men were relieved to have found Christopher. He greeted them somberly, as the whole Jarret business had been weighing heavily upon him. To ease Christopher's mind, Mr. Bleasdell took no time in sharing the good news.

"Christopher, I have just come from Salem with Mr. Carr and Mr. Foster, whereupon we met a man who has given us a written account of Dixie Bull, including a well-detailed description. Mr. Carr had been informed of the man by our town clerk and took no time in making arrangements for the three of us to set off for Salem."

"This is, indeed, good news," said Christopher, with relief. "I could scarcely believe that a man with whom I had only recently become acquainted, would attempt to stir up trouble for me. Moreover, I had been informed that you were away on business and that the day of your return was unknown. Thus, as there was not another person on the board of selectmen who could give testimony on my behalf, I have been expecting the constable to come at any moment."

"Mr. Carr is, at this very moment, calling for a meeting of the board. We must hasten back to town, as he will be awaiting our arrival," said Mr. Bleasdell.

Charles accompanied Christopher and Mr. Bleasdell back to town as a demonstration of his support.

Madeline and Elizabeth had not yet been informed of whether the trip to Salem had been a success. Furthermore, they were not aware of Mr. Bleasdell's return and imminent meeting with the board of selectmen.

After hearing of the unrest in town regarding Christopher, Madeline asked in disbelief, "Elizabeth, who would believe such a ridiculous story about Christopher?"

"I am of the opinion that with the assistance of a sufficient number of busybodies, Jarret has kindled such a flame as will not be easily quenched," replied Elizabeth. "However, if Mr. Bleasdell and the others are successful in their mission to Salem, Jarret may rue the day he made such an accusation."

Upon the arrival of Mr. Bleasdell, Christopher, and Charles to the meetinghouse, they found it to be so full of men that they could scarcely get in. About the outside of the building were scores of women, many of whom were the selectmen's wives with a desire to know what would become of the accused. Once it was made known that Christopher was in their midst, many of the townsfolk hurled insults at him. It was as if his guilt had already been firmly established.

"Gentlemen, this meeting will come to order," demanded Mr. Carr, as he motioned for everyone to sit down. "Anyone demonstrating a lack of respect for my position as the moderator will be removed from the building. As the accusations against Christopher Osgood originated with Jarret Ormsby, he will now stand and state them plainly before this body."

At that point, Jarret stood and addressed the board. "I believe Christopher Osgood and the pirate, Dixie Bull, to be one and the same."

"And what, may we ask, is the basis for such a claim?" inquired Mr. Carr.

"Well ah . . . well, he comes from Pemaquid, which is the last known location of the pirate," replied Jarret. "And his description agrees with that of Dixie Bull."

"Is that the entirety of your *supposed* evidence?" asked Mr. Carr.

"Indeed, as it is sufficiently compelling," Jarret retorted, with apparent agitation.

"Gentlemen," said Mr. Carr, "I, and two other witnesses, have just returned from Salem, whereupon we made the acquaintance of one Thomas Corbitt, an eyewitness of the events at Pemaquid during the dread pirate's infamous attack."

After hearing the name of Thomas Corbitt spoken, Jarret, with his mind racing, stared angrily frontward. He remembered that Thomas Corbitt was the uncle of a woman he had been involved with in Salem. *He must have made a full disclosure to Mr. Carr and the others,* he thought, as he began to, once again, listen to the conversation.

"I have in my hand an affidavit signed by the aforementioned, which includes a detailed account of his dealings with the pirate," said Mr. Carr confidently.

After Mr. Carr read the testimony, he requested that Christopher, Mr. Bleasdell, and Mr. Foster stand with him at the front of the meetinghouse. At that point, the four men stared sternly into Jarret's face in order to deter him from any further attempts at accusing Christopher. Jarret ascertained from their expressions that the information regarding the woman in Salem had most likely been disclosed, and that he would do well to drop the whole matter or live to regret it.

Mr. Carr declared, "An ample and reliable description of one, Dixie Bull, has now been read aloud. Fix your eyes on upon Christopher Osgood and judge for yourselves whether his appearance matches that of the pirate. It is my contention that Jarret Ormsby's accusations are wholly without foundation. If any man is to be accused of a vile thing, such as piracy, ought not there first to have been a collection of indisputable evidence rather than the flimsy sort to which we have been subjected?"

The meeting came to a close with the mood altered. Now in the eyes of most of the men, Jarret Ormsby had falsely accused Christopher Osgood. Additionally, as it turned out, having taken his side they had become willing accomplices in his folly. Thus, after the meeting, many of the selectmen's wives were rebuked for inciting their husbands against Christopher.

"It is highly unlikely that Jarret will again find such favor amongst the townsfolk," reasoned Mr. Bleasdell. "Furthermore, he deserves to be dealt with severely for his actions."

"Oh, I would not count on that, Mr. Bleasdell. Jarret has a charming way about him and will likely talk his way out of any disfavor," replied Mr. Foster.

"Well, Christopher, let us return to the island now that this unhappy mess has been put to rest," said Mr. Carr, with an attitude of contentment.

"Yes, but first allow me to say how grateful I am to all of you for your support during this trying time. You have been true and faithful friends," said Christopher, in all sincerity.

"I must return home as well, for Madeline and Elizabeth are sure to be anxious for news," said Mr. Bleasdell. "Christopher, you must come by for a visit."

"I shall, and very soon," replied Christopher, with a pleased expression upon his face.

Chapter 11

The Misunderstanding Abated

Early one day, Henry got it into his head to go down to the river and skip stones across its surface. He dearly loved the pastime from the time when Madeline had originally given him instruction. Madeline was happy to oblige him, as it was to her, also, a very agreeable amusement.

Christopher chose this particular day in which to come calling at the Bleasdell's home. Upon his arrival, he found Mr. Bleasdell working in the field.

"Good day to you," Christopher called out as he moved in his direction. "May I lend a hand?"

"Oh, it is good to see you, Christopher," said Mr. Bleasdell. "No, no, you must not. I daresay that Elizabeth would be disappointed if I kept you out here with me. Moreover, I am in need of a short rest."

"Good day to you, Christopher," said Elizabeth with delight, as the two men entered the house. "It is good of you to come. I trust that you will stay awhile. Madeline and Henry have gone off somewhere and would be sorely disappointed to have missed seeing you."

Christopher also felt quite disappointed that Maddie was not at home. He comforted himself with the thought that she might arrive before it was time for him to go.

"How is Maddie? I have not seen her ever since our chance encounter on the island. She was in the company of another young lady and Jarret Ormsby. I had not the faintest idea that meeting Jarret that day would lead to such trouble."

"Yes, all of that business with Jarret was deplorable. Our heart ached for you and what you were going through. Thank God it all turned out all right in the end. As for Madeline, I daresay you caught her quite by surprise that day. She had not been made aware you had moved to the island. She and her friend Bridget had been looking forward, for some time, to visiting the island when an opportunity finally came along for them to go. Madeline seemed very pleased to have discovered you out there," said Elizabeth.

"I was delighted to see her as well," replied Christopher, with a dejected expression.

Mr. Bleasdell, sensing Christopher's concern over Jarret and Madeline, said with a reassuring voice, "Yes, she talked of nothing else aside from her annoyance with Jarret. He seems to pop up at the most inopportune moments. He has been a bother to her ever since we arrived in this town. What is more, after all he has done to you, Madeline would not wish to ever be in his company again."

Mr. Bleasdell decided that it was best not to divulge too much, as Madeline had implored him not to make her feelings known to Christopher.

Christopher's mood improved a little upon hearing of Maddie's feelings toward Jarret. He knew in his heart that his friendship with Maddie would have been more important to her than to remain friends with Jarret Ormsby after all he had done. He began to wonder why he had even questioned Madeline's feelings. However, he thought it best not to go on with the conversation regarding Madeline, for fear of exposing his true feelings. Rather, once again, he determined to express his gratitude for Mr. Bleasdell's friendship.

"I am forever in your debt for what you have done for me with regard to Jarret's accusations. Only a true friend would have done so much."

"Christopher, I believe that you will find that you have many friends here in Salisbury. Mr. Carr and Mr. Foster, in particular, think very highly of you," replied Mr. Bleasdell. "Mr. Foster, just today, has informed me of the town's desire to offer you a land grant. I believe there are many who feel simply awful about what has taken place and wish to demonstrate their desire to make amends."

"It has been my wish to settle here, although, what has transpired of late has dampened that desire a bit," replied Christopher.

"Christopher, if you are willing to give the town another go, I believe that you shall be very happy here. Jarret is the only one who truly desired for you to leave; thus, he played on the fears of the whole town to accomplish his goal," said Elizabeth.

"No doubt you are right, and so I shall consider what you have said with regard to remaining in Salisbury. I have enjoyed this visit a great deal, but I must take my leave, as there is much yet to do today. Please convey my disappointment to Maddie and Henry at not finding them at home today," requested Christopher, who seemed in a happier mood than when he had arrived.

"Do take care of yourself, and come again soon," said Elizabeth.

Christopher nodded in agreement, as he rose to leave.

"I shall walk out with you," said Mr. Bleasdell.

With that, Christopher was off with a promise to return very soon. Mr. Bleasdell and Elizabeth each hoped, without having been too obvious, they had eased Christopher's concern over Madeline and Jarret. Though they doubted he could believe, if there had been anything between them, it would continue after Jarret's deplorable behavior.

Soon after Christopher had left, Madeline and Henry returned. Henry was bubbling over with excitement as he recounted the events of the afternoon. "My stones skipped at least four or five times. Madeline said that I am becoming an expert stone skipper."

"Indeed, you are quite the expert, Henry," giggled Madeline. "You are becoming much better at it than I."

Elizabeth and Mr. Bleasdell hesitated to tell Madeline that Christopher had come to call. They knew that she would be deeply disappointed to have missed him. However, once Henry was asleep, they decided to inform her of his visit.

"Madeline, we had a visitor today," said Elizabeth. "Christopher came to call."

"Oh, I wish I had been here. I have not seen him ever since that day on the island or his meeting with the selectmen. Did he make any inquiries about me?"

"Yes, he wanted to know how you were, and he was genuinely disappointed that you and Henry were not at home," answered Elizabeth.

"He did not seek after any information concerning Jarret and me?" asked Madeline. "He must not still believe that I would have anything to do with someone who had treated him so abominably."

"He did not question us regarding you and Jarret; however, he did mention that he had seen you and Bridget with him on the island," replied Elizabeth.

"Oh, and were you able to discover whether he had the wrong idea about Jarret?"

"We could not be sure; however, his countenance was rather downcast," replied Elizabeth. "We did tell him that you seemed happy and surprised to see him that day. We also mentioned your annoyance at having seen Jarret there. In addition, Mr. Bleasdell informed him of the bother Jarret is to you in general, but we dared not speak anything more on the subject, for fear of divulging more than we ought," explained Elizabeth.

"Madeline, I did not have the opportunity to explain fully about Jarret, but I believe that he left with a better opinion than the one with which he came," said Mr. Bleasdell.

"Oh, I am glad, then, that I was not here, as my presence would have hindered the conversation," said Madeline with relief. "As I desired, you were restrained, but he must have understood your meaning. How will I ever thank you? You are both such a blessing to me. I do not know what I would do without you."

"You are a blessing to us as well," replied Mr. Bleasdell with Elizabeth in agreement.

***

The following day, Madeline met up with Bridget in town on her way to Emma's house. "Good morning, Bridget, and how are you? I have not had the pleasure of your company in what seems like a very long time. I am on my way to call on Emma. Would you like to come along?"

"Yes, I would be delighted. We can talk on the way. Have you seen Christopher since that day on the island or the meeting of the board?" asked Bridget. "I have thought of nothing else than my poor dear friend's broken heart."

"You are a dear," said Madeline. "No, I have not seen him, but he has come to call at the Bleasdell's. In fact, he came just yesterday while Henry and I were down by the water skipping stones."

"So you were not there when he came?" inquired Bridget.

"No, but I have a good report to share. He inquired after me affording Mr. Bleasdell and Elizabeth an opportunity to inform him of my mood upon seeing him on the island, that I had been surprised and happy to see him. They went on to explain that I had been annoyed at finding Jarret there, but dared not to say very much more on the subject."

"How wonderful. They have declared just enough to set the matter straight without betraying your true feelings!" exclaimed Bridget. "You must have been very happy to find out what was said in your absence."

"I cannot deny that I was. And, though he continues to be unaware of my feelings for him, at least now he should not believe that my affections lie elsewhere," said Madeline, with a sigh.

"Do you not think that he must have known if there had been anything between you and Jarret, you would have ended it after what Jarret has done?" inquired Bridget.

"Yes, I had begun to believe that he must have realized I would never betray our friendship. Which, of course, did serve to relieve my worry a bit regarding his thoughts about Jarret and me," replied Madeline. "But I wanted to be sure that it was, indeed, clear to him."

"At any rate, what did you think about the ridiculous accusations that Jarret made against poor Christopher?" asked Bridget. "The moment I heard about it, I had no doubt but that Jarret was acting out of jealousy. I so wanted to talk with you, as I could not share my opinions with anyone else."

"The whole matter was so distressing," replied Madeline. "Elizabeth and I were aware that Mr. Bleasdell was going to Salem to obtain the testimony that, in the end, exonerated Christopher. However, we could not share the news with anyone, as Jarret might have learned of it. We were concerned that if Jarret had foreknowledge of the mission to seek the testimony of the man who had seen the pirate, he may have been able to find a way to discredit him, rendering his testimony worthless."

"Oh, I understand," replied Bridget. "You surely did the right thing."

Emma greeted Bridget and Madeline with a hug and a kiss. "Will you not sit down? It is so good to see you, my dear girls. And how have you been?"

"In light of the recent events, we have been tolerably well," replied Bridget.

"What has happened is precisely why I am so opposed to gossip," replied Emma, as she poured some tea. "This time, baseless accusations almost destroyed a young man."

"You are so right, Emma," replied Bridget, "and Christopher is such an amiable young man. It stirs the emotions to think about what he has gone through."

"You are very quiet, my dear," said Emma to Madeline.

"Emma, it has all been too much given that Christopher is a good friend. I became acquainted with him aboard the *Angel Gabriel*. In fact, he was the one who rescued me from the ocean the night the ship went down in a storm. It grieves me to think of what he must have suffered at the hands of Jarret Ormsby, and all of his false accusations. He has been treated cruelly and must wish he had never come to this town," uttered Madeline, in a somber voice.

"I am aware that you are acquainted with Christopher," replied Emma. "As you know, Mr. Foster accompanied Mr. Carr and Mr. Bleasdell on their mission to Salem. He has since informed me of the connection between you. Do not concern yourself any longer about Christopher, for there are many men in town who wish to make up to Christopher the wrongs that have been done to him. He shall find out soon enough that he has several friends here."

"Oh, I hope that you are right," replied Madeline, in a hopeful voice.

Bridget and Madeline felt more at ease as they visited with Emma. Her calm demeanor had always been a bit contagious. Though they were enjoying the day, the time came for the young ladies to take their leave.

"It was kind of you to allow us to drop in for a visit," said Madeline to Emma.

"Thank you for the tea," said Bridget, as they turned to leave.

"Come again, soon," said Emma, as she waved goodbye.

Chapter 12

Maddie Takes a Stand/All Is Well with Christopher

It was a beautiful Sunday morning when everyone eagerly flowed in to the new church for worship. On her way in, Madeline met up with Bridget and her husband, John.

"Good morning, Bridget. How are you on this beautiful morning?"

"Just fine, Madeline. Have you been informed of where you are to be seated?"

"No, but I am guessing by your expression, we are seated next to each other," replied Madeline, squeezing Bridget's hand. "Elizabeth and Mr. Bleasdell have already gone in. I was running a little slow this morning. I am so happy to be in your company, for I saw Jarret not far behind. Thus, I was attempting to make my way here as quickly as possible. I have not seen Christopher as yet; however, he may already be inside."

Bridget let go of John's arm, as they said their goodbyes until after the service. John hurried in to the side of the church, which was allocated for the men, as Bridget and Madeline took their seats in the women's section. Madeline's mind was racing as she tried, to no avail, to focus her attentions on Reverend Worcester's sermon.

I hope I have the opportunity to speak with Christopher after the service. I wonder if Jarret will again interfere. Surely, after what he has done, he could not believe he still had a possibility of winning my affections. Knowing the kind of man that he is, however, he would not allow anything to stand in his way. If he comes near to me, I shall simply walk away from him. Oh, I must focus on the reverend and quit this silliness.

The morning service was over. Bridget and Madeline were eager to be outside where they could freely converse.

"Oh, Bridget, I could by no means focus on the sermon today," said Madeline, with frustration. "I am so ashamed of myself, thinking such selfish thoughts at a time when I should have been attentive."

"Madeline, you are much too hard on yourself," replied Bridget. "John will be out soon, and I shall have to be going. Be careful of Jarret on your way home. Maybe you should wait for Mr. and Mrs. Bleasdell."

Madeline decided to follow Bridget's advice and wait for the Bleasdells. However, while she waited, Jarret emerged from the church and sauntered her way.

"Good morning, Miss Maddie. How are you today? You rushed off so quickly before, I did not have the chance to speak with you."

As he was coming out of the church, Christopher caught sight of Jarret speaking with Maddie. He walked slowly so as to observe the exchange between the two in the event that Madeline should have need of his assistance.

"If you will excuse me, I am waiting for Mr. and Mrs. Bleasdell," she said, as she turned away.

"Oh come now, Maddie. I will keep you company while you wait," insisted Jarret.

Madeline was quickly becoming cross with Jarret as she attempted, once again, to be rid of him. "Jarret, I beg you excuse me. I have not the need of your company. I must be going."

"I shall escort you home," asserted Jarret, in an annoyed tone of voice.

By now, Christopher was becoming angry at Jarret's unwanted advances toward Maddie so he decided it was time to come to her defense. "Good morning, Maddie. May I escort you home? The Bleasdells have invited me to dine with you this afternoon."

Jarret was fuming at the sight of Christopher and Maddie. "Excuse me, Mr. Osgood, but Maddie already has an escort."

"I beg your pardon, Jarret, but I have not consented to having you for an escort," replied Madeline. "Furthermore, seeing as Christopher has been invited by the Bleasdells to dine with us today, there is no need."

"Well, I shall take my leave of you then," replied Jarret angrily.

"I am obliged to you, Christopher," said Maddie, with her heart beating loudly. "My own attempts to be rid of him failed miserably. At no time have I ever been desirous of his company. Moreover, after what he has done to you, he is the last person in the world I would wish to have as an escort. Well anyway, it is so good to see you. I was sorry to have missed you on your last visit to the Bleasdell's."

"I am happy to be of assistance," replied Christopher with a smile. "I was sorry to have missed seeing you as well. A lot has transpired since we last met. As you say, it is plain to see that Jarret has not been dissuaded by the outcome of his attempts to be rid of me."

"Yes, he has always been presumptuous when it comes to me. I do not understand his persistence, as I have never encouraged it. But let us talk about something other than Jarret, shall we? Have you decided to settle in Salisbury?" inquired Maddie.

"Yes, in fact Mr. Carr spoke to me, only this morning, informing me that the town has granted me a plot of land for a home and another to farm," replied Christopher, with a happy tone in his voice. "I shall continue working for Mr. Carr with his ferry service and shipbuilding; however, I shall soon have my own home and land here in town."

Madeline was so filled with happiness at the thought of Christopher's decision to remain in Salisbury, she could scarcely keep from expressing it.

Christopher and Madeline were strolling along so slowly that Mr. Bleasdell, Elizabeth, and Henry soon caught up and joined them for the rest of the walk home.

"Christopher, we are so glad that you could come home with us today," said Mr. Bleasdell, patting Christopher on the shoulder.

"We shall truly enjoy your company, for we have so little time with you," said Elizabeth.

"It was kind of you to invite me," replied Christopher.

Madeline and Christopher conversed easily throughout the afternoon. Every now and then, as they caught each other's eye, Mr. Bleasdell and Elizabeth smiled at the sight of the two of them looking so happy together. However, soon it was time to set off for the evening service.

I wish this day would never end, thought Madeline, as they strolled along. She was content in knowing that Christopher understood clearly that she had no affection for Jarret.

"Thank you for the lovely afternoon," said Christopher, with contentment.

As they approached the church, Bridget caught sight of Madeline coming toward her in the company of Christopher. Barely able to contain her excitement as Madeline came near, she said with delight, "Good afternoon, Madeline, Mr. Osgood."

"And to you," replied Christopher.

"Maddie, I had a very enjoyable day," said Christopher, with a smile. "I hope to see you again very soon."

"Thank you, Christopher. It was a good day for me, as well," replied Maddie.

Bridget and Madeline gave each other knowing glances as they entered the church, anxious to be able to discuss the events of the day. But for now, it would have to wait.

Jarret, upon observing Maddie entering the church, reasoned with himself that he must make a show of being friendly to Christopher Osgood if he was to have a chance with Maddie. He also thought that if he could get close to her again, he may well convince her that he was only trying to protect her and the rest of the town from danger when he made the accusations against Christopher Osgood.

Following Reverend Worcester's sermon, as he conversed with many of his parishioners, Jarret strolled up. Being a good and forgiving man, he decided to welcome him in spite of the fact that he had tried to have him removed from his post.

"Good evening, Jarret. It was so good of you to join us today."

"And to you, sir, and thank you. I am happy to be here," replied Jarret shamelessly.

Once outside, Jarret waited for Christopher until he emerged from the church, at which time, Jarret came up to speak with him. "Good evening, Mr. Osgood. How did you like the sermon? The reverend can surely preach a good message."

Christopher wondered why Jarret seemingly had waited for him. What is more, why was he being so cordial? "Good evening, Jarret," acknowledged Christopher, quickly moving past.

Madeline and Bridget observed the exchange and thought it odd. Bridget reasoned that Jarret must now own to being completely wrong about Christopher, to which Madeline responded, "I am convinced that Jarret was always aware that what he said about Christopher was a lie, and I suspect he surely has some twisted plan for his cordiality."

Chapter 13

A New Man in Town/Haven't I Seen You Before?

Madeline and Bridget were coming out of Emma's house one day when they were met by a young stranger who introduced himself to them as Anthony Hall. He was an amiable and handsome young man who spoke to them in a friendly manner.

"You may call me Anthony, as I dislike being addressed as Mr. Hall," insisted Anthony. "I am honored to make the acquaintance of two such lovely young ladies."

"How do you do," replied Madeline. "I am Madeline Pike and this is Mrs. Bridget Dudly. You must be new to our town."

"Yes, I have just arrived from Norwich, England. I am lodging over at the town ordinary," replied Anthony.

Just then, Madeline caught the eye of Jarret who had begun to move in their direction. *I do hope he does not come over while we are making a new acquaintance,* thought Madeline.

However, his direction changed rather quickly once he locked eyes with Anthony.

Madeline found this to be a rather strange occurrence, as Jarret usually saw other men as a challenge, not something from which to run. Brushing away any thought of Jarret, Madeline returned to her conversation with Anthony and Bridget.

"Are either of you acquainted with the man who was headed this way a moment ago?" inquired Anthony. "I am only asking because he looks very familiar."

"His name is Jarret Ormsby," replied Bridget disgustedly.

"Oh," said Anthony, realizing that this was, indeed, a former acquaintance. He decided, however, that for now it might be best not to mention anything more about it.

"It was very nice to have met you, but I must be off," said Anthony. "I hope to see you again when there is time to become better acquainted." With that, he headed off down the road.

Bridget and Madeline remarked on what a handsome and pleasant young man they thought Anthony to be. With his dark hair and tall stature, he was sure to draw the interest of many a young lady in town. As they were walking along speculating about which of the ladies might be most suitable, Madeline remembered the look that passed between Jarret and Anthony.

After stopping for a moment, Madeline remarked, "There was one very odd thing that happened back there, Bridget. Did you happen to notice how quickly Jarret changed direction after seeing Anthony?"

"Indeed. I thought we would have to put up with Jarret's irritating presence, but when I looked again, he was gone," replied Bridget. "Jarret has never allowed another man to speak with you without getting in the middle of it. It was so unlike him to behave in that way."

"You are right. He is usually so self-assured and unyielding when in my company. Moreover, the way he continues on as though what he has done to Christopher is inconsequential is so infuriating," Madeline responded, visibly frustrated.

"Precisely. He is truly shameless," replied Bridget.

"Another thing, Bridget, did you happen to notice that Anthony inquired after his name?" asked Madeline. "It seemed, to me, he may have recognized him. Perhaps we will find out more when Anthony is not in a hurry to be somewhere."

"Maybe you are right," replied Bridget. "Well, I must be going, as John is expecting me at home."

"Goodbye, Bridget," said Madeline, as she, too, set off for home.

***

The next day, Christopher and Anthony happened to meet down by the river just as Christopher was climbing out of Charles Banister's canoe.

"Good day to you," said Anthony. "My name is Anthony Hall, and whom do I have the pleasure of addressing?"

"Christopher Osgood. It is nice to make your acquaintance. I have not seen you around here before, though I have not been here long myself. Are you new to the town?"

"Yes, I have recently come over from Norwich," replied Anthony. "Are you just returning from Carr's Island?"

"I am, and this is my good friend, Charles Banister," replied Christopher. "He carries me out to the island and back."

"Nice to make your acquaintance, Mr. Banister," said Anthony.

"I am headed into town," said Christopher. "Anthony, I hope to see you again, and I thank you, Charles. I shall see you in the morning."

"Goodbye, Christopher. I shall be here," replied Charles.

"Well, Christopher," said Anthony, "I was just having a look around. I am heading back into town myself so I shall accompany you, if you do not mind."

"I would appreciate the company," replied Christopher.

The two conversed over many things concerning the town as the strolled along. Christopher also informed Anthony of his work on the implementation of the ferry service and the shipbuilding, both of which he informed were in the employ of Mr. Carr.

"I have had various professions," replied Anthony. "A shipwright, fisherman, and house carpenter, just to name a few. Can you tell me; are they in need of more men for the completion of the ferry service and the shipbuilding?"

"Perhaps Mr. Carr could do with another man. I shall make the introductions, if you like," replied Christopher. "In the meantime, where are you staying?"

"At the ordinary in town," he replied. "I hope, in the near future, to purchase a piece of land. Only yesterday, I made the acquaintance of a man over at the ordinary with knowledge of an available property. Moreover, if I were to secure that one in particular, it has a house already situated upon it. It seems that the previous occupants have returned to England. It would certainly save me a lot of work not to have to build a house."

"Mr. Carr is on the board of selectmen," replied Christopher. "He may be of assistance in that as well."

The two men had become easy acquaintances by the time they reached town.

"Anthony, would it be convenient for me to come by the ordinary in the morning?" inquired Christopher.

"For sure," replied Anthony.

"I shall take you to meet Mr. Carr tomorrow, then."

"I am much obliged," replied Anthony.

The two men parted company with Christopher continuing on to his property. He could scarcely believe that he had his own lot on which to build a home. He began to think of his beloved Hannah, knowing how happy she would have been. He also wondered if he would have been instructing children with Hannah, by now, had she survived.

Back at the ordinary, Anthony, again, caught sight of Jarret. However, just as before, he ducked out of sight.

As acquaintances from the same hometown, I should think I deserve at least a cordial greeting, thought Anthony. Once more, he began to wonder why Jarret was so obviously avoiding him unless the rumors he had heard back in England, regarding Jarret, were true.

Morning came, and Christopher, as promised, was at the ordinary to meet Anthony.

"Good morning, Anthony, are you ready to set off for the island?"

"Absolutely. I am obliged to you for taking the time to do this for me," replied Anthony.

The two men made their way to the river where Charles was waiting to convey them over to the island. "Good morning, gentlemen," said Charles.

"And to you," replied Christopher. "Anthony may require a return trip earlier than my regular time of departure."

"Very well, as I have business with Mr. Carr, I had planned to remain a while," replied Charles.

Upon their arrival to Mr. Carr's estate, Christopher made the introductions. Mr. Carr was genuinely pleased to make Anthony's acquaintance and assured him that he would have need of him for some of his ventures. He also assured him that he would assist him in his purchase of a property, as it would require the town's approval before any land might be purchased; after which, Anthony met again with Charles for his return trip. "Charles, this has been a good day."

"Did things turn out well with Mr. Carr?" asked Charles.

"Indeed. In view of the fact that he has work for me and shall assist me in the purchase of a property, I would say it went very well," replied Anthony.

"A very successful day, then," smiled Charles.

Back at the Carr estate, Christopher and Mr. Carr were conversing about Anthony and his diverse work experience. Mr. Carr remarked, "Anthony is a man of many talents. I am sure he will prove to be indispensable to me."

Christopher was pleased with how things had turned out for Anthony. Though he had not known him long, he thought he would enjoy having him around.

"I must set off for town, as there is still so much to be done on my own property. I am not complaining, mind you," Christopher said with a chuckle.

"Yes, I too have many things to do today," replied Mr. Carr.

Chapter 14

An Unexpected Blessing

Madeline and Elizabeth were busily working around the house when Mr. Bleasdell stopped off home to verify that Elizabeth was presently in good health. He had been concerned about her, as she had not been quite herself as of late.

"Are you feeling well today, my dear?" asked Mr. Bleasdell, with concern.

"Just a little tired," replied Elizabeth, with a smile. "Do not be concerned, as it is, no doubt, simply my age catching up with me."

"If you are sure. However, if you begin to feel poorly, send Madeline to find me, and I shall go for the doctor," he replied, while kissing her on the brow.

"Do not worry. I shall come straight away if we have need of you," assured Madeline.

Later in the day, while churning the butter, Elizabeth became a bit faint. Madeline caught sight of her just as she was about to collapse. She quickly caught her arm and helped her to a chair.

"You must take a seat and leave off from doing any work for the rest of the day. I am going to fetch Mr. Bleasdell," said Madeline, with a look of concern.

"Madeline," said Elizabeth. "There is nothing at all to be concerned about. I am not ill. I have not informed Mr. Bleasdell of this, as yet, for I wished to be sure before mentioning it. But I believe that I am with child, as I am having similar feelings to when I was expecting Henry."

"Oh Elizabeth, that is wonderful news!" exclaimed Madeline. "You must not overdo. There is not a thing, in the way of chores or taking care of Henry, that I cannot do in your stead."

"Madeline, indeed I may be in need of some assistance with certain of my duties, but as for the better part of them, I shall function as usual," replied Elizabeth.

"As you wish, though, I shall be keeping a close watch to be sure that you are not burdening yourself with too much," replied Madeline.

The following day, Madeline set off for Emma Foster's home to exchange a portion of Elizabeth's newly churned butter for some of Emma's freshly baked bread. Madeline was happy to be doing something to lighten Elizabeth's load. However, an additional purpose for her visit was to seek advice from Emma regarding Elizabeth's condition, as Emma was presently serving and had served as a midwife for many years. As such, she had delivered many a child during that time.

Upon arriving at Emma's, Madeline was greeted in Emma's usual affectionate and friendly manner. As she was most anxious to discuss Elizabeth's condition with Emma, she hurried inside. Madeline knew that Elizabeth did not yet wish to share her news with their general acquaintance, but she was sure it would be all right for Emma to know.

"Good morning, Emma. I am so happy to see you today. I have with me the butter from Elizabeth."

"Thank you, Madeline. I have some bread cooling on the table for you to take back with you. And how are you today, my dear?" asked Emma, sensing that Madeline had something on her mind.

"Well, Emma, I am in need of your counsel on a matter, the nature of which is confidential," replied Madeline.

"All right, Madeline. How may I help?"

"Elizabeth is with child, and has not yet shared the happy news with Mr. Bleasdell."

"Oh, I am so pleased for her," replied Emma.

"Indeed; however, I am concerned that she plans to continue with most of her usual duties. I do not believe this to be a good idea, for I have observed that she is weak, and at times even faint. This cannot be right," insisted Madeline. "Perhaps if you were to come, she may heed your advice regarding her condition."

"I shall pay her a visit tomorrow, but as this is not the first time that she has been through this, she must be aware of her limitations," replied Emma. "Therefore, do not be too concerned."

"It shall put me at ease knowing she is in your care," replied Madeline. "She means the world to all of us. We could not bear it if anything were to happen to her. Now, I must make haste to return home to Elizabeth. I shall see you tomorrow."

"Good bye, dear, and try not to fret so," replied Emma.

The following day, Emma stopped by to look in on Elizabeth. "Good morning, Elizabeth," said Emma. "How are you feeling today?"

"I am quite well and not much in need of all of this attention. Nevertheless, I am happy to have you here. After Madeline divulged to me that she had informed you of my news, I decided to wait to talk to Mr. Bleasdell until you and I have consulted," replied Elizabeth.

"Let me take a look at you," said Emma. "Madeline informs me that you have been having dizzy spells. Have you experienced them before?"

"Indeed, while carrying Henry," replied Elizabeth. "Thus, I am not at all troubled by them."

"Even so, you must not take any unnecessary risks," replied Emma. "Madeline is willing and able to take up the slack so that you may rest. You must allow her to help."

"Elizabeth, I see Mr. Bleasdell approaching the house. He is nearly at the door. Do you wish for us to step out so that you may speak with him?" inquired Madeline, with glee.

"That may be best," replied Elizabeth. "I am obliged to you, Emma. It is a comfort to me that you will be the one to see me through the many months that are ahead."

"Well then, I shall call on you in a few days," replied Emma, patting Elizabeth's hand. "Remember, do not overexert yourself."

"I shall walk out with you," said Madeline. "Oh, good afternoon, Mr. Bleasdell. Emma and I were just leaving."

"Oh, do not leave on my account, for I shall be here but a moment," replied Mr. Bleasdell.

"You may be here a bit longer," said Elizabeth, with a smile. "See you in a few days, Emma."

With that, Emma and Madeline were out the door leaving Mr. Bleasdell alone with Elizabeth.

Mr. Bleasdell observed that Elizabeth seemed anxious to speak with him. Thus, he came in and sat down, pulling a chair up next to her. "Now what is this all about?"

"I wanted to be certain before I said anything, but I believe that Henry is going to have a little brother or sister."

"Are you quite sure?" Mr. Bleasdell asked with joy.

"Yes, reasonably, as this is not my first go at this."

"This must be the reason for your weak physical condition of late. I am delighted that we are to be blessed with another child. What is more, this happy news brings relief to my mind, as I have been quite concerned believing you to be ill."

"I am quite well, and Emma will see to me as the months progress," said Elizabeth. "Furthermore, Madeline is sure to be incessantly fussing over me so you need not concern yourself any longer, as I am in good hands."

Madeline walked Emma half of the way home in order to give Mr. Bleasdell time to digest the good news. "What is your opinion, Emma, is Elizabeth going to be all right?"

"Indeed, as it is not too unusual for someone in Elizabeth's condition to experience a bit of weakness," replied Emma. "Madeline, she is blessed to have a friend on which she can depend, but you must allow her to decide, within reason, what she feels she may do with regard to her responsibilities."

The following day, Elizabeth informed Henry of the news. He was so excited he could scarcely contain himself. He had grown up so much in the few years that had passed since their arrival from England; however, Elizabeth was still surprised to hear him express a desire to be of assistance to her until the baby arrived.

"Thank you, Henry. I know you shall be a great help to me," replied Elizabeth. "With you and Madeline to lend a hand, there shall be little left for me to do."

Henry smiled at his mother's words of affirmation, knowing he had pleased her by offering to help out.

Chapter 15

The Confrontation/Madeline and Emma Travel to Ipswich

Early one Sunday morning, Anthony caught up to Jarret just as he was about to enter the church. "Good morning, Jarret. It seems every time I have observed you in town, you are off somewhere before I can speak with you. Why have you not come over to greet me? After all, we have both come from Norwich, have we not?"

"You must be mistaken. I have not met you before today," replied Jarret abruptly.

"Are you not from Norwich, England?" asked Anthony, with full knowledge that he was.

"I am not. You must take me for someone else," Jarret huffed.

"Am I to believe that there is someone who not only bears a remarkable resemblance to you, but also answers to the same name? That seems, to me, to be a bit too much of a coincidence; would you not agree?" Anthony asked sarcastically.

"I would not," replied Jarret, as he darted into the building to avoid any further scrutiny.

Anthony stood a moment, bewildered by the conversation. *There can be no other reason than Grace, for which Jarret should not wish to be known,* he reasoned. *It is just too despicable to be believed, and yet it must be true.*

105

Just then, Christopher came walking up. "Good day, Anthony. Did I see you conversing with Jarret Ormsby?

"Indeed," replied Anthony, looking disconcerted.

"I must say that I am not at all surprised to see that you appear to be taken aback by something he said. I do not wish to pry, but I would be careful where that individual is concerned. He is not to be trusted. Considering that Jarret has said something to distress you, may I inquire as to the nature of your conversation?"

"You may, however, what I have to divulge shall take longer than the few moments we have before service. May we meet afterwards? I must speak with you in confidence regarding Jarret," replied Anthony.

"Very well, then. I shall meet with you after the service," replied Christopher with concern.

"I am much obliged," said Anthony.

Following the service, Christopher and Anthony met to discuss the situation.

"Christopher, the strangest thing has occurred. I am confident that I was acquainted with Jarret while living in Norwich, England. However, every time that I have observed him in town, he scurries off before I am able to speak with him."

"That is very odd," replied Christopher.

"I caught sight of him, the first time, while I was becoming acquainted with Madeline Pike and Bridget Dudly. I was sure that he was coming our way when he quickly turned and walked the other direction," said Anthony.

"That is without a doubt peculiar behavior, for Jarret, as he has never missed an opportunity to ingratiate himself with Maddie," replied Christopher. "You say that you are acquainted with Jarret?"

"Indeed, for as I had mentioned, we hail from the same town in England," replied Anthony. "The most disturbing bit of information I have not, as yet, made known to you is that Jarret is married, or at least he was when last I saw him."

"What! He is married? How can this be? He has never mentioned a wife, not even when he was in Salem after he first arrived from England. What do you suppose has become of her?" inquired Christopher, with a dazed look.

"I believe I have the answer to that question," grimaced Anthony. "He left her in England. It was well known, in Norwich, that Jarret had set off for the new land, and that he was to have sent for his wife, Grace, once he was settled. How hard it must have been for her once she came to the realization that he was not going to send for her. She may have even believed him to be dead."

"Is there no end to Jarret's chicanery?" scowled Christopher.

"Christopher, how would you advise me? I am unsure as to what can be done. He would certainly, if confronted, deny everything," insisted Anthony. "It would be my word against his and after so short an acquaintance with me, the town would most likely take his word over mine."

"I assure you, there would be some who would accept what you say as true. Jarret's reputation has had a few black marks against it. But we must obtain proof, as it is by no means certain that he would not be believed given that he is one of the cleverest of men," replied Christopher.

"We will speak on this again after we have had time to think on it a while," said Anthony.

"In view of the fact that he has been portraying himself as an unmarried man, we better not be too long in deciding how best to deal with the situation," warned Christopher.

"Agreed. I shall meet with you again very soon to discuss this further."

The following day, Madeline and Elizabeth received an unexpected visit from Emma. "Good morning, ladies," said Emma, "I have come to inquire after Elizabeth."

"Good morning, Emma," replied Elizabeth. "Do take a seat. It is good of you to come by to see how I am getting along. Would you like some tea?"

"I cannot stay long. I must confess that I have an added purpose for my visit. I truly had planned to call today. However, I have just received disturbing news from my daughter, Jane," sighed Emma.

"Of what nature is this news?" inquired Madeline.

"My daughter has sent word that her husband, Nathan, is near death. He is extremely ill and has been informed that it is not likely he shall recover. In fact, the dreadful event may have already taken place in the time that it has taken to receive word."

"How dreadful!" exclaimed Elizabeth. "Emma, you must feel so helpless. Is there anything that we can do for you?"

"Well, I have a proposal to make, which you must not hesitate to decline if it does not meet with your approval," replied Emma.

"We are happy to hear you out, Emma," replied Elizabeth.

"Very well then. I have taken the liberty of speaking with Bridget about daily assisting you, Elizabeth, with all of Madeline's responsibilities. Furthermore, I have requested of Mrs. Rebecca Sewall that she call on you a few times a week, as she has assisted me in many a delivery and is well acquainted with the whole of midwifery. You see, I was in hopes that you might be able to spare Madeline for what should be no more than a fortnight, to accompany me to Ipswich. It is my desire to be available to Jane in whatever manner she requires. As Madeline is near to Jane's age, and has had a similar experience, it was my belief that she may be of some comfort to her."

"When is this trip to take place?" inquired Elizabeth sympathetically.

"It is my desire to set off tomorrow, as I am sure that she wishes for me to be there even now," replied Emma. "I am aware that what I am requesting is difficult, and I have left you with little time to decide. Please accept my most humble apologies for placing such a burden on you, but I truly felt that Jane would benefit greatly from this arrangement."

Elizabeth nodded to Madeline giving her consent; thus leaving the decision in Madeline's hands. Madeline acknowledged Elizabeth's gesture and quickly responded to Emma.

"Emma, I would be happy to accompany you to Ipswich. I only hope that you are right and I can be of some comfort to Jane, as I know full well the pain she suffers."

"I am truly blessed to have the two of you as friends," replied Emma, with a sigh of relief. "The shallop on which we shall travel is that of Captain Barnes. Mr. Foster will see us off in the morning. I am indebted to you both. I shall be off now as I have much to do before tomorrow."

Elizabeth and Madeline said their goodbyes and went to work preparing for Madeline's departure. "Elizabeth, are you certain that the arrangements are to your satisfaction?" asked Madeline. "I am concerned that if I am not here to look after things, you will do too much for someone in your condition."

"Bridget and I will make out just fine. Between Bridget, Henry, and Mrs. Sewall, I shall receive every possible attention. You are not to worry," replied Elizabeth.

The following day, Emma and Madeline were off with heavy hearts to Ipswich. "Madeline, I am grateful to you for accompanying me on this trip," said Emma.

"Emma, you have done so much for me," replied Madeline. "It is time for me to give back a little. Besides, though I am not acquainted with Jane, my heart breaks for her just the same. I would have wished to be there with you even if you had not asked me."

Chapter 16

A Journey to England/A Secret Mission/Regretful Goodbyes

The ferry service was almost ready to commence when Mr. Carr called for a meeting with Christopher. "Christopher, it is my plan to journey back to England, as I am in need of some final supplies for the completion of the ferry service and the ongoing shipbuilding. In addition, I wish to collect more of my belongings now that I am permanently settled."

"Is it your desire that I should accompany you to England?" asked Christopher.

"I see that you have anticipated me," replied Mr. Carr. "I am aware that what I am asking is a rather large request."

"How soon before we are to set off on this journey?" asked Christopher.

"It is my desire to embark on our journey in a few days while the weather is still agreeable. There is a ship leaving for England at that time, and I would like us to be on it," replied Mr. Carr. "If the idea meets with your approval, I shall set one of the men to work on your property whilst we are away so that you do not fall behind. You may speak with him about your desires for what is to be done in your absence. Remember, the trip is not obligatory; you may decline it."

"How long shall we be away?" asked Christopher.

"Allowing for the length of the voyages, over and back, as well as a few weeks stay in England, I should estimate it to be approximately six or seven months."

"What is our destination?" inquired Christopher.

"Harwich, as it is the location for the supplies of which I am in need. From there, I shall travel on to London, the place from whence I came," replied Mr. Carr. "You are from Bristol, are you not?"

"Indeed, but my family is no longer living. However, I do have business in Norwich to attend to if time permits," replied Christopher, with anticipation at the thought of discovering whether Jarrett has a wife he abandoned in England.

"Harwich is more or less the halfway point between London and Norwich. Whilst I am in London, you shall have time to travel on to Norwich," replied Mr. Carr. "Am I to take it, then, that you will be accompanying me to England?"

"Indeed, and I am obliged to you for seeing to my property while we are away," replied Christopher.

"No doubt you have much to do before we leave; therefore, take the days leading up to our departure. I can get by without you until then."

"Perhaps I shall take tomorrow," replied Christopher.

"All right, and thank you for your willingness to accompany me on such a lengthy journey," replied Mr. Carr.

"I shall head off to make preparations," replied Christopher.

As Christopher made his way down the road, he was astonished at such a turn of events. He believed the trip could possibly be the answer to the dilemma with which he and Anthony had been presented. Therefore, he decided he must speak with Anthony before departing, and he knew that he could not leave without calling on the Bleasdells and Maddie.

"Anthony, I am so happy to have found you in town. Mr. Carr has you doing so many different tasks, you might have been just about anywhere. I have news to share of a most unexpected nature," said Christopher, excitedly.

"What news?" Anthony inquired with anticipation.

"What seemed to us a hopeless business has now a prospect of being resolved," replied Christopher. "I am to accompany Mr. Carr to Harwich, England, for supplies for his ferry service. Furthermore, while we are in England, he intends to travel on alone to London, from which he came, to collect more of his belongings. As Harwich is close to the halfway point between London and Norwich, I shall travel on to Norwich at that time to see what can be found out regarding Jarret."

"I am astonished at this news," replied Anthony. "I had supposed that we had not the power to stop Jarret from snaring some unsuspecting lady into an unlawful marriage. We must be in prayer that you will be successful in your attempts to gain the information needed to set things right."

"Indeed, but I must now be off as I have much to do before the voyage," replied Christopher.

"Goodbye, then, and safe journey. Oh, and how long will you be away?" inquired Anthony.

"I shall return, God willing, in about seven months," replied Christopher, as he rushed off down the road to the Bleasdell's home.

Mr. Bleasdell was coming out the door just as Christopher was approaching the house. "Good afternoon, Christopher. It is good to see you. And how have you been?"

"Just fine, Mr. Bleasdell, and you?"

"We are all very well. Moreover, there is happy news to report," replied Mr. Bleasdell.

"What news?"

"In a few months, there shall be an addition to our family. Elizabeth is with child," replied Mr. Bleasdell with glee.

Just then, Bridget came walking out the door calling back, "I shall return early tomorrow, Elizabeth. Oh, hello, Christopher. It is so good to see you. Have you heard the good news?"

"Indeed. In fact, Mr. Bleasdell has just informed me," replied Christopher. "Are Maddie and Elizabeth inside? I must speak with them and with you, Mr. Bleasdell."

"Christopher, I am sorry but Maddie has accompanied Emma to Ipswich. Her daughter's husband is not expected to live. He has an extremely bad case of pneumonia," replied Mr. Bleasdell. "It is likely that they shall be away a few weeks."

"Oh, I am sorry to have missed her," lamented Christopher. "I am to be away for several months to England. Mr. Carr shall be journeying there in a few days and has asked me to accompany him. I should like to have seen Maddie before we set off."

"She will be sorry to have missed you as well," replied Mr. Bleasdell. "However, you must come in and see Elizabeth."

"Very well, lead the way," replied Christopher, trying to sound cheerful.

"Well, Christopher, it is so good to see you. Undoubtedly, Mr. Bleasdell has informed you of the happenings around here," said Elizabeth.

"What happy news for the two of you and for Henry," replied Christopher. "Elizabeth, I have come to tell you that I am to be away about seven months. Mr. Carr has asked me to accompany him to England."

"Oh, that is a very long time," replied Elizabeth. "You shall be greatly missed by each and every one of us."

"I too, shall miss all of you. I so wish that I could have spoken with Maddie before we leave. Please convey to her my disappointment."

"To be sure," replied Mr. Bleasdell. "We will be praying for a safe journey for you and for Mr. Carr. Though things have improved somewhat for people who hold to our beliefs in England, you must take care whilst you are there."

"I shall, and I am obliged to you for your prayers on our behalf. Let me now express my indebtedness to you and Elizabeth for all that you have done for me. I have felt myself to be a part of your family since the day we embarked on our first journey. Though it is my intention to return, at times our plans do not come to fruition, as the sea has swallowed up more than a few on the journey. We know all too well. Thus, I could not have left without expressing my feelings," declared Christopher.

"Christopher, you must know that we look on you quite as our own son. Consequently, any help we have offered has been for no other reason than for your wellbeing and happiness," responded Elizabeth affectionately.

"Yes, you are, indeed, a cherished member of this family," expressed Mr. Bleasdell.

"I must be on my way. I have not even begun to prepare for the journey," sighed Christopher. Knowing he would be away for so long a time without having seen Maddie was beginning to weigh heavily upon him.

"Goodbye, Christopher," said Elizabeth, her voice cracking as she attempted to hold back her tears.

"Goodbye, young man," said Mr. Bleasdell, as he walked Christopher to the door.

Chapter 17

An Unexpected Loss/A Move to Salisbury

Emma and Madeline arrived in Ipswich where they were greeted by a friend of Jane's with distressing news. "You must be Emma. And who might this be?" the woman said, gesturing toward Madeline.

"I am Madeline, a friend of Emma's."

"I am happy to make your acquaintance? I am Sarah Stevens. Whilst you were yet on your journey, Nathan passed from this life to the next. Jane is doing tolerably well considering all that she has been through. However, as she has many visitors at the moment, I have come in her place."

"What dreadful news. We are obliged to you for meeting us," said Emma, sorrowfully. "Poor Jane! What she must have been through. But I am afraid that the next few months may be yet more difficult as she adjusts to the loss."

Madeline spoke not a word as they walked on to Jane's home, as the experience was all too familiar.

"As I am sure you know, Emma, Jane is settled about a mile from the body of the town. We should be there directly," said Sarah. "She will be very happy to see you."

The three ladies arrived at Jane's, whereupon a crowd of somber faces greeted them.

"May I ask where Jane is at the moment? I am Emma, her mother, and this is my friend Madeline Pike."

"We are delighted to make your acquaintance though it is under such unhappy circumstances," spoke one of the neighbors who had come to offer her sympathies. "It was a very sudden and awful death for such a young man in the blossom of his youth. So tragic! Just so tragic!"

Madeline sensed that Emma wished to be done with the conversation and to be at Jane's side, so she addressed the lady hoping to distract her while Emma moved by and into the house to find Jane.

"It was so nice of you to pay your respects, but I must excuse myself and see to Jane," said Emma, as she went into the house.

"Certainly, we shall take our leave," replied the woman. "Come, let us be off and let these ladies alone to comfort Jane."

"I am much obliged to you," said Madeline, as she moved her way to the door to follow after Emma.

"Come in, Madeline. This is my daughter, Jane."

"It is nice to meet you," said Madeline, with a look of sorrow.

"I am happy to make your acquaintance," replied Jane. "It was so good of you to come with Mamma."

"Jane dear, is there anything that we can do for you?" asked Emma. "Have you had anything to eat today?"

"Do not worry yourself over me, Mamma. I shall be all right. I was in great distress at the beginning of Nathan's illness; however, God has given me added strength and a great sense of peace these past few days."

"Madeline and I are so happy to find you in such a frame of mind. It often takes many months or even years to arrive at the place you now find yourself," expressed Emma, with some relief.

Jane nodded and smiled at her mother's comforting words. "I was thinking that I may accompany you and Madeline back to Salisbury for a visit. I have so much to consider with regard to the future. I feel that I need to be with my family while I make such weighty decisions."

"I am so happy to hear that. Though, I had thought I should have a time convincing you of it, as I have been of the same mind," replied Emma, with delight.

Though she bore it remarkably well, the next few days were difficult for Jane as she said goodbye to Nathan, for she knew that their lives together on this earth were over. However, it was comforting to her that he was now in God's care, and that they would see each other again when it was her turn to take that final journey.

Madeline and Emma assisted Jane in packing up her belongings. "Have you everything that you wish to take with us?" asked Emma.

"Indeed, I am ready to be off," replied Jane. "Getting away from the home that Nathan and I shared shall be good for me. I fear that in this place, the grief might be too overwhelming."

The ladies were off to the shallop for their return trip to Salisbury. It was not long before they caught sight of their destination. They gave a sigh of relief knowing they would very soon be disembarking.

Mr. Foster met the ladies to carry them back to the homestead. "Dear Jane, how happy I am to see you. Let me help you with your things."

"Oh, Morris, I am happy to see you too. I have missed you," replied Jane.

"We were hopeful that you would decide to come to Salisbury," said Mr. Foster, as he put his arm around Emma. "I have missed you too, Emma. It is good to have you home. And, Madeline, how was your trip?"

"In the company of two such wonderful ladies, how could I help but to have a pleasant trip," replied Madeline with a smile, attempting to lighten the mood. For the trip had, indeed, been a sorrowful one for Jane.

"Let us be going. I am sure that Jane could do with a nap," said Emma.

"You are so right, Mamma," replied Jane. "I feel as if I have not slept for a month."

As they approached the Bleasdell's home, Madeline said her goodbyes as the others continued on to the Foster homestead.

"Well, Madeline, it is good to have you home," said Elizabeth, as Madeline came in the door. "And how was your time away with Emma and Jane?"

"It was surprisingly uplifting, as Jane was in good spirits when we arrived. She is a most impressive young lady with a very strong faith," replied Madeline. "I believe that she shall be quite all right."

"Her character must be very similar to that of her mother's, as Emma, too, is an extraordinary person," replied Elizabeth.

"Well, let us speak about all of that later. Have you been quite well while I have been away?" asked Madeline.

"I could not have been otherwise with Bridget, Henry, and Rebecca looking after me," replied Elizabeth. "They have scarcely let me lift a finger around here."

"Good. That is what I like to hear," replied Madeline. "And Mr. Bleasdell, is he well?"

"Indeed he is," replied Elizabeth. "His feet have scarcely touched the ground since he learned of our happy news."

"Where is Henry?" inquired Madeline.

"He is off with Bridget. I expect that they shall return very soon. She has been a blessing. Henry has enjoyed nights away at the Dudly home more than once whilst you have been away," replied Elizabeth.

"That must have been a real adventure for him and a nice break for you I am sure," replied Madeline.

"Has Christopher come to call while I have been away?" inquired Madeline.

"I have news that concerns Christopher. He has accompanied Mr. Carr to England for supplies," replied Elizabeth. "They left soon after you had gone to Ipswich."

"How long will they be away?" inquired Madeline, with a stunned expression.

"When he came to bid us farewell, he said he believed it to be no longer than seven months," replied Elizabeth. "Madeline, he seemed exceedingly disappointed when he asked us to convey to you his regrets at not having seen you before he left."

"I had no idea of his taking a journey. He had not mentioned anything about it," said Madeline glumly.

"He was not aware of it until just a few days before they were to set off," replied Elizabeth.

Just then, Bridget and Henry returned. "Madeline, what a surprise! It is so good to see you," said Bridget.

"And you, dear Bridget. I have been informed of your extraordinary efforts on behalf of Elizabeth and Henry," smiled Madeline. "I am obliged to you for being so dutiful to our fine lady. And, Henry, have you missed me?"

Henry came running over to Madeline to give her a hug. "Madeline, I am so happy you are home. I had hoped you would not be gone for long."

"How is Jane?" inquired Bridget.

"She has come to Salisbury," replied Madeline. "Oh, Bridget, she is so much like Emma—such a fine lady with a strong faith. I had thought to comfort her. However, her words spoke more comfort to me than any I might have had for her."

"I shall be delighted to make her acquaintance, but only when the time is right," replied Bridget, "as she will surely, for a spell, be in need of some rest and solitude."

Chapter 18

New Friends and Bad Company

Emma and Mr. Foster were delighted to have Jane at the homestead. They thought to make her stay as comfortable as possible, for they hoped that she would make Salisbury her permanent home. Mr. Foster met Anthony in town one day when the idea came to him that an addition to his home would lend more space for Jane.

"Good day to you, Anthony," said Mr. Foster, with a smile. "I would imagine that things are a little slow for you with Mr. Carr away."

"Indeed they are," replied Anthony. "He has asked me to oversee a lot of the goings on out on the island. However, things are a bit stalled while we wait for the supplies from England."

"I could do with a bit of help on my homestead if you are in need of some additional work," said Mr. Foster. "You see, our daughter, Jane, will be staying with us for a while."

"I was informed of the unhappy news just this morning. Mr. Bleasdell was in town for a meeting and passed on the sad news. What a terrible loss to your family," replied Anthony. "I shall be delighted to help out. If you would like, I shall come by tomorrow."

"Until tomorrow then," replied Mr. Foster.

Early the following day, Madeline came to call on Jane and Emma. Elizabeth had sent her off to Emma's in hopes that she might spend some time with Jane. "Good morning, Emma and Jane. Are you all settled in, Jane?"

"Indeed, Madeline," replied Jane. "Morris and Mamma have been so kind. Morris has even hired someone to help him build on to the homestead. He is of the opinion that I am in need of more space for my things. I have tried to reassure him that I am completely fine and that he need not go to any trouble. However, as is his way, he would have none of it. He has such a generous nature."

"Indeed he does, but in this case, I believe that he is right," replied Emma.

"Jane," said Madeline. "I thought perhaps you might care for a walk?"

"Yes, Jane, go with Madeline and enjoy the fresh air," insisted Emma.

"I see that the two of you have decided my plans for the day," replied Jane, with a smile. "Very well, let us go."

"Goodbye, Emma, I shall return with Jane in a few hours," said Madeline, as the two set off.

Once outside, Jane lifted her face to the sun, determined to enjoy the day. "Thank you, Madeline. I do believe that a walk will do me good."

"If you like, we could go down to the river and sit a while," said Madeline. "It is always so beautiful and peaceful there."

"Yes, I would like that," replied Jane.

The new friends strolled along conversing about many things. Before long, they came to the realization that they had a good deal in common.

"Madeline, I am so pleased to have you for a friend. You truly understand my situation. I feel strong one moment, but the very next, I am overcome with emotion. I fear we shall never fully recover from the losses we have suffered. However, I am confident that God has not forsaken us as He has seen fit to provide for our needs," said Jane, with a smile.

"Indeed he has," replied Madeline.

They had finally reached the water's edge when Madeline pointed out, "That island, out there, is Mr. Carr's island. Bridget, another friend of mine, accompanied me on a full day of exploring the island. We had a grand time. I shall introduce you to Bridget one day very soon. She is truly a loyal and good friend. I am sure the two of you will get on famously."

"I believe that coming home was a good decision," replied Jane. "I can see that I shall not want for friendship."

"Jane, there is Charles Banister's canoe coming over from the island. He carries people over to the island and back. Soon there will be a ferry service as well. I believe I see Anthony Hall in the canoe with him."

Soon after, the canoe pulled up to the water's edge for Anthony to come ashore. "Good morning, Madeline," said Anthony. "Thank you, Charles, I shall be ashore all day."

"Very well," replied Charles. "Good day, ladies," said Charles, as he shoved off to return to the island.

"I shall have to introduce you to Charles at another time," said Madeline to Jane. "However, this is Anthony Hall. Anthony, this is Jane Dickson, Emma's daughter."

"It is nice to make your acquaintance; I shall be working with Mr. Foster today. I am sorry for the unhappy circumstances that brought you to Salisbury."

"Oh yes," replied Jane. "He did mention your name and thank you."

"And how are you, Madeline?" inquired Anthony. "I have not seen you in a few weeks."

"I am well, and yes it has been a while since we have been in each other's company. I accompanied Emma to Ipswich," replied Madeline.

"Well, ladies, I shall be on my way, as Mr. Foster will be expecting me," smiled Anthony.

"Good day to you, Anthony," replied Madeline.

"He seems a fine gentleman," remarked Jane.

"Indeed, though I have not been acquainted with him long. Shall we take a walk through town?" inquired Madeline.

"I should like that," replied Jane. "I have heard that the new church has been in use."

"Yes," replied Madeline. "It is so grand to see how the town continues to take form. I have often thought, umm well . . . better not to speak of that just now."

"You were thinking of Oliver, were you not?" inquired Jane. "Do not make yourself uneasy on my account. I would not wish for us to be silent on the subject of our dear husbands. Indeed, it makes the heart ache to remember them, but they are happy thoughts as well."

"I know just what you mean," replied Madeline. "They are bittersweet memories, to be sure."

"Your dear mother is a shining example of God's abiding love, as He has given her a second chance at happiness," said Madeline.

"Yes, dear Morris. He has been a wonderful husband and father," replied Jane. "We love him exceedingly."

The two ladies were just coming into the center of town when Jarret Ormsby made haste to greet them. His attempts at winning Madeline had failed miserably, and as he had not seen her in quite some time, he was now searching for other prospects.

Now that his interest in me in waning, Jane is sure to attract his attention along with many of the other young ladies of the town, thought Madeline as he was approaching.

"Good day, ladies, and this must be, Jane Dickson. I was informed that you had come to Salisbury. I am Jarret Ormsby; happy to make your acquaintance."

"I, too, am happy to make your acquaintance," replied Jane. "We are on a walk through town. It is lovely to see how it has grown. We are headed in the direction of the new church. I so wished to see it, and Madeline was agreeable to the idea."

"Well then, what a happy coincidence as I had hoped to speak with Reverend Worcester about a matter today," replied Jarret. "I shall accompany you, if you like?"

Madeline remained silent as Jane conversed with Jarret while they strolled along. She decided she must warn Jane about Jarret but realized that now was not the time.

Reverend Worcester was standing in the doorway of the church as Jane, Madeline, and Jarret approached.

"Good day, and this must be Jane. I am delighted to make your acquaintance, Jane. I am very sorry about your husband, my dear. If you ever have a need to speak with me, I am here for you anytime."

"Thank you," replied Jane, wiping away an unexpected tear. "Although, truly, I am all right."

Reverend Worcester sensed that Jane was a young woman of great strength upon observing her countenance as she fought to regain her composure.

"Jarret, you expressed a desire to speak with Reverend Worcester so we shall leave you now," said Madeline, believing that it had only been an excuse to walk with Jane.

"Oh, no, no. I shall speak with the reverend another time," replied Jarret. "I would so much like to continue to be an escort for you lovely ladies."

"Jarret, I am free to speak with you now if you wish," insisted Reverend Worcester, desiring to be of assistance to Madeline in her obvious bid to be rid of Jarret.

"Another time, Reverend," responded Jarret as he turned to follow behind Jane.

Madeline was becoming more frustrated by the minute with Jarret's obvious advances toward Jane. Though, at the moment, she knew not how to deter him. *If only Jane were aware of his treacherous nature, she would not treat him so kindly,* she thought.

After what seemed to be a very long walk, Madeline was happy they had finally reached the Foster's house. Mr. Foster and Anthony observed Madeline and Jane walking up in the company of Jarret. Glancing disgustedly at each other, they each wondered how Jarret had managed to become acquainted with Jane so quickly.

"Good day, Jarret," said Madeline, with a stern tone.

"I am happy to have met you," said Jane to Jarret.

"The pleasure was all mine," replied Jarret, with his usual charm. "I am sure that we will see each other again very soon."

Not if I have anything to say about it, thought Madeline. *Jane must not remain uninformed regarding Jarret. However, I am confident that there is no immediate danger, as she has just lost her beloved Nathan. She would not be interested in anyone else for quite some time.*

"Madeline, Jarret is such a kind gentleman. It was good of him to see us home," remarked Jane.

"Jane, I must speak with you regarding Jarret," replied Madeline. "However, now is not the time, as you have had a long day and must surely be in need of a rest."

As Jane and Madeline were approaching, Mr. Foster inquired, "Jane, have you had a pleasant day?" He hoped to glean something that would explain the reason Jarret had been along on their walk.

"Indeed, it has been a very pleasant day, though, I am a little tired," replied Jane.

After taking her leave of Madeline and Mr. Foster, Jane went into the house, leaving Madeline alone with Mr. Foster.

"Mr. Foster, I am sure that you observed Jarret as we were approaching."

"Indeed I did," scowled Mr. Foster. "How did he happen to join in on your walk?"

"He caught sight of us as we were walking toward the church," replied Madeline.

"And, of course, he came right over. Once he saw the two of you, you were unable to be rid of him, were you not?" replied Mr. Foster.

"You are right. He was a real bother. Mr. Foster, I am very concerned that Jane is unaware of his true nature, and may be taken in by him. I know that she would not have a thought of any man, at present, but we would do well not to underestimate Jarret, as he is sure to ingratiate himself with her during this vulnerable time," grimaced Madeline.

"You are quite right," replied Mr. Foster. "It might be best if we warn her of his character, though, I dislike having to burden her with such a report at this time."

"I agree that it is a shame to have to tell her now. She seems so happy to be in Salisbury, and I should hate to alter her favorable view of the town," responded Madeline.

"Perhaps we should delay speaking with her whilst we observe Jarret to see if he makes any further advances. Besides, between the two of us, we should be able keep her otherwise occupied, and he may not have another opportunity," said Mr. Foster.

"I am amenable to your suggestion," replied Madeline with a sigh of relief.

"Then we are in agreement. We should wait until such a time as it becomes necessary to inform her about Jarret," replied Mr. Foster.

"Yes. I shall be off for home now. Goodbye, Mr. Foster."

"I am much obliged to you, Madeline, for taking such good care of our girl," Mr. Foster called after her.

As Anthony was in earshot, he listened intently to the conversation between Mr. Foster and Madeline wishing he had news from Christopher to share. He could see now more than ever the importance of learning the truth regarding Jarret.

Chapter 19

Quilting Experts/Adjustments/ Anthony's Concern

Elizabeth and Emma met for tea one day without any of the younger ladies to join them. "It is rather nice having tea alone with you today, Elizabeth," remarked Emma. "Not that I dislike the company of our young friends, but a little peace and quiet does the body good every now and then."

"I know just how you feel," replied Elizabeth, with a giggle. "Madeline may be almost ten years Jane's senior, but she has not lost a bit of her energy. Emma, how is Jane really doing? She appears happy enough, but I suspect she suffers greatly."

"I have been truly amazed at her strength. However, I have seen many sorrowful looks come upon her face when she thinks that no one is watching. I remember too well the loneliness that ensues during the first few months. I am so grateful to you and Madeline for your friendship to her, as I know that it has helped immensely."

"I believe that her friendship has been good for Madeline too. Madeline suffered so over the loss of Oliver. In bringing comfort to Jane, I believe, she has healed a part of herself as well," replied Elizabeth.

"Where is Henry today?" inquired Emma.

"He is with his father. It is Mr. Bleasdell's desire that Henry work with him each day now that he is almost ten. Of course, this is to be after he does his schooling. Soon, Madeline and I shall have the new baby to contend with so it is good that Henry shall be spending more time with his father. Furthermore, there is so much he can learn from Mr. Bleasdell even beyond essential skills. His character, for instance—there is no one better than Mr. Bleasdell for Henry to pattern himself after."

"Indeed, Henry could have no better guide than Mr. Bleasdell," replied Emma.

Jane and Madeline were together at the Foster's homestead while Emma spent a few hours with Elizabeth.

"Jane, your mamma had been instructing me in the art of quilt making when I had more time to lend to it. I do wish I had the talent to make a quilt to present to Elizabeth upon the birth of the child, but I am not, as yet, confident enough in my ability to attempt it on my own."

"Madeline, if you like, I should be delighted to help. Mamma taught me as well, and at a very young age. Thus, I have been making quilts for many years," replied Jane.

"Oh, thank you, Jane."

"We will begin right now," insisted Jane. "Mamma has a box of scraps. I am sure she would not object if we were to rummage through it. I shall go and fetch it."

"Elizabeth will be so happy to have a warm quilt with which to swaddle the baby," replied Madeline. "Jane, were you aware that Elizabeth lost two babies in their infancy?"

"No, I did not know. How awful that must have been for the Bleasdells," replied Jane.

"Yes, it must have been a terrible time for them. However, this new little one is certain to bring great joy to their hearts," remarked Madeline.

"Without a doubt. But as time is short, let us get started on the quilt. You may search through this box for whatever scraps you like," Jane insisted as she pushed the box over in front of Madeline.

Just then, a knock came at the door. "Oh, good day, Bridget. Come right in," said Madeline, with delight. "Jane, this is my dear friend Bridget. Bridget, this is Jane."

"I am happy to make your acquaintance," replied Jane. "Madeline has spoken of you so many times, I feel as if I know you already."

"I, too, am pleased to make your acquaintance," replied Bridget, "though I am sorry for the circumstances for which you have come."

"Thank you," replied Jane, "but no more unhappy thoughts. Madeline desires to make a quilt for Elizabeth's baby. She has informed me that, though she had commenced with her instruction, she has not followed through, owing to a lack of time. Would you be of a mind to aid us in this endeavor?"

"I shall be delighted. As a result of Emma's instruction, I am happy to inform you both that I am quite the expert at quilt making," laughed Bridget.

"With the two of you assisting, it shall be finished in no time," remarked Madeline, with a smile.

"I had hoped you would not mind my unexpected visit," said Bridget. "Elizabeth directed me to you insisting that I come."

"No, no. We are happy that you have come," replied Madeline, with Jane in agreement.

"Jane, have you had a tour of the town?" inquired Bridget.

"Indeed, we had a lovely walk through town just the other day," replied Jane. "I had the happy occasion to meet a couple of the folks, the Reverend Worcester and Jarret something or other."

"Jarret Ormsby," scowled Bridget, glancing over at Madeline.

"Yes and Reverend Worcester," replied Madeline, changing the subject while shaking her head to alert Bridget not to say anything about Jarret.

Bridget gave an inconspicuous nod, as she perceived that Madeline did not wish to discuss Jarret. "Well, what are we waiting for? Let us get started with the quilt."

Jane and Bridget assisted Madeline, joyously chatting away the afternoon.

Mr. Foster and Anthony were busily working outside while the young ladies were conversing inside the house. Anthony could not help but chuckle, as he could hear the conversations taking place. Mr. Foster smiled at the thought of Jane having fun with her new friends.

"Anthony, I am delighted to hear Jane laughing. They must be having a good time in there," remarked Mr. Foster.

"Yes, I daresay they are, as I have heard laughter many times this hour," replied Anthony.

"With the loss of her father and now her husband, poor Jane has dealt with much for someone so young," remarked Mr. Foster.

Upon hearing more of the sufferings of Jane, as Morris talked on, Anthony was even more determined that Jarret must be kept away.

"Anthony, Emma has instructed me to invite you to dinner, and it would make her very unhappy if you were to decline her invitation," said Mr. Foster, with a smile.

"I should not wish to make Emma unhappy," replied Anthony, "so I shall accept."

Meanwhile, inside, the ladies concluded their quilting.

"Jane, I must be getting back to Elizabeth," said Madeline.

"And I must be going too. John will be wondering what has kept me so long," said Bridget.

"I am grateful to the two of you for such a joyous day," said Jane. "I know we shall all be great friends. We will continue the work on the quilt whenever it is a convenient time for both of you."

"To be sure," replied Bridget as she and Madeline rose to leave.

"Goodbye, Jane," said Madeline. "I am sure that Emma will be home soon."

Just as Bridget and Madeline were on their way out, Emma strolled up.

"Well, Bridget, I see that you found them."

"Indeed, and what a joyous time we have had," she replied.

"I am much obliged to you both for spending the day with Jane. She is in need of companionship more than ever," said Emma.

"Emma, it brings us pleasure as well," replied Madeline. "Jane is a delight to be with. We must be going now. Goodbye, Emma."

"Goodbye, ladies," replied Emma.

Emma made her way to where Mr. Foster and Anthony were working. "So good to see you, Anthony. Has Mr. Foster invited you to dine with us tonight and for that matter any night that you are here?"

"Yes, he did. I am much obliged to you," replied Anthony.

"Well then, I shall call for the two of you when supper is ready," said Emma as she was entering the house.

"Well, Jane, and how are you?" inquired Emma. "I met your guests as they were leaving."

"We had such a good day," replied Jane. "Madeline wishes to make a quilt for the new baby. However, it is a secret so you must not let on to Elizabeth."

"Oh, I shall not say a word about it," whispered Emma, as if she might be overheard.

"I did not think you would mind if Madeline made use of some of your old scraps of material," said Jane.

"I am happy that someone has a use for them," replied Emma. "However, if she has need of something other than what is in the box, you might make a visit to Mr. North's shop. He is a proprietor in town that, amongst other things, carries cloth. I believe he has a daughter about your age."

"Very good," replied Jane. "We may pay a visit to Mr. North's shop, then."

"I have invited Anthony to dine with us today and any day that he is here working. I hope that meets with your approval, as I do not wish to make you uncomfortable," said Emma.

"Indeed, he should stay and dine with us," replied Jane. "He seems to be a fine gentleman and I am happy to have so many new friends near to my age; what with Madeline, Bridget, Jarret, and now Anthony, I shall not be lacking."

"Indeed, there are many fine young people in Salisbury. However, after so short an acquaintance, take heed not to trust in all so implicitly," replied Emma, upon hearing Jarret's name in the list of new friends and acquaintances.

Chapter 20

Midwifery/Jane Discovers the Truth

It had been a few weeks since Jane's arrival to Salisbury. During which time, Emma had been called away several times to visit her expectant mothers. Whenever she returned home from a visit, Jane was very inquisitive as to how the mothers were getting along and how much longer before their babies might arrive. After a time, Jane decided to accompany Emma on many of her visits, as she found the whole thing to be extremely fascinating.

"Jane, it has been a joy for me that you have displayed such an interest in midwifery," expressed Emma. "There is only one other midwife close by and she is getting along in years. Someday the town will be, again, in need of a midwife. As you have already learned most of the duties that are involved, you are sure to be accepted."

"I have never known anything as wonderful as assisting you with the mothers," replied Jane. "Our first delivery together ran through my mind for days. I can still see her little face as she entered the world. What a miracle of God."

"I remember the excitement of my first delivery. I felt just as you do now. The joy of it all remains for some time," replied Emma. "Oh Jane, do you think you could be happy here in Salisbury? You have seemed so in recent weeks."

"Indeed, I believe that I shall be quite happy. Remaining in Ipswich would have been too much of a reminder of Nathan, though my lonely heart persists even here in Salisbury. However, God in His mercy has seen fit to keep me otherwise occupied with the midwifery and new friendships, so I have had little time for such thoughts," replied Jane.

"Tomorrow I should like for you to take a day for yourself," said Emma. "You and Madeline ought to work on her quilt, as it shall not be long before Elizabeth's new little one will arrive."

"Yes, and perhaps Bridget will be free to join us," replied Jane.

***

The following day, Jane came to call on Madeline. "Good day, Madeline, and, Elizabeth. Mamma said you might be free today, Madeline."

"Indeed she is," replied Elizabeth. "Emma is going to call today. I shall be quite all right here until she comes. Off with you now, the two of you."

"Very well. I do have some things I need to do today. Elizabeth, the chores are done, thus, all you need do is rest until Emma arrives," insisted Madeline.

"I shall simply sit here with the mending. Now the two of you go and enjoy the day," replied Elizabeth.

While Jane and Madeline were making their way to Bridget's home, Jane confided that she had news she had not, as yet, shared with anyone. "You see, Madeline, my news is happy news in a way, but troubling as well."

"Go on, I am listening."

"Now that enough time has lapsed for me to be sure, I have to acknowledge the reality of my situation," replied Jane, with her head low.

"To what are you referring?" inquired Madeline.

"Madeline, I believe that I carry within me a part of Nathan."

"Are you telling me that you are with child?" inquired Madeline.

"Yes, I believe that I am."

"You have not said a word about this before," said Madeline, with a puzzled expression.

"I began to wonder about it a few weeks ago, but passed the signs off as relating to the strain of so many changes that have taken place in such a short time. However, of late I have become quite convinced and had to tell someone."

Attempting to be cheerful regarding Jane's situation, Madeline said, "This is good news, is it not?"

"It is, in that I shall always have a part of Nathan with me; however, I am concerned that I shall be placing an added burden on Mamma and Morris."

"I am confident they would not wish for you to feel that a new baby would be a burden," replied Madeline.

"Perhaps, but regardless, it is another mouth to feed."

"Jane, what would you have said to me if our roles were reversed?" inquired Madeline. "Would you not have insisted that God is always faithful, and we should trust Him in this as well?"

To that, Jane gave a smile and a nod. "You are a good friend, Madeline. Let us keep the news between us for now. I shall soon share it with Mamma and Morris, but not just yet."

"Very well, but I do believe that Emma should know, as she is to be your midwife," responded Madeline.

"Just think of that, me needing a midwife," said Jane, with a smile. "I am happy, Madeline, truly I am. However, I cannot help but to be a bit apprehensive."

"Everything will be all right," replied Madeline. "There is Bridget's house," said Madeline.

"Remember, not a word," insisted Jane.

"I have not forgotten," replied Madeline. "However, you shall not be able to hide it for long."

Upon their arrival, Bridget greeted them with excitement. "How are my two fine friends today?"

"Good day, Bridget. We are just fine. Are you able to get away today? We will be spending much of the day at Jane's working on the quilt," said Madeline.

"In truth, I had intended to call on each of you; thus, I have been swift in my work," replied Bridget. "I am ready to go."

The three ladies strolled along until reaching the Foster's, whereupon they were kindly greeted by Mr. Foster and Anthony Hall.

"Morris, we will be here most of the day working on the quilt for the baby. In a while I shall bring you and Anthony out some refreshments," said Jane.

"I am much obliged, my dear, as Emma will be away today," replied Morris.

Anthony nodded and smiled as Jane, Madeline, and Bridget entered the house.

"I shall prepare some tea and bread," said Jane.

The ladies shared many secrets as they worked along on the quilt. Madeline decided, as Jane was becoming so close a friend, it was time she confided in her regarding Christopher. Moreover, she believed that Jane could do with the distraction.

"Jane, I have not told you, as yet, of Christopher Osgood. He is away in England at this time, but shall be returning in a few months. As you have become a dear friend, I thought you should know of my feelings for him," divulged Madeline.

"What is this?" asked Jane, with a look of surprise. "You have been keeping such news all to yourself?"

"I did not think it appropriate, until now, for me to inform you at a time when you have suffered such a loss," replied Madeline.

"Do not be anxious about that, as news of this kind pleases me greatly. Tell me all about him," said Jane, excitedly. "He is the one on the journey with Mr. Carr, is he not? I have heard Morris speak of him."

"Indeed he is," replied Madeline. "I have not seen him in a couple of months and shall not see him for yet another four or five. We first met on the journey over from England as we traveled on the same ship, the *Angel Gabriel,* which wrecked just off the coast at Pemaquid. He lost his wife, Hannah, and son, Zackary, that day."

"Mamma had informed me of the wreck of your ship," said Jane. "Have you and Christopher an understanding with regard to a future together?"

"No, we have never spoken of our feelings. I have to admit that I am not even certain of his," replied Madeline.

"What is that you say?" inquired Bridget, playfully. "Jane, you only need to be with the two of them for a moment to realize that he has feelings for her as well. Madeline has been endeavoring to keep her feelings from him owing to the notion that it has not been long enough since the passing of her husband for her to find happiness with another."

"Madeline, it has been six years, has it not?" inquired Jane, stunned.

"Indeed it has," replied Bridget.

"Bridget, you do tease me so," chuckled Madeline. "I do believe that I am finally ready to let go of the past for a future with Christopher. However, Jane, you must never mention any of this, as I would be mortified if Christopher was certain of my feelings before declaring his."

"I can see that Bridget has done well to protect your secret, as she has not even given a hint up to now," said Jane.

"Yes, she has been a faithful friend," replied Madeline.

"You can count on me as well," assured Jane.

"Well, though I have enjoyed this day immensely, I must be going, as it is getting on toward time to prepare the evening meal for John," said Bridget.

"I must be going, too," replied Madeline.

"Thank you, ladies, for a joyous day," said Jane. "Bridget, if you like, I shall walk with you, as my legs are in need of a little stretch."

"Enjoy your walk, ladies," replied Madeline. "I shall see you soon."

With that, Madeline was off for home while Jane and Bridget headed the other way through town in the direction of Bridget's house.

"Jane, there is no need to walk me all the way to my house. You should not have to travel the entire distance back alone," insisted Bridget.

"Very well. I shall turn back now as it is nearly halfway," replied Jane. "Do take care and I shall see you soon."

On Jane's return trip back through town, Jarret observed her walking alone. "Good day, Jane. What are you doing in town?"

"I was accompanying Bridget to her home," replied Jane. "She has been with me for most of the afternoon."

"And, are you, now, on your way home?" inquired Jarret.

"Yes, that is my plan," smiled Jane.

"Will you do me the honor of allowing me to escort you?" asked Jarret.

"I would not wish to inconvenience you, though I could do with the company," replied Jane.

Jane's acquaintances must not have informed her of their ill feelings toward me, as yet, or she would not be so pleasant, thought Jarret. "It is not an inconvenience," he said, with a smile. "Must you rush home, or shall we take an indirect path and pass by the river on our way?"

"I suppose it would be all right," responded Jane. "It is so pleasant down by the river."

Jarret and Jane were together for quite a while before it crossed her mind that she had been gone long enough to be missed. Therefore, she decided it would be best to return home, immediately.

"It has been a delight simply to be in your company, Jane," said Jarret charmingly, as they walked back in the direction of the Foster's. "May I come to call on you tomorrow?"

"Oh, Jarret, I shall not be ready for that for some time," replied Jane. "However, we shall surely see each other in town and at church."

Jarret decided that for the moment he would not press Jane; however, he was determined not to allow too much time to pass before coming to call.

Jane and Jarret continued on to the Foster's home conversing happily until they arrived at their destination. "Well Jane, I shall take my leave, as you are safely home," said Jarret.

"I am much obliged to you for escorting me," replied Jane as she waved him goodbye.

Jane strolled up into the yard toward the house when Mr. Foster happened to see her.

"You have been gone a very long time. Did you stay and visit at Bridget's house a while?"

"I accompanied Bridget only half the way home," replied Jane, as she was moving toward the door to go in. "On my return trip, Jarret Ormsby, seeing that I was alone, offered to escort me. We decided to walk home by way of the river; however, we lingered there longer than I had intended. I must go in now, as Mamma surely has returned by now."

"Yes, she came back a little while ago," replied Mr. Foster, with a look of concern.

Anthony overheard the conversation taking place between Mr. Foster and Jane; thus, he decided to address the Jarret situation with Mr. Foster. "Mr. Foster, it appears that Jarret is continuing his attentions toward Jane."

"Indeed," he scowled. "I believe the time has come to inform Jane of our dealings with Jarret, though I dislike having to speak ill of another. It seems a shame to have to do it now with Jane adjusting so well to life here in Salisbury," replied Mr. Foster.

"Mr. Foster, I am expecting to have further news, regarding Jarret, once Christopher returns from England, the nature of which is sure to put an end to his preying on the ladies in this town. However, as it may, yet, be another five or six months, it would not be prudent to wait for this additional information," replied Anthony.

"Will you not tell me more?" inquired Mr. Foster.

"I am not at liberty to say anything further as I have, as yet, only my word to offer as proof. I will say, if what I believe is true, it is too despicable for words. Be assured that the moment it can be confirmed, I shall come to you straight away," replied Anthony.

"Until such time as you have more to share, we shall offer what is already known, regarding Jarret, as testimony to Jane to deter her from having anymore dealings with him," replied Mr. Foster. "I shall speak to Emma tonight about how to inform Jane so as not to upset her. Not that she has any feelings for Jarret, but her constitution is still in a delicate state, and I should not wish to distress her."

"You know best," replied Anthony.

Later that night, Mr. Foster spoke quietly with Emma so as not to be overheard, regarding the situation with Jarret. "Were you aware that Jarret escorted Jane home today?"

"Indeed, and I have to say that I was troubled by the news," replied Emma.

"I am of the opinion that we should not put off any longer telling Jane what we know, concerning Jarret," replied Mr. Foster. "Would you not agree?"

"Without question. My only regret is that we have not already done so," replied Emma.

"Jane will probably think us silly for not informing her before now, as it is likely to have less of an effect on her than we have imagined."

"I agree. We do, at times, tend to shelter her beyond what is necessary," smiled Mr. Foster.

"Let us speak with her about it tomorrow," said Emma.

"Very well," replied Mr. Foster.

The following day, Mr. Foster and Emma sat down with Jane and informed her of everything that had gone on with regard to Jarret. "We did not wish to burden you with this, Jane, but it has been increasingly obvious that Jarret has turned his attentions toward you," scowled Mr. Foster. "As you can see by what we have shared, Madeline knows all too well what it means to have Jarret Ormsby's notice. What is more, what he did to Christopher might have ruined his reputation, or worse."

"This is shocking news to be sure," replied Jane. "However, you need not have worried, as it will be a long time before I am of a mind to accept attentions from any man with my Nathan continually on my mind."

"We were sure that you felt this way, but as Jarret is one of the cleverest of men, we did not dare trust that you would be safe," replied Emma.

"It is a wonder that Bridget and Madeline never mentioned a word of this to me," said Jane.

"We had all decided to wait as you are still recovering from the weeks of taking care of Nathan during his illness, as well as the devastating loss that followed. And, as you seemed to be adjusting so well to Salisbury, we did not wish to hinder that in any way," replied Emma.

"I am aware that you all had my best interest in mind when you elected not to inform me, but in the future do not think me so weak as to be so easily distressed," said Jane, with a smile.

"You can be sure that we shall be more forthcoming in the future," confirmed Mr. Foster.

"Now, as we are all in agreement, let us not speak of this again," replied Jane, lightheartedly.

Chapter 21

The Joke/Susanna North a New Acquaintance

A few days had passed since Jane's last visit with Madeline and Bridget when she observed them strolling up to the house. She decided to tease them a bit, regarding Jarret, as they had kept the reports of his character from her.

"Good day, ladies. I am so happy that you have come. Come in, I have news that I wished for my dear friends to be the first to hear," said Jane, with Emma listening intently wondering of what news she could be speaking.

"Do sit down. I shall bring tea," said Emma.

"Thank you, Mamma," said Jane.

"Do tell us your news," insisted Madeline.

"As you know, I accompanied Bridget part of the way home following our last visit. Well, as I was walking back, Jarret Ormsby came out to greet me. He is such a fine gentlemen, and was so kind as to escort me the rest of the way," said Jane slyly, hiding a grin. "Is he not the kindest of gentlemen?"

Bridget and Madeline stared at each other not knowing how to respond.

Jane continued, "He has requested that I allow him to come to call on me, and I have decided to say yes. What do you say to that?" she said, with a smirk.

Emma clasped her mouth to keep from laughing aloud as she peeped over at Madeline and Bridget who sat looking utterly stunned at the news.

"Jane, do you think . . . well, you are ready? I mean, do you think it wise?" stammered Madeline, thinking Jane was making this terrible choice for a future husband because of the child that she was carrying.

"Oh yes, my dear Madeline, after hearing your news when last we met, I thought why wait six years for happiness to come when a wonderful man presently desires to court me?" asked Jane mischievously.

"Oh, Jane, if no one else will speak to you about Jarret, I feel that I must," insisted Bridget, glaring at Emma and Madeline.

At this point, Emma and Jane burst into laughter for several minutes. "I cannot stand the look on your poor bewildered faces any longer," said Jane, holding her aching sides. "I must admit the truth. I am only teasing. Do you wish to know why?"

Madeline and Bridget, looking confused, answered in the affirmative.

"It is because you, my naughty friends, have been keeping things from me. Mamma and Morris recounted to me everything regarding Jarret," replied Jane, still giggling.

"After Jarret escorted Jane home from Bridget's the other day, Mr. Foster and I decided that it was time to tell Jane everything," chuckled Emma. "Oh, Jane, you are too hilarious. I could not keep from laughing when I saw their faces."

"Jane, you wicked girl. What a rascal you are," laughed Bridget. "Your expression did not reveal even a hint of a joke."

The ladies continued to laugh for several minutes. What's more, Madeline felt relieved that Jane did not seem burdened any longer. *She seems so lighthearted, she must now be at peace regarding the baby*, thought Madeline.

Mr. Foster and Anthony laughed as they listened to the joyful ruckus coming from inside the house. "I have to say, Mr. Foster, the ladies are surely enjoying themselves in there," smiled

Anthony. "The news of Jarret does not appear to have harmed Jane in any way."

Mr. Foster nodded, relieved that Jane had taken the news so well.

"Madeline, let me take a look at that quilt," said Emma. "You are almost finished with it. It looks as if all that is left to do is to attach the binding. I am afraid that I do not possess enough left over material for that task. A while back, I suggested to Jane that you ladies go down to Mr. North's store and see what he might have that would suit you. Though, I must say, other than attaching the binding, the quilt has turned out beautifully."

"Jane and Bridget have been a great help to me, as I had not the skills to do it on my own," replied Madeline.

"You have done most of the work yourself," replied Bridget. "A fine job you have done too."

"As you know, Elizabeth is getting closer every day to having the baby, so it might be best if you went to Mr. North's shop today," insisted Emma.

Bridget, Jane, and Madeline took Emma's advice and set off for Mr. North's shop. While they were there, they were introduced to Mr. North's daughter, Susanna. They found her to be a pleasant sort who was of an approximate age to Jane's. They decided they should very much like getting to know her.

"Let us make a point of inviting Susanna to join us for tea someday very soon," said Jane as they sauntered back to the Foster's home.

"Yes, let us invite her sometime when we all get together," replied Madeline. "I am so happy that I shall be able to complete my quilt, now that I have the material needed for the binding. It was good of Emma to suggest Mr. North's shop."

Madeline continued to admire her binding cloth the rest of the way to the Foster's, while imagining Elizabeth's reaction upon receiving the quilt. "Elizabeth is going to be very surprised," remarked Madeline.

"Indeed she will," replied Bridget.

Over the next few days, Madeline was able to steal away a little each day to work on the quilt. Before long, she was nearly finished. Bridget and Jane met with her one last time, at the Foster's, to assist in the final touches.

"Well, I believe that we have finished it," Madeline squealed with delight. "I am much obliged to you all for your assistance. Would it be all right if I were to leave the quilt here until such time as I present it to Elizabeth?"

"Yes, it will be safe here until you are ready for it," replied Emma.

Bridget and Madeline said their goodbyes and were off, leaving Jane and Emma to prepare dinner for Anthony and Mr. Foster.

"Morris, Anthony," called Emma.

"Emma must have dinner ready to serve," said Mr. Foster to Anthony, as he heard Emma calling.

"Are you sure that I am not a bother to your family, eating with you almost every night?" asked Anthony.

"How can you ask such a thing?" inquired Mr. Foster. "We are all delighted to have you. In addition to being a great help to us, you have also become a good friend."

Anthony and Mr. Foster joined Emma and Jane for dinner whereupon Emma told them of the joke that Jane had played on Madeline and Bridget.

"I had to cover my mouth to keep from laughing once I realized what Jane was up to," giggled Emma.

By this time, Mr. Foster and Anthony were holding their sides from laughter. Seeing that Jane made light of the situation, regarding the news about Jarret, everyone felt relieved.

"Jane, to think we were concerned regarding your ability to manage such dismal news," remarked Mr. Foster. "I hope you can forgive us for failing to recognize that you have become quite a strong and very grown up lady."

"I may one day struggle with similar things with my own children, so I shall not hold it against you. If there is one thing I know to be true, what you did, you did out of love for me," said Jane, with a smile. "I am privileged to have such wonderful parents."

Anthony was happy to have stayed again for dinner, as he was blessed by the affection that the Fosters had for each other. Later that night, something that Jane said played over and over in his mind: "I know I shall one day struggle with similar things with my own children."

Not knowing the truth about Jane's condition, he was persuaded that, though her heart must still be grieving the loss of Nathan, she must not be opposed to marrying again. With each passing day, Anthony's admiration for Jane continued to grow.

***

A few weeks had passed since Jane had learned of Jarret's treachery. She had not been to town for anything other than Sunday services. Consequently, in all that time, Jarret had been unable to speak with her directly. Moreover, he had not, yet, felt himself bold enough to call at the Foster's homestead knowing that it might provoke them to inform Jane of his shortcomings.

One particular sunny morning, Jarret thought, *No matter how the Fosters react to my coming, I shall call on Jane today, as it has been weeks since last we met. I cannot wait any longer for a chance encounter to occur.*

Jarret sauntered over to the Foster's homestead whereupon he was met by Mr. Foster and Anthony. "Jarret, what may I ask are you doing here?" inquired Mr. Foster, with Anthony standing close by.

"I have come to call on Jane," replied Jarret.

"Jane is not accepting visitors today, for that matter any day where you are concerned," replied Mr. Foster.

"And do you presume to speak for her?" retorted Jarret, in a defiant tone.

"Indeed I do," replied Mr. Foster. "You are not welcome here so I should not return if I were you, as you will not be permitted entrance."

"I shall take my leave, but you cannot prevent me from speaking with her when she is in town," Jarret demanded as he turned to leave, sputtering to himself.

Anthony expressed some concern to Mr. Foster over Jarret's threat. "It is my opinion that we have not heard the last of Jarret on this matter, as he is not so easily dissuaded."

"We shall just have to keep Jane close by whenever we are in town. He will eventually move on to some other poor unsuspecting soul," replied Mr. Foster.

The following morning, Mr. Bleasdell stopped by to speak with Mr. Foster. "I am on my way to call on an old friend, Mr. Bailey, for I have not seen him in all of my time here in Salisbury. He moved here a short time before we came to Salisbury. He is a good man, though he has had his troubles since leaving England. Elizabeth has been insisting for quite some time that I locate the residence of Mr. Bailey. However, until just recently we had not heard tell of him by any of the townsfolk. Finally, just the other day as I happened to be in town, I overheard his name spoken in a conversation. I inquired after his whereabouts, and was told where he may be found. In truth, had I come right out and asked, someone could have told me where to find him. I am ashamed that I have neglected him for so long. If you have the time, would you be inclined to accompany me?"

"Very well, as he is a friend of yours it will be my pleasure to make his acquaintance," replied Mr. Foster.

"Anthony, we will return in a few hours," said Mr. Foster.

"I shall look after things around here today," responded Anthony.

"Thank you, Anthony," replied Mr. Foster, as he headed in to inform Emma that he would be away for a good part of the day.

Mr. Bailey had procured a plot of land from the town near the Merrimac River. He made his living as a fisherman, for he was one of only a few men supplying the surrounding towns. Mr. Bleasdell had been informed by the one who had disclosed Mr. Bailey's whereabouts that he had yet been unsuccessful in convincing his wife to come over from England with their other children. Knowing this to be a great strain on Mr. Bailey, he wished to offer his support and any counsel of which he may have need, regarding his predicament.

Providentially, Mr. Bailey was just returning home when Mr. Foster and Mr. Bleasdell approached. "Good day to you, Mr. Bleasdell. It is very good to see you."

"And you," replied Mr. Bleasdell. "How have you been, my friend?"

"Oh, tolerably well," replied Mr. Bailey.

"This is, Mr. Foster, another friend of mine," said Mr. Bleasdell, motioning to Mr. Foster.

"So good to make your acquaintance," replied Mr. Bailey. "As I am not often in town, I have not had the pleasure of becoming acquainted with many of the people."

"Mr. Bailey, I should have been here to see you long ago," said Mr. Bleasdell shamefacedly. "I was informed that your wife remains in England."

"Yes, and I am at a loss as to what to do," replied Mr. Bailey. "I cannot fault my wife, as I too am frightened to, again, cross the ocean."

"Mr. Bailey, this is a tragic situation to be sure," replied Mr. Foster. "How hard it must have been for you out here alone missing your wife and children."

"Well, thankfully, I have had two of my children here with me," replied Mr. Bailey. "John Jr. and Joanna accompanied me over from England."

"Oh, I was unaware of that," replied Mr. Foster. "That is some comfort, then."

"Joanna has recently married," said Mr. Bailey. "However, John Jr. remains here with me, at present."

"Is there any way that we can be of assistance to you in this matter?" inquired Mr. Foster.

"If I only knew in what way you might assist me," replied Mr. Bailey, "but I fear that there is no remedy to be found for my quandary. If only I had remained in England."

"John," said Mr. Bleasdell softly. "We will pray on this matter for as long as it takes to find a solution; however, you must not stay out here alone, excepting your children of course, as there are folks in town who should enjoy becoming acquainted with you."

"I am much obliged to you for your friendship," replied Mr. Bailey. "I, too, should have sought you out before now; however, the next time I am in town I shall come to call."

"We must take our leave now," said Mr. Bleasdell. "We will call again, soon."

"It was nice to make your acquaintance," said Mr. Foster, with a smile and a pat on Mr. Bailey's shoulder.

Mr. Bailey gave a nod as Mr. Bleasdell and Mr. Foster turned to leave. Mr. Foster spoke about the sorrowful situation most of the way back. He felt sure that there must be a way to reunite Mr. Bailey with his family. Mr. Bleasdell concurred, but neither had an immediate answer.

Later that night, when Mr. Bleasdell was at home with Elizabeth, he related Mr. Bailey's situation and that it was not much improved since he had left Ipswich. Elizabeth assured that she would remember him in her prayers, as she understood that separation from his loved ones must be a terrible thing. She also insisted that they not allow a great deal of time to pass before calling again on Mr. Bailey.

Chapter 22

Rumors and Lies

It had been a few weeks since Jarret's last attempt at visiting Jane. While in town one day, Mr. Foster heard a rumor that Jarret had been claiming to be courting Jane. He could not comprehend what benefit this could be to Jarret, as Jane was not likely to affirm his lie. Though he was certain that the rumors were not true, he decided he must inform Jane and Emma.

"I heard a strange rumor in town that Jarret is claiming to have been courting you for many weeks, Jane," stated Mr. Foster, with a scowl.

"Did I hear you correctly?" asked Jane, stunned.

"Yes, and I am sorry to say that it was from a reliable source," replied Mr. Foster miserably, knowing he must accept that it must be true. "I am unsure as to why he would say such a thing, as he must surely know that you would set it straight."

"I cannot imagine what he is up to this time," replied Emma angrily.

"God alone knows what goes on in Jarret's wretched mind," replied Jane, as she was becoming distressed at the thought of her condition in relation to this terrible news. "How would you advise me with regard to putting an end to these rumors?"

"I shall discuss this with Mr. Bleasdell, as I have come to believe him to be a man of great wisdom," replied Mr. Foster. "I shall go directly."

"I agree, for we must take action soon," replied Emma, "as Jarret has several powerful friends in town who will surely believe him."

Mr. Foster made haste for the Bleasdell's home, wishing that Anthony had been working with him today, as he would certainly have been of assistance in this situation. As he arrived at the Bleasdell's, Madeline came out of the house to gather some vegetables from the garden with Henry ready to assist her.

"Mr. Foster, to what do we owe the pleasure of your visit?" she asked, with a smile.

"I must speak with you all on a matter of some delicacy," replied Mr. Foster. "Are the Bleasdells inside?"

"Yes, they are," replied Madeline. "Follow me; I shall show you in."

"Mr. Bleasdell and Elizabeth, Mr. Foster desires to speak with us," informed Madeline.

"Come in, Mr. Foster," replied Elizabeth. "Do take a seat. May I offer you some tea?"

"No, but thank you, Elizabeth," replied Mr. Foster. "I have just heard very distressing news. I must seek your advice, as I am unsure as to the best course of action."

"Do go on," replied Mr. Bleasdell.

"There has been a rumor circulated in town in which Jarret and Jane are courting. I believe that it has been initiated by Jarret, but for the life of me, I cannot comprehend what his motive might be."

"What arrogance! Does he truly believe that starting such rumors would compel Jane to consent to such a thing? Are we never to be rid of Jarret Ormsby and his deception?" inquired Madeline furiously.

"I share your frustration Madeline; however, now is not the time to allow it to distract us from the problem. We must try and seek out the motive behind this, as it will surely help us to come up with a solution," replied Mr. Bleasdell.

"You are right. I am sorry," replied Madeline. "There has to be a reason behind this madness."

"You decided in the last meeting of the selectmen what actions to take in instances where there had been fornication, did you not?" inquired Elizabeth.

"Yes, but what has that to do with this situation?" inquired Mr. Bleasdell.

She continued, "Was it not the opinion of the selectmen that our town would take a different course of action than it had on previous occasions regarding the punishment for such things? And was it not, also, decided that the couple should marry rather than be lashed or fined?"

"Indeed it was," replied Mr. Foster, with a look of shock, as he was beginning to take Elizabeth's meaning. "Clearly that must be the motive, as he has certainly been made aware of the decision. However, as yet, no accusation of fornication has been levied."

"If she is right, you can expect just such an accusation to be secretly instigated by none other than Jarret. He only has to set in motion a little gossip among certain of the woman in town, to force the board of selectmen to take action," replied Mr. Bleasdell, with a scowl.

"We must take steps to prevent him from going any further with this," replied Madeline, aghast, as it occurred to her what people might think once Jane's condition became known.

"I do not believe that we should alert anyone to this, as yet, for we may be mistaken. Moreover, if we are wrong, we might be planting ideas into Jarret's head," said Mr. Foster. "What is your opinion, Mr. Bleasdell?"

"Perhaps you are right," replied Mr. Bleasdell. "When in town, let us keep our ears open for any news regarding this situation and whenever possible squelch any rumors regarding Jarret and Jane."

"I am much obliged to all of you for your concern for Jane," said Mr. Foster, with a sigh. "I must be off now, as Jane and Emma will be eager for my return."

"Do not worry, my friend," said Mr. Bleasdell, as Mr. Foster was leaving. "We will be in prayer for guidance."

Mr. Foster returned home with a heavy heart, knowing that he must divulge what Elizabeth had wisely discerned to be Jarret's motive for the lies he had been spreading. Emma and Jane were of the same opinion as Elizabeth upon learning of the conclusions at the last meeting of the selectmen, regarding fornication.

***

Two days had gone by, when Anthony returned to assist Mr. Foster with the house. He had been in town the day before whereupon he heard of the rumors concerning Jarret and Jane.

"Good day, Mr. Foster," said Anthony. "I have disturbing news."

"I may know of what you speak," replied Mr. Foster. "It involves Jarret and Jane, does it not?"

"I venture to guess that you have already heard the despicable gossip," replied Anthony.

Mr. Foster nodded in response to Anthony. He went on to explain what they had deduced with regard to Jarret's motives. Anthony agreed with their conclusions as well as the course of action on which they had settled.

The following day, Emma and Jane came to call at the Bleasdell's home to see how Elizabeth was getting along.

"Elizabeth, how are you feeling today?" inquired Emma.

"I am very well," replied Elizabeth. "It will not be long now, and I shall be holding a new little one in my arms. And how are you, Jane?"

"I, too, am well, considering," replied Jane. "Though the matter with Jarret did make me a bit low, I am determined not to allow the rumors to upset me any longer."

"That is good, as I am sure this will all be settled very soon," replied Elizabeth.

"Madeline, perhaps you would care for a walk," said Jane. "Mamma will be here with Elizabeth."

"I am happy to," replied Madeline as she rose to go. "We will return in a little while."

"Take your time; we are not in any hurry," replied Emma. Madeline and Jane decided in order to avoid Jarret, it was best if they walked away from town. They did not wish to add any credibility to his rumors by allowing Jane to be seen in his company.

"Jane, tell me the truth; how are you really?"

"Madeline, I must admit that this whole business is a bit disconcerting, especially under the circumstances. I am glad that I have taken you into my confidence, regarding the baby."

"We may be wrong about Jarret's motives and nothing will come of this," assured Madeline.

"We can only pray that you are right," replied Jane. "Is that not Anthony coming our way?"

"I believe you are right. He must be heading into town," replied Madeline.

Anthony approached from the direction of the Merrimac, for he had been out on Carr's Island.

"Good day, ladies. How are you this fine day?" asked Anthony, attempting to be cheerful.

"We are tolerably well considering that our walks will now be limited to this direction, as it is away from town," replied Madeline.

"If you wish to walk into town, I shall be your escort," replied Anthony. "Jarret would not dare show his face in my presence."

"And why is that?" inquired Madeline, with a smile. She had always had a suspicion that Anthony held some bit of knowledge of which Jarret was afraid.

"Well, it is just that Jarret seems to come up amongst the missing whenever he sees me," replied Anthony, with a look that seemed to suggest that there was more to the story.

Madeline decided not to press Anthony on the subject any further, for she was just glad to have him escort them into town.

"We should be delighted to walk with you," replied Jane, with a determined tone in her voice that demonstrated her defiance against Jarret's rumors and the busybodies who believed them.

Thus, they set off where they eventually came upon Bridget who, out of concern for Jane, had been searching for them. "Oh, Jane, I hear that Jarret is up to his old tricks. Please do not be concerned over Jarret, as there are sure to be many who refuse to believe such rumors," insisted Bridget.

Jarret emerged from Mr. North's shop as Jane and her friends were outside conversing with one another. Without saying a word, he quickly turned away and went in the direction of his house.

"You were right," said Jane to Anthony. "He surely would have come over to speak with us had you not been here."

"Let us go in to Mr. North's shop and have a look around while we are here," said Madeline.

"Why not," smiled Jane, heaving a sigh of relief that things seemed to be going well with Anthony along.

Once inside the store, Madeline went searching for Susanna North.

"Good day to you, Susanna," said Madeline, with a smile. "It is very nice to see you again."

"And you," replied Susanna, happy that Madeline had come over to converse with her. "Have you come with Jane Dickson?" she inquired.

"Yes, she is with me. Do you wish to speak with her?" asked Madeline.

"No, but I must speak with you regarding Jane," whispered Susanna, ushering Madeline over to a secluded corner. "A man by the name of Jarret Ormsby has just been in the store seeking out a gift for your friend. He said that they had been courting for some time and that they were soon to be married. I have to say that I believed this to be a falsehood owing to the facts with which I had been presented, regarding Mr. Ormsby. Facts that my father had divulged in an effort to protect me from being taken in by his attentions. Furthermore, as Jane is clearly still grieving the loss of her husband, I did not find his story to be credible."

"Susanna, you are a faithful friend," whispered Madeline. "I must confirm that you are correct in your assumption regarding Jarret and Jane. Furthermore, I am persuaded more now than ever, Susanna, that our suspicions regarding his motives for such lies are closer to the truth than we knew. A final word for your benefit; as the town has not, as yet, bestowed on him the honorable title of 'Mr.' you may simply call him Jarret."

Susanna laughed at Madeline's last remark, but then became quite serious as she cautioned, "This is not the first I have heard of this. Whenever certain of the ladies in town are in the store, Mr. Ormsby, I mean Jarret, makes a point of speaking with them regarding Jane. It seems as if he is rallying people who will stand by his story. But what could he hope to gain from all of this?"

"I am indebted to you for making this known to me. As for what might be gained from instigating such rumors, our town has decided that the penalty for fornication is that the couple in question must marry," grimaced Madeline. "Many of us are of the opinion that he intends to force Jane into marriage by stirring up the town with his lies regarding their relationship."

"Oh, now I understand," replied Susanna. "How desperate he must be to force a woman into marriage."

"Indeed," replied Madeline. "We know of no other reason for his lies. He must know that she shall never be prevailed upon to marry him unless forced to do so. In view of all of this, I shall say, again, how much I appreciate your willingness to involve yourself on behalf of Jane. We must not breathe a word about our suspicions."

"You can depend on me to keep silent," replied Susanna.

"I must go and speak with the others regarding all that you have disclosed," replied Madeline. "We must get together for tea and happier conversation."

"I should like that," replied Susanna.

Madeline rushed Jane and the others out of the store so that she could reveal the information that she had acquired from Susanna. Upon hearing the news, they thought it best to return home and discuss it with Mr. Foster and Emma.

Chapter 23

Birth Anomalies/Jarret's Wicked Scheme/ Waiting for Proof

Jane accompanied Emma on a visit to an expectant mother by the name of Mary Haddon who lived just outside of town. As the ladies were approaching, Mary's husband, Thomas Haddon, hastened them inside; she had commenced with her labor before they had arrived.

"Dear Mary, do not be anxious. Jane and I are here to assist you," said Emma softly.

"Oh, Emma, you came in time," replied Mary. "It has been going on a few hours now. I wished for Thomas to go and fetch you, but he did not want to leave my side."

"It will be all right," answered Emma.

Mary struggled for a few more hours before delivering a son. At first glance, the lad appeared to be robust and healthy, but upon closer inspection, Emma noticed that he had been born with anomalies that would surely mean his death. She ushered Jane aside and requested that she ask Thomas to come inside, as he had removed himself to the out of doors to wait upon the arrival of the child. Once Thomas had returned, Emma whispered to him the sorrowful news. She expressed her desire that he remain to bring comfort to Mary once she learned the truth.

Just as Emma had anticipated, the baby died within a few hours. The mother and father were left in despair at the loss of their firstborn son. Emma expressed her sorrow over the loss, and set off for home knowing that she could do little to comfort them at such a time.

Later that night, after Emma and Jane had returned home, they recounted the events of the day to Mr. Foster. He shared in their sadness and offered his assurance that there was nothing that could have been done to save the little lad.

"I know that all such things are in God's hands; however, I felt extremely helpless as the baby lay dying in the arms of his mother," cried Emma. "I know that this is not the first birth in which I have assisted that has ended in a loss, but one never gets used to it."

"Jane, you have not spoken a word," remarked Mr. Foster.

"I have been silently praying for the family."

"That is good," replied Emma. "Only God can mend their broken hearts."

"It is not only the loss of the Haddon's baby," confessed Jane. "There is more on my mind I have not disclosed. I am carrying Nathan's child."

"Oh, Jane, I had hoped you would say something to us," replied Emma. "I did not wish to inquire about it until you were ready to tell us."

"What, you knew?" inquired Jane, stunned.

"Jane, after all, I am a midwife," responded Emma, with a smile. "Are you not happy about the baby?"

"Yes, but I did not wish to burden you and Morris further than I already have in coming here."

"Burden us!" exclaimed Morris. "You and your baby, my grandchild, could never be a burden. I am overjoyed. Never let me hear you say such a thing again. Do you hear me?"

"Yes, Morris, and I thank you for your kind words. But do you not see that the rumors could not have come at a worse time?" inquired Jane. "It shall only exacerbate the situation once it becomes obvious that I am heavy with child."

"Try not to worry. I sincerely believe that he shall not prevail. The truth will be known, before long," insisted Mr. Foster.

***

A few days had passed since the loss of the Haddon baby had taken place, when Susanna North came to call on Madeline. "Madeline, I must speak with you directly," Susanna insisted with a solemn face.

"Elizabeth can hear whatever it is that you have to say," assured Madeline.

"Very well," replied Susanna. "I dislike having to always be the bearer of bad news."

"Go on," replied Madeline, with concern in her voice.

"When Mr. Haddon was in town to see the Reverend Worcester, Jarret approached him outside the church. I happened to be outside, myself, just as this was taking place; thus, I overheard Jarret consoling Mr. Haddon over the loss of his son. I thought this to be a kind deed until he implied that Emma was somehow responsible and that she had assisted in other births in which there were anomalies resulting in death."

"This is the most vicious attack, yet, brought on by Jarret," replied Elizabeth. "Is there no one who can put an end to the devastation that he continually brings upon this town?"

"Susanna, once more you have proven yourself a true friend," said Madeline, with a sigh.

"I wish that, for once, I could demonstrate my friendship in some other way," replied Susanna.

"Once again, I am puzzled as to what might be his motive," insisted Madeline.

"I venture to guess that it is his intention to tarnish Emma's reputation, therefore, rallying people to believe whatever he says with regard to her daughter," replied Susanna.

"Jane and Emma must be told, at once," insisted Elizabeth. "Susanna, are you willing to accompany Madeline to the Foster's home to offer a firsthand account of what you have heard?"

"Certainly," replied Susanna resolutely.

Once Madeline and Susanna reached the Foster's home, they were greeted by Anthony and Mr. Foster who escorted them in to speak with Emma and Jane.

"Mr. Foster and Anthony it might be best if you remained to listen to what Susanna has discovered while she was in town," requested Madeline.

Therefore, they remained listening intently to Susanna; after which, Mr. Foster and Anthony rose to their feet in anger. "I am going to speak with Reverend Worcester!" blurted Mr. Foster. "He must be informed of what has been taking place, as he is sure to give counsel regarding the situation."

"If you like, I shall accompany you," said Anthony.

"If you have a mind to, then come along," replied Mr. Foster.

With that, the two men were on their way to seek counsel from Reverend Worcester while Madeline and Susanna remained for a time with Emma and Jane.

Along the way, Mr. Foster filled Anthony in on Jane's condition.

"That will surely add fuel to the fire," cautioned Anthony. "And it causes me added concern for Jane's health, as the stress is sure to be detrimental to her and the baby."

As they approached their destination, Mr. Foster warned not to speak of the news regarding Jane.

"Of course, however, everyone will know soon enough," warned Anthony.

"True, but let it not be today."

A knock came at the door of Reverend Worcester's home. He was surprised to find Mr. Foster and Anthony standing there. "Come in, gentlemen. To what do I owe the pleasure of this visit?"

May we speak with you regarding a very serious matter?" inquired Mr. Foster.

"Well certainly, and what might this be about?" replied Reverend Worcester.

"Surely you have heard the rumors in town regarding Jane and Jarret," insisted Mr. Foster.

"No, I must admit that I have not," replied Reverend Worcester. "What are the rumors of which you speak?"

Anthony sat quietly as the conversation went on, ready to assist Mr. Foster in the delivery if necessary.

"You are aware, are you not, of the decision at the last meeting of the selectmen regarding the penalty for fornication?" inquired Mr. Foster.

"Well yes, I was in attendance and had given some counsel on the matter before the meeting," replied Reverend Worcester. "I believe this to be a more compassionate form of punishment than what had been done previously on such occasions. Why, is there some question as to whether we should have moved in this direction for such situations?"

"No, no. I share your opinion on the matter," replied Mr. Foster.

"Very well then, I shall keep silent and let you explain," responded Reverend Worcester.

"Thank you," replied Mr. Foster. "What I have to say may come as a shock, though I am not sure why we should be shocked any longer by any of Jarret's antics. We believe that Jarret is using the decision of the board to further his own interests. Despite the fact that he was rejected by Jane, he has been circulating around town a falsehood in which he claims to be courting her and that they intend to be married. Moreover, we believe that he intends to force her hand by way of the board of selectmen."

"Is it your opinion then that he intends to say that fornication has taken place between the two of them?" inquired Reverend Worcester, shocked.

"That is precisely what we believe," replied Mr. Foster.

"That is an extraordinary claim. Not that I disbelieve that he would do such a thing, but have you any proof?"

"Only that we have witnesses to the fact that he has made false claims regarding their courtship and intent to marry," replied Mr. Foster. "As he has lain the groundwork, all that is left for him to do is make the final claim of fornication. Furthermore, we are sure of Jane's disinterest in Jarret, as she has been with us every moment and has refused to allow Jarret to call."

"This may, yet, be his most despicable act," replied Reverend Worcester, with concern.

"There is more," insisted Mr. Foster. "You are aware of the Haddon baby, are you not?"

"Of course, as I have been continually with the family ever since the tragedy occurred," replied Reverend Worcester.

"Today, as Mr. Haddon was arriving to speak with you over at the church, Jarret approached him with the pretext of consoling him only to follow it with accusations against Emma. He claims that she is the cause of the death of their baby as well as the deaths of certain others born with peculiar anomalies!" exclaimed Mr. Foster.

"What is your opinion as to the reason for such claims against Emma?" inquired Reverend Worcester.

"If he can discredit Emma by exploiting the superstitious types, others may be apt to believe his lies against Jane," replied Mr. Foster. "In fact, it was Susanna North who wisely pointed out that the discrediting of Emma might serve to besmirch Jane as well."

"Susanna North, what has she to do with this?"

"She has been a witness to many of the events to which we are referring," replied Mr. Foster.

"Reverend Worcester, Mr. Foster, I have news of which I had hoped to have obtained proof prior to making it known to anyone," said Anthony.

"Of what nature is this news?" inquired Reverend Worcester. "And from where do you expect proof to come?"

"I shall explain," replied Anthony. "Upon my arrival to Salisbury, I observed Jarret Ormsby in town one day. I recognized him right away as having come from Norwich, my hometown in England."

"Oh, you came from the same town," said Reverend Worcester, with surprise.

"Yes," replied Anthony.

Continuing on, he explained that upon seeing him, Jarret had hastened away, and that he continues to do so every time they meet.

"Very interesting," said Mr. Foster.

"There is more," continued Anthony. "One day I caught up with him and inquired as to why he had not greeted me whenever he had seen me in town. I explained that, after all, we had come from the same town. At which point, a very peculiar thing happened; he denied ever having met me or that he had even come from Norwich. Well, I knew that there was something amiss, which was confirmed to me when I learned that he was presenting himself as never having been married. You see, he has a wife in Norwich that he was to send for once he was settled. That was many years ago. Unless I am mistaken, he has abandoned his marriage to Grace and never intended to send for her."

"I am in utter and complete shock," replied Mr. Foster. "He has pursued women, not only here, but in Salem, knowing full well that he has a wife in England. The poor dear soul, how she must be suffering. Can she even be aware of any of this? Or maybe she believes that he is dead."

"Yes, I have also wondered about that, Mr. Foster. I have so longed to make this known to you; however, it would have been my word against his. As I am new to this town and have but few acquaintances, such an outlandish story might not have been believed," insisted Anthony. "Furthermore, I did not wish to alert him that I was, even now, seeking proof of his marriage, but I cannot remain silent any longer."

"You say you are seeking proof; from where do you expect this proof to come?" inquired Reverend Worcester.

"I am in hopes of substantiating my claims upon the return of Christopher Osgood," replied Anthony.

"Oh, I see," replied Reverend Worcester. "Is he to seek out the truth whilst he is in England?"

"Yes, upon their arrival in England, they shall be disembarking in Harwich. From there, Christopher plans to travel to Norwich while Mr. Carr sets off for London," Anthony explained.

"You were wise to wait for proof before making this known to the town," replied Mr. Foster. "However, I am pleased that you have decided to share this information with us. Rest assured, we will not divulge any of this unless it becomes absolutely necessary in the defense of Jane."

"I am in complete agreement," replied Reverend Worcester. "Anthony, it is good that you have made all of this known to us, as it shall surely help to direct our actions in the future."

"I am happy that it is out, if only to the two of you," sighed Anthony.

Chapter 24

Arriving in England during a Time of Unrest/Mr. Carr's Wedding Plans

Mr. Carr and Christopher had finally reached the end of their long journey to England; at which point, they disembarked in Harwich where they were conveyed to their lodgings.

"Mr. Carr, thank the Lord, we have arrived at last," said Christopher, utterly exhausted. I am happy that our lodgings are an easy distance, for I feel as if I might sleep for a week."

"Christopher, we shall rest a day before traveling on, you to Norwich and I to London. Once my business is concluded there, I shall return to inquire after purchasing the implements of which I am in need. I shall be gone but a few days," said Mr. Carr.

"Very well. I could, indeed, do with a rest before setting off. I am in hopes that my business shall not require a great amount of time, and that I too shall arrive back here in a few days," replied Christopher.

However, Mr. Carr and Christopher soon learned that there was much unrest in England that might interfere with their plans, as a conflict between King Charles and Parliament had been brewing for some time.

"Mr. Carr, there was a kindly gentleman who observed us as we disembarked from the ship. Knowing that we had only just arrived, he inquired as to whether we were aware of the danger not far off from Harwich. He disclosed to me that Parliament recently adopted something called 'the Grand Remonstrance' in which they recite the evils of the king's reign and insist on church reform as well as parliamentary control over the army. The result of which split Parliament, as many of the moderates moved to the Royalists side. It appears that England may be headed for civil war," informed Christopher.

"Yes, I had heard rumors before we took leave of Salisbury of the intensity of the power struggle between Parliament and the king," replied Mr. Carr. "However, this 'Grand Remonstrance' must have been adopted whilst we were yet on our journey. It is sure to have heightened the tensions even further. It is my belief that many from the colony shall return to England to fight on the side of Parliament, should a war break out."

"I truly hope it does not come to that," replied Christopher.

"Agreed," replied Mr. Carr in all sincerity, for though he had removed from England, he continued to be burdened for its people. "We shall need to take great care as we travel on to London and Norwich."

As anticipated, after a day of rest, Mr. Carr set off for London with a warning to Christopher to be vigilant as he traveled to Norwich. Christopher procured a packhorse, and within two days, he reached his destination. Despite the fact that he was a bit uneasy over the unrest as well as the prospect of meeting Jarret's abandoned wife, he was pleased that things were moving ahead as planned.

What am I to say to a lady who has suffered so? he thought as he unburdened his horse at the stables. *I do not wish to add to her distress by bringing to light this whole unhappy situation.*

Later at the inn, he made the acquaintance of an elderly gentleman by the name of Henry Jacobs who had long been living in Norwich. After some conversation, mostly about the situation in England, Christopher ventured to ask whether Henry was acquainted with Jarret Ormsby, explaining that Jarret had once been a resident of Norwich.

"Indeed," grimaced the old gentleman. "He has long been over across the ocean in New England. Are you acquainted with him?"

"Yes, I have had the misfortune I am sorry to say," replied Christopher. "I am, in truth, here to find his wife."

"The poor soul has been treated contemptibly by the scoundrel, as he abandoned her some years ago," replied Henry. "She thought to join him over there once he sent for her. However, he never did, though she held out hope for ever so long."

"My purpose in coming to Norwich is to speak with her regarding Jarret, and his misrepresentation of himself in Salisbury, the town from whence I came. Had it not been for another of your former townsman, who is presently residing in Salisbury, we should not have found out that he is presently married," said Christopher. "It is not my intention to cause his wife additional pain, but I must set things right in my town. You see, Jarret has attempted to pursue more than one young lady, knowing all the while that he is not free to do so."

"Perhaps I might accompany you," replied Henry. "In as much as she is a friend and a neighbor of mine, it may not be quite so much of a shock if I am with you. I shall initiate the conversation by informing her of the reason for your visit; after which, you may make your inquiries."

"I would be most grateful," replied Christopher. "I have been uneasy about this whole business; thus, it would greatly ease my mind to have you with me when I speak with her. Henry, might you tell me her name? It escapes me at the moment, and it would not do for me to speak with her regarding something so personal without first addressing her properly?"

"Her name is Grace," replied Henry. "She is a lovely young lady. She moved in with her sister and her sister's husband once it became apparent that she had been abandoned."

"As it is too late today, shall we meet tomorrow?" inquired Christopher.

"Yes, tomorrow would be best," replied Henry. "I shall collect you in the morning."

"Until tomorrow, then," replied Christopher.

Christopher went to his room where he was to lodge for the night. He felt as if he should sleep for a week. However, knowing what he must do the following day, sleep did not come so easily.

Early the next morning, Henry came to the inn. "Are you prepared to go and speak with Grace?"

"Indeed, but I take no delight in it, as it is likely to cause her pain," replied Christopher.

"It may, nevertheless, it appears to be necessary. We shall be there before long, as it is not a long distance. In fact, you can see the house at the top of that hill," Henry pointed out.

The two men were quickly approaching, when they noticed a slender figure out in the yard. "Christopher, Grace is out in the front of the house," said Henry. "I shall introduce you."

Grace noticed the two men as they were coming into the yard; thus, she strolled over to greet them. Henry spoke up first. "Good day to you, Grace. I should like to introduce you to Christopher Osgood, a new acquaintance of mine. He wishes to speak with you on a matter of some delicacy."

"How do you do. I am Grace Ormsby." Grace had long desired to be rid of the name of "Ormsby," as it was an unwelcome reminder that she was a married woman who had been abandoned.

"Delighted to make your acquaintance," replied Christopher.

"Grace, may we find a quiet place in which to talk?" inquired Henry.

"If you will follow me, we may speak privately over there in the garden," replied Grace directing them.

The two men followed after her until they came upon an exquisite little garden. She ushered them to the benches that were situated facing each other amongst a lovely well-groomed row of hedges.

"Do sit down," said Grace.

"Grace, I must speak plainly, as I find that there is no easy way of commencing with this conversation," said Henry. "What we have come to speak to you about concerns Jarret."

Christopher was grateful that Henry had delivered the shocking nature of the visit before he made his inquiries.

"Grace, pray forgive me, but I must know some things, regarding Jarret, that only you can answer. I assure you that I would not have come were it not necessary for the protection of many a young lady in my town."

"I believe that I know in which direction this conversation tends. Jarret has been living the life of a bachelor, has he not?"

Upon meeting such a sweet and lovely young lady, Christopher hesitated in answering the question put before him.

"Do not make yourself uneasy, for I have long wondered if this had been the reason for the forsaking of our marriage," said Grace, with a smile so as to ease Christopher's discomfort. "The only other possibility was that he had died, but I guess I did not really believe that to be so. You see, he was not like the others who journeyed to New England, as the largest part were motivated by their beliefs. Jarret saw it simply as an opportunity for gain. He was not, or should I say *is* not, a man of many principles."

Seeing that Grace was not very much moved by the discussion, as yet, he continued, "You see, a man by the name of Anthony Hall, who had once lived amongst you in Norwich, moved to Salisbury whereupon he observed Jarret in town. When confronted, Jarret denied ever having met the man before or having come from Norwich. We had deemed it almost impossible to verify that he was, indeed, married until I was presented with an opportunity to return to England on business. Once we learned of this forthcoming trip, Anthony and I decided that there was now a possibility of setting things right. I would not have burdened you had there been another way."

At this point, Christopher and Henry's eyes were fixed upon Grace to observe whether she was becoming too distressed by the news to continue. They suspected that she might simply be putting forth a strong front.

Endeavoring to restrain her emotions, Grace entreated Christopher not to suffer regret for having confirmed her fears as she was now happily settled with her family. She went on to explain that she had been much happier living with her family than she had ever been with Jarret.

"I am convinced after knowing Jarret, you truly are in a more agreeable situation," insisted Christopher.

Grace doubted that she could be of assistance, as she was in England and they were across the ocean in Salisbury. "Have you a way for me to verify, short of coming to Salisbury, that I am Jarret's abandoned wife?"

"It is my belief that an affidavit comprised of your testimony, to be signed for verification by the officials of your town, would be enough to preclude any doubt," replied Christopher. "You may think it strange, but we have had a similar experience, with Jarret, in which we had to obtain an affidavit. However, in that instance, I happened to be his victim of choice."

Henry and Grace nodded in agreement that this was, indeed, a very odd situation in that twice an affidavit had been required with regard to Jarret.

"Perhaps I might be of additional assistance in this matter," said Henry. "You see, I hold a position of influence in this town; thus, I shall have an affidavit drawn up and signed by those in authority; at which point, it shall be presented to Grace and her family for their signatures by this time tomorrow," assured Henry, with satisfaction.

"I am indebted to you both," replied Christopher, with a sigh of relief that things had gone so well. "Grace, it has been a delight to have made your acquaintance, though I wish it had been under happier circumstances. Moreover, I believe Jarret is a fool to have treated you so contemptibly. He is not worthy of such a respectable and lovely young lady."

"My only hope in all of this is that he is not sent back to me, as I should not want him back for the world," confessed Grace. "Will you send word of the outcome?"

"Indeed I shall," replied Christopher. "Furthermore, whenever there is news, with regard to Jarret, I shall send word, as you are entitled to be informed of anything pertaining to Jarret."

Just as their conversation came to a close, a lovely little girl came strolling up. With a look of distress, Grace quickly glanced over at Henry before confessing to Christopher that the child belonged to Jarret.

"Christopher, since all connection between Jarret and myself seemed dissolved, I did not wish for him to learn of Esther. Otherwise, he may have had a notion to take her away. Moreover, given that he is prone to stray, cheat, and lie, I thought better of allowing Esther any contact with him."

"Mamma, I have been searching for you," she said, as she climbed into her mother's lap.

"I have been right here, Esther," replied Grace, kissing her on the cheek. "Now run along and play. I shall be but a little while longer." With that reassurance, she was off.

"Jarret was unaware, then, of your condition before departing from England," said Christopher.

"It is doubtful that it would have deterred him from departing," replied Grace.

"Henry, I see none of this is news to you, as you have been her confidant."

"Yes, Grace speaks with me on such matters as one would speak with a father," replied Henry. "It was my belief that Grace would not have wished for me to reveal to you the truth regarding Esther."

Christopher hastened to assure Grace that her secret was safe and that there was no need for further explanation as to why she did not wish to inform Jarret. He understood Jarret's character far too well.

"Grace, you are truly a brave soul, looking after your child without the assistance of a father," expressed Christopher, with admiration.

"I am not so brave, for God in His mercy has seen fit to provide me with an extraordinary family from which I have a great deal of support," replied Grace.

"We shall take leave of you now," said Christopher. "Once more, allow me to say that I am grateful to you for your willingness to speak with me."

Grace bid them farewell and they were on their way. However, Christopher could not cease from thinking about Grace and little Esther and the difficult position in which Jarret had left them. *Though he knew not of Esther, there can be no excuse for his treatment of Grace*, thought Christopher.

The following day, Henry met up with Christopher at the inn. "Good morning. Here is the affidavit. I am delighted that for Grace there is finally some bit of closure. However, having Esther she will forevermore be reminded of Jarret. I only wish that she were free to marry again, though she insists she has no such desire."

"If you only knew the half of it, Henry, for there is more to be said with regard to Jarret. However, it is sufficient to say that it appears that Jarret has consistently been leaving pain in his wake," replied Christopher.

"Well then, the good news in all of this is that this affidavit should squelch any of his further attempts to harm anyone else," replied Henry.

"Indeed it shall," acknowledged Christopher. "And, Henry, I am especially grateful to you, as I could not have accomplished any of this without your assistance."

"You must take care as you return to Harwich. Rumors are that the king has been secretly securing some of the seaports. You may find it difficult to return to New England," warned Henry.

"Thank you for alerting me, Henry," replied Christopher.

Henry's warning troubled Christopher throughout the night. However, with the dawning of a new day, Christopher decided to trust that all would be well. As he set off for Harwich to meet up with Mr. Carr, he said a prayer. "God, I thank You for granting me success in Norwich. I leave the details of the remainder of our journey in Your capable hands. As always, I entrust to You our safety," whispered Christopher, as he loaded up his packhorse for the trip.

Along the way, Christopher could not help but think of Grace and Esther. *In most situations for justice to be carried out, a wayward husband and father would be sent back to fulfill his duty to his family,* he thought; *however, with such a man as Jarret, it would be cruel to compel Grace to allow his return. Jarret would surely bring her additional anguish, as he is such a scoundrel. Although I dislike absolving him of the responsibility, I shall have to make the recommendation to the town that he not be sent back to England.*

A few days after Christopher's arrival in Harwich, Mr. Carr arrived back at the inn. They conversed about the events that had taken place in each other's absence.

"Mr. Carr, I have been warned that the king may be surreptitiously securing certain seaports. It might be difficult to secure passage for our return trip," cautioned Christopher.

"Yes, I too have heard the rumors," replied Mr. Carr. "We shall need to be discreet regarding our plans. The ship on which I hope to travel, the *New Englander*, happens to be the one on which an emissary to the king shall be traveling. The rumor is that he is to repress any support for Parliament in the colonies if a war breaks out in England."

"In that case, the ship shall be permitted to leave port," said Christopher, with a hopeful tone.

"Precisely," whispered Mr. Carr.

"Oh, I see," replied Christopher, with a smile, realizing that Mr. Carr hoped to arrange their plans accordingly.

"And now let us keep silent on the subject, as it would not do for us to be overheard," insisted Mr. Carr.

"You are right, besides there is so much to share with you regarding my trip to Norwich," sighed Christopher.

"I did not think that you wished to divulge the nature of your business in Norwich, as you had never spoken of it," replied Mr. Carr. "Let us go in and take food and rest and tomorrow we shall speak of your news."

"That is most agreeable to me," replied Christopher, "for I am as tired as an old dog."

The following morning, Mr. Carr and Christopher met up early, at which time, Christopher commenced with the revelations regarding Jarret in relation to his secret mission to Norwich. However, as he had promised Grace, he determined that he would not share her secret concerning Esther, even with Mr. Carr.

He began, "I was not at liberty to speak on this before, as I had first to confirm the facts of the situation with which I had been presented," insisted Christopher. "Anthony Hall shared with me a while back that while living in Norwich he had been acquainted with Jarret. It seems that it was from there that Jarret came. The most shocking bit of news he divulged was that Jarret is married."

"That is extraordinary. Can you be sure of this?" replied Mr. Carr.

"We had not the proof until now," replied Christopher. "This trip opened up an opportunity that Anthony and I had not thought possible. You see, Grace, Jarret's wife, resides in Norwich. As we had hoped and prayed, I was able to meet with her while I was in Norwich. God truly granted me favor in that He brought a gentleman by the name of Henry Jacobs to assist me. He happened to be Grace's neighbor and was all too happy to introduce me upon hearing the whole, sordid story. He believed that it might bring some closure for Grace to have some news of Jarret."

"Is there no end to this man's perfidy?" grimaced Mr. Carr. "This time, he will not be able to wriggle out of being publicly set down as he should have been long before now."

"That is my earnest desire," replied Christopher.

Mr. Carr and Christopher procured all of the needed supplies within a few days during which time they spoke openly regarding their plans to establish a ferry service. They also made it known that there would be a benefit to the Crown if travel in New England were to be less difficult.

In fact, their strategy was successful, as they easily secured passage on the *New Englander* and were, once again, on the long journey across the ocean.

Their first night aboard the ship, Mr. Carr, once again, warned Christopher not to make known the presence of the emissary. "To do so may well put us all in peril, as he would surely know that the king's secrets might be made known abroad," insisted Mr. Carr. "Therefore, let us travel much as we did on our journey over, making new acquaintances and staying out of trouble."

"Very well," replied Christopher. "However, once we return home, we shall have to decide what is to be done."

The second day aboard ship, Mr. Carr was introduced to a woman by the name of Elizabeth Oliver. Elizabeth was a slender pretty woman with blonde, silky hair, which she kept neatly pinned low at the back of her head. Since the death of his wife many years back, Mr. Carr had been disinterested in forming any new attachments. However, with each passing day aboard the ship, he found himself more and more looking forward to seeing and talking with Elizabeth. Their conversations were of great interest to him, as she had a vast array of knowledge on many subjects. Although she was many years his junior, at but five and twenty, she seemed to him a wise and courageous woman whom he grew to admire greatly in the short time he had known her aboard the ship.

Christopher was delighted to see the interest that Mr. Carr was taking in the young lady, as he knew full well the broken heart he had suffered with the loss of his first wife. Christopher was reminded as well of the young lady that held his interest, and their times together on his first voyage. He wondered what she might be doing this very minute so far away. He so wished he had been able to bid her farewell before embarking on his journey, and hoped she understood that he should never have rushed off without seeing her had it not been for the distance between them, as she had been in Ipswich when the time came for his departure.

At an opportune moment with Christopher, Mr. Carr divulged his feelings for Elizabeth. "I wish to ask for her hand in marriage before we reach the end of our crossing," said Mr. Carr, with trepidation.

"Well, that is wonderful news," replied Christopher. "But what is this mood of apprehension I am sensing?"

"Do you think it is too soon, as we have only known each other a short while?" inquired Mr. Carr.

"Ah, now I understand the source of it. You are concerned, are you not, that she may not accept you, as you have held such a short acquaintance?" inquired Christopher.

"Indeed, and as I am almost twenty years her senior, she may not think me a suitable husband," replied Mr. Carr.

Christopher smiled and reassured Mr. Carr that from what he had observed of her countenance whenever she was in his presence, the chances of her accepting him were very much in his favor.

"I do not wish to let this opportunity pass, as she shall be living in Ipswich and not in Salisbury. Hence, continuing a courtship, though not impossible, would present some difficulty," sighed Mr. Carr, as he was mustering up the nerve to approach Elizabeth. "As we are about halfway through our journey, tomorrow shall be the day that I inquire after her feelings with regard to marriage," he said, resolutely.

"I shall beseech the Lord to steady you as you speak with her, for your nerves seem to be in great need of calming," chuckled Christopher.

The following afternoon, Mr. Carr approached Elizabeth and requested an audience with her. "Elizabeth, we shall be disembarking in a few weeks; therefore, I believe this to be a fitting time to express to you my regard and admiration. Although there is a great deal of difference in our ages, if you will accept my hand, I shall endeavor to do my very best to make you happy. Furthermore, I shall provide very well for you, especially once the ferry service gets underway. Elizabeth, let me say it clearly; I love you and wish to marry you."

"Mr. Carr, I need not be convinced of your worthiness, as I have found you to be one of the most worthy gentlemen in all my acquaintance," replied Elizabeth, with a smile. "I shall be honored to accept your hand."

"Elizabeth, you have made me a very happy man!" exclaimed Mr. Carr. "To think, I should never have met you had I not returned to England for supplies. We must share our news with Christopher, as he is sure to be very pleased."

The joyful couple sought out Christopher to convey the happy news. Christopher was overjoyed, though, observing them together made him think of Maddie. He thought about the fact that he had never given her any indication that he wished to marry her, as he had held conflicting emotions for so long regarding that subject. He had even entertained thoughts of speaking with her before setting off for England, but he knew that he was, at that time, not altogether prepared to do so, and she was away at the time. However, the long separation from her had served to settle it for him. He now longed to explain the battle that had been raging within, and at long last request her hand in marriage.

But for now, a few weeks remained until the end of the journey. *What is more, she may not even return my feelings*, he thought.

Chapter 25

Jane's Nightmare/Reputations Destroyed/Reassurances

Although the warm weather had come early that year and there had been very little snow, all the same it had been a hard winter for two of the ladies of Salisbury. Madeline had been growing more and more anxious for Christopher's return and, for Jane, the constant worry over the situation with Jarret had become almost too much to bear.

Early one morning, Jane was awakened by a dreadful dream in which she saw herself married to Jarret and forced to live in his home. She sighed with immense relief upon waking to the reality that she had not married Jarret and was safely in her own home with her dear parents. She decided she had to get up quietly, so as not to wake anyone, and move to the door. She thought that the fresh air blowing on her face might serve to calm her.

She made her way out into the yard without disturbing any of the other sleeping occupants. Finding her favorite tree to recline under, she prayed for strength and for the truth to come out regarding Jarret's lies. Before long, she heard someone coming up behind her. She turned with a start, only to find that it was Anthony.

"You scared me half out of my wits!" she exclaimed, grasping her chest as if to prevent her heart from flying out.

"Pray forgive me," replied Anthony, gently touching her arm. "I did not expect to find you out here so early."

Attempting to distract from being asked the reason she was out so early in the morning, she said, "Anthony, you are too good to us, coming here every day as you do. You have helped Morris immensely, what with adding on to the house amongst many other things. I shall miss you when you return to working for Mr. Carr full time."

Anthony smiled upon hearing Jane say that she would miss him.

Realizing what she had just disclosed, Jane felt a bit embarrassed. "Well, you take my meaning, do you not? I um . . . I mean we are just very accustomed to having you here," she said, trying to lessen the possible impact of her previous comment.

Averting her gaze away from Anthony, she felt her cheeks flush. "I must be going inside now," she said, as she hastened away leaving Anthony standing there staring after her.

Anthony remained by the tree a while thinking about what Jane had said, wondering if she had truly meant it or if she was simply making conversation. *She did appear to be caught off guard by her own words as though she had not intended to speak them*, he thought. Whether she truly meant it, he knew not, but he was sure of his own feelings. He would miss her when he was not needed by Mr. Foster any longer.

I must get back to work and leave off from contemplating over this any longer, he decided. However, as he walked toward the barn, he continued to think about Jane. *I wonder if she realizes that I am aware of the baby. When she was speaking the other night with regard to future children, she must have been referring to the baby that she is now carrying. However, she may well desire to be married again and have other children.* Shaking his head so as to disrupt any further thoughts of Jane, he launched into his work.

Once inside, Jane began to wonder why she had said that to Anthony. Did she really feel that way? *If only I had not said aloud that I shall miss him*, she thought. *Now I shall be uneasy whenever he is present.*

Emma and Mr. Foster had awakened shortly after Jane returned to the house. "You are up bright and early today, my dear," said Emma.

"Oh, I am sorry if I woke you," replied Jane. "With all of this Jarret business, I was having a bit of trouble sleeping. In fact, I had a terrible nightmare in which I was married to him."

"Oh, that is terrible to be sure. I should imagine it would be difficult to sleep with everything that has taken place," replied Emma, with a sympathetic tone. "Perhaps a walk might take your mind off things. However, if you go, remember to go in the opposite direction from town."

"No, I do not believe I shall take a walk just now, for I do not wish to run into Jarret. I am a bit fearful of being away from the house no matter the direction, as Jarret tends to pop up in the most unlikely places," uttered Jane. She also felt uneasy about seeing Anthony, but could not mention that to Emma.

"In a short while I shall be setting off to call on one of our mothers. Perhaps you ought to accompany me, as it has always been a good distraction for you."

"Indeed, that is precisely what I need to keep my mind more agreeably engaged."

Mr. Foster joined Anthony outside just as he was finishing up some of the morning chores.

"Good morning, Anthony. I am indebted to you for all that you have done to assist me over the past few months."

"It has been my pleasure. Being with you and your family has kept me from missing my relatives back in England," replied Anthony. "Thus, it shall be difficult to do without the constant companionship that I have so enjoyed."

"As our friend, you are always welcome," replied Mr. Foster, "so you need not be lonely."

"I must confess that, if she is agreeable, I should like to call on Jane when the time is right," divulged Anthony. "I have come to greatly esteem her, as I have daily observed her character. I find her to be a caring and courageous young lady."

"I could not wish for a better man for Jane," replied Mr. Foster.

"In that case, have I your approval?"

"Certainly."

"We need not mention any of this to Jane just now," said Anthony, "for though I am eager to commence with courting, it is too soon for Jane."

Emma and Jane came out of the house just as Anthony had finished speaking with Mr. Foster regarding his desire to court Jane.

"To where are you ladies off?" inquired Mr. Foster.

"We have an expectant mother who is in need of a visit, as it has been a few weeks since we last we saw her," replied Emma. "From there, we shall walk over to call on Elizabeth."

"Be sure to keep your distance from Jarret," warned Mr. Foster.

"We shall," replied Emma.

Jane and Anthony glanced at each other as Emma said goodbye. The easy manner with each other they had previously enjoyed seemed now to be far out of reach. To their dismay, it had been replaced by an unexpected awkwardness.

"Jane, you did not even speak to Anthony. Is there anything amiss with you today?" inquired Emma.

"Not a thing," replied Jane, "I could not think of anything I wished to say."

"You should have at least bid him goodbye," replied Emma, with a sigh.

Emma wondered what could have happened to change the friendly way in which Jane and Anthony had always gotten along together, as it seemed apparent that neither wished to address the other.

Jane and Emma arrived at the home where they were to execute their usual duties, only to be turned away by the woman's husband. He met them at the door with the following words: "In view of the fact that the most recent birth in which you assisted ended in the death of the child, we find that you are ill qualified to assist in the birth of our baby."

"Am I to understand that you are blaming me for the death of the Haddon's baby?" inquired Emma.

"Yes, that is precisely what I am saying," he replied.

"May I inquire after your wife's opinion on this matter, and whether she remains in good health?" asked Emma, concerned that it was getting close to the woman's time. "She must not be left unattended, or you may indeed lose the baby, and then it shall be on your head."

"It is no longer your concern. She is being cared for by another and is certainly receiving every possible attention," replied the man.

"I shall not intrude any longer, as it is plain to see that we are unwelcome," replied Emma, while walking away in utter disbelief at what had transpired.

"Oh, Mamma, Jarret is sure to be the ruin of us all if he is to be so easily believed," cried Jane.

"It is by no means certain that Jarret is the cause of our having been turned away," replied Emma. "Though I shall admit that it is highly probable that he is."

"I feel quite unwell and wish to return home," uttered Jane sadly.

"Very well. I shall see you home before I call on Elizabeth; I know I shall not be turned away from the Bleasdell's," replied Emma.

Jane and Emma hastened back home, as they had no desire to be stopped by anyone for conversation along the way. Once home, with tears spilling from her eyes, Jane made haste for the door.

Mr. Foster and Anthony inquired after the reason for the ladies' swift return, as they had intended to be out most of the day. Emma explained what had taken place while endeavoring to remain composed.

"Jane is greatly troubled by this, is she not?" inquired Anthony, upon observing her countenance as she hastened inside.

"Indeed, and she is terribly concerned that Jarret shall be believed regarding anything he asserts about our family," replied Emma.

"The man will stoop to any level to get Jane with no regard for her wellbeing or happiness," said Mr. Foster.

"Mr. Foster, I am of the opinion that Emma and Jane are in need of the confidential information of which I am in possession, regarding Jarret," expressed Anthony. "It is sure to ease their minds."

"If that is your wish, Anthony," replied Mr. Foster, with a nod. "You can be sure that they shall not disclose the news to anyone."

Anthony explained everything to Emma regarding Jarret and his wife as well as his hopes upon Christopher's return for obtaining proof to present to the town.

"Oh, Anthony, this information is certain to cheer Jane," replied Emma, with a sigh. "She must be informed directly. Mr. Foster and I shall go inside and ask Jane to come out to speak with you. I am obliged to you for giving us this hope that all of this may soon be over."

As Mr. Foster and Emma went in to speak with Jane, they found her sitting quietly in a corner gazing up at a wall as if it were some faraway place. Mr. Foster spoke softly to her explaining that Anthony had some news that was sure to encourage. Jane did not move or even acknowledge that she had heard him speaking; thus, Emma walked over to her and began stroking her hair while whispering that she must hear what Anthony had to say. She finally turned her eyes to Emma. Conceding to her request, she rose and moved toward the door.

As she stepped out in the yard, Anthony said, "Jane, I must speak with you." Taking her by the arm, he led her over to sit under the tree he had seen her reclining under many times before. "I have information regarding Jarret that I hope shall set your mind more at ease. I have not spoken to you about it before now, as I had not the proof to support my claims."

Jane sat emotionless as Anthony began to tell her everything regarding Grace, his hometown, his encounter with Jarret, and that he was hopeful that Christopher would return with the proof.

Upon hearing all that Anthony had disclosed, Jane finally spoke. "Anthony, can this be true? Jarret has a wife in England? I should not doubt it, as he is the kind of man that would be so horrible as to abandon a wife. Is it truly your belief that Christopher will have obtained proof?" she inquired, with a sense of relief slowly sweeping over her as she gazed into Anthony's eyes.

Waiting for her to absorb all that he had divulged, Anthony replied to her questions, "Jane, I believe that Christopher shall make every effort to find Grace and secure proof of her existence. If, however, he is unsuccessful, I shall never allow Jarret to force you into marriage. If it should become necessary, I shall steal you away from here. Though, I believe that it shall not come to that, as there is every reason to hope that Christopher shall be successful."

"You are too kind," replied Jane. "However, there are things about me of which you are unaware."

"If you are referring to the baby, I already know," replied Anthony, while taking hold of Jane's hand.

Stunned by all that Anthony had said, Jane dared to glance in his direction, whereupon she observed a gentleness in his expression. Seeing this, she felt a warmth come over her and, for the moment, all of her fears melted away. She knew that come what may Anthony would protect her from Jarret.

Chapter 26

The Return Voyage/Decisions and Confessions/New Acquaintances

Christopher looked intently out over the vast blue ocean deeply absorbed in his thoughts of Maddie. He was beginning to wonder what he might say to her upon his return to Salisbury. His recollection of how she had always conducted herself toward him whenever they were together suggested that her feelings must be similar to his own. Thus, he finally settled in his mind that upon his return he intended to ask for her hand.

Shaking his head, he thought, *I must speak with Anthony concerning Jarret before I attend to my own wishes and desires. Heaven knows what disastrous events may have taken place in the time that we have been away.*

Just then, Mr. Carr approached. "Good morning, Christopher. Did you sleep well?"

"Tolerable, and you?" replied Christopher.

"Very well," replied Mr. Carr, with a smile. "Christopher, as I was speaking with Mr. Winsley last night, I learned of his intention to settle in Salisbury. It is curious, but in all this time with him aboard ship, I was unaware that we shall be neighbors. George Martin shall be settling in Salisbury as well as work for Mr. Winsley. Given that they are great friends, Mr. Winsley desired to pay for George's passage, free of obligation. However, George insisted on working for his fare. He insists that Mr. Winsley not pay for his services until such time as his debt for the passage is paid in full."

"Mr. Winsley made him a very kind offer," replied Christopher. "Were you aware that Mr. Winsley spoke with me just the other day regarding George Martin? He informed me that George's parents, Christopher Martin and Marie, his stepmother, came across the ocean on the *Mayflower* only to die the very first winter. As George was still a small child, he remained in England with his aunt, Christopher's sister. Upon her death, Mr. Winsley, being a friend of the family, took him in. It seems that he is more like a son, to him, than a servant."

Just as Mr. Carr and Christopher were concluding their conversation, George Martin strolled up.

"Good day to you," smiled George.

"And to you," replied Mr. Carr. "We were just speaking of your parents and their voyage over on the *Mayflower*. Once settled, they were to send for you, were they not?"

"Indeed, they were," replied George. "I was living with my aunt in England at the time. She was to allow me to come over to be with my father. My father and stepmother had a dream similar to many others who have journeyed to the 'new land.' My greatest desire is to carry on that dream."

"They would have been proud, to be sure," replied Christopher.

Mr. Carr, George Martin, and Christopher talked on for another hour; at which point, George was called away by Mr. Winsley.

"Pray excuse me, but I must speak with George," said Mr. Winsley.

"That is quite all right," said Mr. Carr, as Mr. Winsley and George walked off together.

Christopher thought about what George Martin had said regarding his parents' dream and his desire to carry it forward. He thought, once again, about his first crossing and the dreams that had spurred him on. He decided that he should like becoming better acquainted with George Martin.

"Please excuse me, too, Christopher," said Mr. Carr as he headed off to find Elizabeth.

Early the next morning, Christopher inquired of the captain his opinion as to how much longer before they would reach Ipswich. The captain reassured him that within a fortnight they should be arriving at their destination. Christopher could scarcely contain himself at the thought of seeing Maddie again. Moreover, he knew he would finally be able to address the matter of Jarret.

***

Back in Salisbury, while working out in the garden, Maddie's thoughts went to Christopher. Growing more and more concerned over his wellbeing with each passing day, she longed for his return. She thought of the illness and the shipwreck that had robbed her of her Oliver and Christopher of his Hannah. She prayed that she would not suffer the loss of Christopher as well.

Even as Maddie was deep in thought about Christopher, Jane arrived with Emma. She observed Madeline out in the garden and hastened out to greet her.

"Good day, Madeline. Mamma has gone inside to Elizabeth."

"And how are you today?" inquired Madeline. "You seem very cheerful."

"I must confess that my mood has improved a bit since the other day when I went along with Mamma on one of her visits. Upon our arrival, the husband came out to send us away. He did not wish for Mamma to continue caring for his wife."

"Why did he turn on Emma in such a dreadful way?" inquired Madeline.

"It seems they had heard about the Haddon baby and blamed Mamma for the death. However, I do believe that I see Jarret's hand in this. Until now, they had always seemed confident in Mamma's service to them."

"Had I known that all of this had taken place, I would have come to comfort you," replied Madeline, with concern.

"Mamma surely would have informed you of all of this had she come to call that day as she had intended. After we had returned to the house, she decided not to leave me, for I was in an awful state."

"Anyone would have felt as you did under such dreadful circumstances. Even so, I am sure that you were more temperate than I should have been if confronted by such a man," replied Madeline. "And how was Emma after such an ordeal?"

"A bit shaken, but she has a strong constitution," smiled Jane. "She does not allow such things to remain on her mind for long. I, however, fret over things long after they have occurred."

"Not so, for you are here today in a most cheerful mood," replied Madeline.

"There is a reason for my improved mood," whispered Jane, with a grin.

"Do tell." She could sense that Jane had good news to share.

"Madeline, I am at a loss as to where to begin."

"Well, you must begin somewhere as I am eager to hear," laughed Madeline.

"Very well," replied Jane. "When I returned home with Mamma following that terrible confrontation, I ran inside to avoid Morris and Anthony, for my eyes were swollen and red from weeping. Shortly thereafter, Morris and Mamma came into the house whereupon they shuffled me out to speak with Anthony, stating that he was eager to share a bit of news with me. Though I did not wish to go out, I eventually acquiesced. Once outside, Anthony ushered me over to sit under my favorite tree; at which point, he disclosed something regarding Jarret that he believed would set my mind at ease."

"Do go on," replied Madeline, with anticipation.

"I am not at liberty to share the whole of it with you; however, I will say that if what he disclosed can be proven, no one shall ever believe Jarret again, and I will no longer be in danger of falling prey to his schemes."

"You have me intrigued beyond measure," replied Madeline. "Can you not say more?"

"Only this—it involves Christopher and his trip to England," whispered Jane. "Upon Christopher's return, you shall understand all, that is, if he has been successful."

"You must tell me more," insisted Madeline.

"I cannot, for I have been told in confidence," replied Jane. "However, I shall share something of my own news with you that you must not tell to anyone."

Madeline nodded in agreement, thus, Jane continued, "After Anthony left off from telling me of the information he possessed, he went on to say that if he is unsuccessful in his endeavors regarding the proof he seeks, he shall not allow Jarret to force me into marriage. He said, to prevent Jarret he shall take me away from here."

"Jane, he must love you," insisted Madeline, with a look of surprise. "There can be no other reason for such a promise."

"It appears to be the case. Even so, I could barely keep my countenance upon hearing his plan."

"How did you respond?" inquired Madeline.

"I was at a loss for words, at first, for I was in such utter shock. I never suspected that Anthony might care for me. However, I knew I had to inform him of the baby, to which he replied that he already knew."

"That is too wonderful. And do you care for him?" inquired Madeline.

"It is too soon," replied Jane. "Would you not agree?"

"Jane, I caution you not to follow in my footsteps, for it is a lonely path I elected to take," replied Madeline.

"You have regret, then?" inquired Jane.

"I do indeed," uttered Madeline, knowing that Christopher could be lost to her forever.

"I have come to believe that it should not simply be a matter of time; it should also depend on the heart. If you love Anthony, do not wait for some arbitrary or proper time for your grieving to end. It shall never fully end, and you should not wish for it to be so, for contained within our grief are the treasured memories of our lost loves."

Chapter 27

Jarret's Scheme/Confessions

While in town one day to make a purchase at Mr. North's store, Anthony overheard an elderly woman, known to be a gossip, speaking about the "appalling behavior of Jane Dickson," and how she had "thrown herself at Jarret Ormsby who with so great a temptation could not help but surrender to it." The woman in whom she was confiding was of the same opinion offering up still more details for the story. She claimed that she had heard tell of the news by two other people.

Anthony glared at them as he marched past, determined not to speak to two such condemnatory women. Susanna Martin quickly ran after Anthony hoping to catch him.

"Anthony, may I speak with you a moment?" inquired Susanna, calling after him as he hurried down the road.

Anthony stopped in his tracks. Whirling around in anger, he found that it was Susanna. "Oh, I am sorry I did not know that it was you calling," said Anthony.

"That is quite all right," replied Susanna. "I only wished to inquire as to whether or not you are going to the Foster's home, as I believe that it is imperative that Jane be informed, immediately, of what is being said regarding her and Jarret."

"You can be sure that I am about to do just that," replied Anthony. "If I were not a Christian man, I would wring Jarret's despicable neck."

"Anthony, there shall come a day when he will answer to God for all of this," remarked Susanna. "I should not wish to be in his shoes on that day."

"If only he would end his deception," insisted Anthony, in a calmer voice. "I thank you for reminding me that it is not for me to judge; however, I am going to do my very best to protect those he wishes to harm."

"Of course. That is as it should be. All I am saying is that you not wish him harm or you are no better than he. Do tell Jane that Father and I are on her side in this matter, and we will do whatever we can to defend her," insisted Susanna.

"I am much obliged to you for cautionary words, and your defense of Jane is commendable. Please tell your father that we are grateful," said Anthony. "I must be off to the Foster's, though I take no pleasure in the task."

"Goodbye, then. We shall continue to entreat the Lord on Jane's behalf," replied Susanna.

With a heavy heart, Anthony made his way to the Foster's home to speak with Jane. Mr. Foster caught sight of him as he was approaching. "Well, Anthony, I am happy to see you, though, I thought you were to be out on Carr's Island today?"

"I had a purchase I needed to make in town, so I went by Mr. North's store. Mr. Foster, I have come with news of a most unpleasant nature."

"Very well, Anthony. Is it for my ears alone, or shall I take you in to speak with Emma and Jane?" inquired Mr. Foster.

"I must speak with all of you," replied Anthony.

Mr. Foster and Anthony went in to Jane and Emma who were surprised by the visit, as they had not thought to see Anthony until the following day.

"Good day, Anthony," said Emma, with a quizzical look. "Were you not to be on the island today?"

"I have come from Mr. North's store whereupon I had the misfortune of overhearing a conversation regarding Jarret and Jane. The lie we anticipated, from Jarret, regarding the extent to which his relationship with Jane has progressed, has come to pass."

"Has he, now, made the claim that their relationship has become physical in nature?" inquired Emma.

"He has," uttered Anthony somberly, glancing over at Jane.

"Oh, this is grave indeed," replied Emma. "If only Christopher were here with the proof that Jarret is already married, he would surely not be so easily believed."

Jane sat quietly as if in a state of shock while Anthony, Emma, and Mr. Foster fixed their eyes upon her, waiting for some kind of a response. She finally rose to her feet and moved slowly across the room to the door. She turned for a moment as if to say something before stepping outside. She then strode across the grass until she felt far enough away that she might be alone to weep.

Emma, Anthony, and Mr. Foster were unsure as to what to do so they waited awhile, vehemently discussing the matter.

"I am convinced that Christopher shall return very soon with the proof we need, and then Jarret shall at long last be publicly set down," Anthony reassured.

"He is a devil of a man to be so cruel as to cause Jane to suffer so," replied Mr. Foster.

"I can no longer just sit and wait for Jane to return," stated Anthony, in an unsettled tone, "I must go and find her."

"Do whatever you think is best," replied Emma.

Anthony hastened out the door and across the yard hoping to find Jane sitting under her favorite tree. However, as Anthony surveyed the spot where he had thought to find her, she was not there. Feeling anxious, he quickly searched around the property to see if he might catch sight of her in some other location. At last, he spied Jane off in a far corner of the yard; at which point, he made haste to catch up with her. Jane glanced up with tear-filled eyes as Anthony approached. She quickly wiped away the tears and smiled, hoping to conceal her emotions. Anthony settled down beside her, placing his hand over hers.

Speaking softly to her, he said, "Jane, though it is difficult, you must not be so troubled by all of this. As I have already stated, I have every confidence that all will be set right very soon.

Christopher shall return any day now, and Jarret will rue the day he decided to make such accusations."

As before, Jane felt more at ease as Anthony spoke soothingly to her. "I am very grateful to you, Anthony. I know not how I should have stood another day of this had you not been here to speak words of comfort to me," whispered Jane.

"It is my desire to be at hand whenever you have need of me. Jane, assisting Mr. Foster has made it possible for me to become well acquainted with your family. In that time, I have come to admire and respect all of you. You, most of all, Jane," said Anthony. "You might have discerned by now that I possess feelings for you of a most tender and adoring nature. Do not misunderstand me; I do not expect that you should return such feelings, as this situation with Jarret, together with the loss of Nathan, is surely to have made such confessions displeasing to you at present."

Jane's heart was racing upon hearing Anthony's revelations spoken so plainly. As she had suspected, given that he was willing to whisk her away from Jarret, he had feelings for her. However, she had not thought it possible that she would feel so strongly for another man so soon after the loss of Nathan. Nevertheless, she had become exceedingly fond of Anthony. She too had come to admire him over the weeks that he had been a constant at the Foster home. The care he took in looking after her, with regard to the Jarret situation, endeared him to her more with each passing day. Coming to herself, she realized that she had not spoken a word to him following his declaration.

"Anthony, I too have come to possess feelings for you, the nature of which I am, as yet, attempting to discover. You have been a constant friend. I depend on you, greatly. Simply being near to you brings me hope that, in time, all will be well," replied Jane.

Anthony smiled as Jane spoke. "Jane, you must not believe that I require a response to what I have expressed. I only hoped to share my heart so that there would be no doubt but that I would always be here for you."

Jane wished to say more to Anthony but knew not what more to say. Holding out his hand for Jane, they rose and strolled back across the yard to the house where Emma and Mr. Foster were anxiously awaiting their return.

Upon seeing Jane and Anthony entering the room, Emma said sadly, "Jane, your suffering has brought us much sorrow. Coming to Salisbury must seem to you to be a mistake after all that has happened."

"I would not say that it has been a mistake," uttered Jane. "It has been difficult to be sure; however, there have been many good things as well. Besides, with the baby coming, I should not wish to be anywhere else."

Mr. Foster detected a change in Jane after she returned from the yard with Anthony. He wondered if Anthony had made his feelings known to Jane. The thought of the two of them together made him smile.

Later that day, Anthony and Mr. Foster set off for Mr. Bleasdell's home to inform him of the latest gossip. After which, Mr. Bleasdell advised that a meeting with Reverend Worcester was in order.

"Very well. I shall speak with Reverend Worcester tomorrow as to the best time for a meeting," replied Anthony.

Thus, the following day, Anthony made his way into town to speak with Reverend Worcester while Madeline came to call at the Foster's home.

"Good day, Emma, Jane. I thought, perhaps, Jane could do with a walk as well as the company of a friend. If you like, we might walk over to Bridget's. We have not called on her in a while."

"I should enjoy a day with my two friends," replied Jane, with a smile.

Jane and Madeline said their goodbyes to Emma with the promise to return in a few hours. After which, they made their way through town and over to Bridget's.

"What a delightful surprise to see the two of you today," said Bridget, ushering them inside. "I was just contemplating coming to call on you, Jane. I have been eager to find out how you are getting along, what with all of the rumors whirling around."

"It has been a trial," replied Jane. "However, I am blessed to have such wonderful friends to see me through."

"I thought I might go over to Mr. North's shop today," said Bridget. "I need a few things. Would you care to come along?"

"Susanna North has proven herself a friend these past weeks," remarked Jane. "I should like to see her."

"It is all set, then," replied Madeline. "Let us go, as it is sure to be a pleasant diversion. All of us together might quiet the gossips for at least today."

Off they went, though Jane was a bit apprehensive as they strolled through town. She felt sure that Jarret must be close by. Just as they were in sight of the store, Jane observed a couple of the chief gossips in town entering the store. Her heart was beating so loudly she could scarcely hear a word that Madeline and Bridget were saying. As they reached the entrance to the store, Jane made an excuse to wait outside, insisting that they go in and she would soon follow. As Madeline and Bridget had seen the gossips going into the store, they were content to allow Jane to remain outside, cautioning her to hasten in at any sight of Jarret.

Unnoticed by the ladies, Jarret had been observing their exchange. Consequently, once Madeline and Bridget entered the store, he quickly moved toward Jane. Unaware that he was coming straight for her, Jane continued to stare off in another direction, vigilant for any glimpse of Jarret.

"Good afternoon, Jane," came a very unwelcome voice. It was too late for Jane to make her escape as Jarret was, already, directly beside her.

"Jarret, what are you doing here?" inquired Jane, as she began to shake uncontrollably.

"I observed you over here at the store, and thought it only polite that I should come out to greet you," replied Jarret snidely.

Jane began to move away from Jarret in the direction of the entrance to the store; at which point, the two women Jane had noticed earlier were coming out of the store. Jarret, placing his arm around Jane's waist, pulled her to him. Without a word to Jane, the ladies hastened by whispering as they passed.

Just then, Anthony was approaching from the direction of the church. From a distance, he could see Jane struggling to get away from Jarret. Catching sight of Anthony, Jarret let go of Jane and swiftly made his escape. Unsure as to whether or not to chase after Jarret or go to Jane, Anthony decided that Jane was at that moment his main concern.

"Jane, are you all right?" inquired Anthony, with a worried look on his face.

Jane was unable to respond as she was in a state of shock. Anthony led her by the arm into the North's store whereupon Madeline, Bridget, and Susanna, seeing that she was as white as a ghost, rushed over to her.

"What has happened?" inquired Madeline, with a bewildered look.

"Jarret held Jane against her will as the two selfsame gossips, I had overheard speaking about Jane on a previous occasion, were coming out of the store. It must have appeared to them as if Jane and Jarret were in an embrace," replied Anthony. "Jane is shaking and is in need of a place to rest."

"Take her to the back of the store. You will find a spot there," replied Susanna.

Madeline and Bridget stared at each other in disbelief as Anthony escorted Jane to the back of the store.

"Oh, why did we leave her out there all alone? This is sure to bolster Jarret's claim regarding Jane," insisted Bridget.

"I am afraid of myself and what I shall do to that reprobate," thundered Anthony, as he sat down attempting to console Jane.

Observing Anthony's anger, Jane finally spoke, concerned for what he might do. "Anthony, I could not bear it if something happened to you because of me. You must promise not to retaliate against Jarret, as he would surely make it look as if you were at fault in any confrontation."

"Do not be anxious for me," replied Anthony. "Though I have a strong desire to throttle Jarret, I shall not, as Christopher is soon to return and Jarret shall finally be seen for the scoundrel that he is."

Just then, Jane began to experience severe pain; the kind she had observed so many times before on her visits with Emma to the homes of expectant mothers. She whispered to Anthony, "I need to return to the house. I feel unwell."

Grabbing Madeline by the hand, Anthony said with concern, "Madeline, we must get Jane home as soon as possible. She is unwell. Though she has not said as much, I believe it has to do with the baby."

Susanna overheard the conversation and offered to lend a wagon in which to transport Jane, to which they appreciatively agreed and were soon on their way.

As they approached the house, Emma came out to see who was approaching in a wagon.

"Jane, what is the trouble?" inquired Emma, with concern.

"The baby, something is wrong."

Anthony carried Jane into the house and over to the bed to lie down. Then Emma asked Anthony and the others to wait outside while she saw to Jane.

After a few hours, Emma finally came out and informed them of the terrible news.

"Jane has lost the baby," she said, with tears in her eyes.

Madeline and Bridget came up on both sides of Emma to console her, asking what could be done for Jane.

"She is resting at the moment. The ordeal has left her completely exhausted," replied Emma.

"I did not know about the baby," cried Bridget. "Poor Jane."

Madeline and Anthony filled Emma in on what had taken place at the store. The more Anthony talked about it, the angrier he became. He began pacing back and forth, insisting that he must have it out with Jarret once and for all.

"Anthony, Jane would not wish for you to put yourself in jeopardy on her behalf. Nothing good can come of a confrontation with Jarret whilst you are feeling this way," insisted Emma. "I too am angry, but we need to be here for Jane."

Anthony agreed that being there for Jane was of more importance than anything else. For now, confronting Jarret would have to wait.

Susanna had closed the store the moment Jane was having difficulty and followed along after Jane and the others. "No one need know of this. I fear that if Jarret were to learn of it, he would surely see the advantage," cautioned Susanna.

"I do not know if we should hide such a thing, for the baby shall need a burial," cried Emma.

Just then Jane, in a weakened state, appeared in the doorway.

"I am aware that you are simply attempting to protect me, but we shall not keep silent about the baby."

Anthony hastened to Jane, "Take care Jane; you must return to your bed."

Observing the pain in Jane's eyes, Emma said softly, "Whatever you wish."

"The baby is worthy to be acknowledged," she cried.

"We shall acknowledge the dear little one," replied Emma, with the others in agreement.

With that, Jane was satisfied and returned to her bed to rest. However, Emma hoped that news of the baby would not be disclosed until after Jane had been cleared of any wrongdoing.

Chapter 28

Formal Accusation/Christopher's Return/The Arrival of Rebecca Bailey

A few weeks had passed since Jane's last confrontation with Jarret and the loss of her child. Once again, she demonstrated great strength while recovering from yet another tragedy.

Although she continued to grieve over the loss of the baby, she was beginning to feel somewhat at ease regarding the whole business with Jarret, for the rumors seemed to have subsided. To honor Jane's wishes, no one intentionally kept the child a secret; however, as not a soul had spoken about it to anyone who had not been directly involved, the news had not spread. Even the little service that Reverend Worcester had performed went unnoticed by the town.

Anthony had been by, frequently, to call on the Fosters, though he and Mr. Foster had concluded their business regarding the work on the house a few weeks earlier. He had not spoken to Jane again regarding the sentiment he had previously expressed. Being acutely aware of the stress she had been under, he determined that, for now, what she needed most was time to recover. Nevertheless, their friendship continued to grow throughout the weeks following the heartbreaking loss.

One evening as Anthony was visiting the Foster's home, Reverend Worcester came to call. "Good evening to you all," said Reverend Worcester. "I am sorry to say, but I have come bearing bad news."

Jane's heart sank as he spoke, for she anticipated what he might disclose. Her fears were confirmed as he went on to explain that a meeting, regarding Jane and Jarret, had been called for the following week.

"It seems that some of the townsfolk are up in arms over Jane's supposed involvement with Jarret, insisting that their relationship had become physical. I am convinced that Jarret is wholly unconcerned about Jane's reputation as he spreads his wicked lies. I assure you that, to no avail, I have spoken on behalf of Jane and to the absurdity of these accusations," insisted Reverend Worcester.

"Has there been any mention of the child?" inquired Mr. Foster.

"No, as the news has not spread beyond your most devoted friends," replied Reverend Worcester. "That is a blessing, at least."

"We have a week, have we not, in which to prepare ourselves for this meeting?" inquired Anthony.

"Yes, a week," replied Reverend Worcester, regretfully.

"We shall beseech the Lord regarding Christopher's safe return, and that it may come to pass before the event," said Anthony.

Reverend Worcester made his apologies before bidding everyone farewell; whereupon Anthony requested that Jane walk with him a bit, as he wished to have a private audience with her.

After walking for a while, Anthony directed Jane over to sit on a fallen tree he had observed. "Jane, I want to reaffirm to you that I shall not allow Jarret to succeed. As I have vowed, if it becomes necessary, I shall whisk you away from here and out of his grasp. You must know that I love you and desire to have you for my wife, though the timing of this declaration is not of my choosing. I should like to have waited until such a time as you were fully recovered from all of this Jarret business. It may also be too soon following the devastating losses you have suffered. However, in light of the circumstances, I feel that I must speak now with regard to my feelings so there shall not be any doubt but that I shall, indeed, protect you."

Jane replied, "I am honored by your declaration and do accept you, for you have proven your devotion to me over and over again. Furthermore, I too have grown to love you more than words can express. Consequently, to be forced into a marriage with Jarret would have been an even greater torture."

"You have made me exceedingly happy," replied Anthony. "I had not dared to hope that your feelings would be thus. Well then, Jane, if it meets with your approval, we shall await the outcome of the meeting before setting our plan to depart from Salisbury, in motion. If the tide does, indeed, turn utterly against you, we shall not delay in removing from here in all haste. However, if reason prevails, or Christopher returns in time, we may not need to escape. If that turns out to be the case, we shall make plans to be wed in the usual fashion. Let us not breathe a word of this to anyone save for Mr. Foster and Emma, as it is too great a risk to our plan."

Jane and Anthony returned to the house whereupon they informed Mr. Foster and Emma of their plans to be wed one way or the other. Jane's parents were overjoyed at the news, but hoped that everything would work out for them to be married and remain in Salisbury. Anthony cautioned that their plans should not be revealed even to the Bleasdell's or to Reverend Worcester, to which they all agreed.

The next day, Mr. Foster and Anthony spoke with Mr. Bleasdell regarding the upcoming meeting and all it entailed. After which, Mr. Bleasdell entreated the Lord with them that the truth would become known and that God would give everyone strength for whatever happens.

Later that afternoon, Jarret went by the North's store whereupon he was met by a couple of the selectmen's wives who had held him to be largely innocent in the whole situation with Jane.

As was the case with sundry others, they supposed her to have charmed him in such a way so as to prevent him from escaping. They reassured him that they would urge their husbands vote to insist that Jane marry him supposing that he desired to do the right thing. Jarret, seemingly humble, thanked them for their understanding of his transgression declaring that he desired to do the honorable thing and be married to Jane as soon as possible.

Having overheard the whole conversation, Susanna—mumbling angrily about Jarret—was approached by a young man. "Are you all right, my dear?" he inquired.

"Oh yes, please excuse me," she replied. "May I help you with something?"

"Forgive me for not introducing myself. My name is George Martin. I have only just arrived from England."

Mr. North was smiling from behind the counter as he witnessed the awkward exchange between his daughter and her new acquaintance. George Martin, a young widower of just three and twenty, was instantly taken with Susanna and her beautiful smile.

"Did you say that you have just arrived from England?" inquired Susanna.

"Yes."

"Well, let me be the first to welcome you. Welcome to Salisbury."

"Much obliged," replied George. "I must be off now as Samuel Winsley, an acquaintance of mine, shall be expecting my return."

Susanna was unaware that Jane and the others were awaiting the very ship on which George had arrived. Samuel Winsley and George Martin came on ahead of Mr. Carr and Christopher, for they had remained in Ipswich for Mr. Carr's wedding to be held in a couple of days.

***

Back in Ipswich, Mr. Carr was eagerly awaiting his marriage to Elizabeth. He and Christopher had followed behind Elizabeth to the home to which she was expected to arrive. The family was unaware that the ship had come into the harbor on this very day.

Upon Elizabeth's arrival to the family home, she was happily greeted by loved ones who had been praying for her safety throughout her journey from England. They were pleasantly surprised by the additional guests Elizabeth had brought along, particularly when they heard the news of the proposal. Mr. Carr could not have been more cheerfully received than he was by Elizabeth's parents.

Christopher, too, was greeted warmly by all of Elizabeth's relatives. He was happy to have the opportunity to see his friend married, though he longed to be in Salisbury. He was aware that Anthony had been awaiting news of his mission to find Grace, for many months. Moreover, he wondered whether Maddie had thought of him while he was away or had she become attached to another in his absence.

The following day, Mr. Carr and Elizabeth went before the magistrate to affirm their vows. They were wed in the presence of Elizabeth's family and Christopher. As they were to remain in Ipswich for a few days, Christopher hastened on alone to Salisbury.

Once aboard the shallop, Christopher was surprised to see one of the passengers that had been aboard the ship traveling back from England. She was a kindly middle-aged woman by the name of Rebecca Bailey, whom he had become very little acquainted with in the weeks at sea. He inquired after her reason for traveling to Salisbury, whereupon he learned of her connection to Mr. Bailey. She informed him that Mr. Bailey was her brother and that she had come to live with him.

Rebecca was astonished to learn that Christopher was an acquaintance of Mr. Bailey's from the time of his first journey across the ocean.

"When last I saw Mr. Bailey, he was living with two of his children in Ipswich," replied Christopher. "I had been informed of his move to Salisbury; however, I have not had occasion to see him there."

"You are aware, then, that his wife remains in England," said Rebecca, with a sigh.

"Yes, I am aware of the unhappy situation," replied Christopher, in a sorrowful tone. "However, you shall cheer him considerably, I am sure."

"I am in hopes of that, for he is the kindest of brothers," replied Rebecca.

"When we disembark, I shall convey you to town where you may be directed to him," said Christopher.

"I am much obliged," replied Rebecca. "Though, I must tell you that he is unaware of my coming, for I had hoped to surprise him. We had spoken of the possibility of my coming, but I had never actually confirmed if or when I might come."

"Then, what a joy it shall be for him to find you here," replied Christopher, with a grin.

***

Mr. Foster stopped in at Mr. North's store to speak with Susanna regarding Jarret and Jane. "Susanna, there is to be a meeting of the selectmen in less than a week. I came to request that if it becomes necessary you speak as a witness on Jane's behalf as to all that you have seen and heard."

"I should be all too happy to do so, as I dislike all that has taken place with regard to Jane."

"I am grateful to you," replied Mr. Foster.

"On a happier note. I would be obliged if you would inform Emma that we have a shipment of cloth that has only just arrived from England," informed Susanna.

"Has a ship arrived from England?" inquired Mr. Foster, with a look of surprise.

"Yes, it disembarked in Ipswich whereupon some of the passengers as well as our shipment were put on a shallop for Salisbury."

"Oh, what wonderful news!" exclaimed Mr. Foster. "I must take my leave and go directly to Jane. Good day to you, dear girl."

Mr. Foster made haste for home, knowing this was sure to be Christopher's ship.

Anthony was rounding the corner to the house just as Mr. Foster hastily approached from the opposite direction. Mr. Foster called out to him that he had good news to share.

"What news?" inquired Anthony.

"Christopher must have returned; a ship from England has arrived," replied Mr. Foster happily.

"Are you certain?" inquired Anthony, while grabbing Mr. Foster by the shoulders.

"Susanna North, over at the store, has just informed me that they have a shipment of cloth in from England," replied Mr. Foster. "It landed in Ipswich where some of the passengers boarded a shallop for Salisbury."

"It must be Christopher," said Anthony, as he turned hastily toward the house. "We must make haste to tell Jane and Emma."

Anthony ran all the way before bursting into the house, startling the ladies half to death.

"Anthony, what has come over you?" inquired Emma, with a chuckle. "You gave us quite a fright."

"Jane," said Anthony, while clutching her hands. "A ship has arrived from England. Christopher must have been on it."

Jane, with a great sigh, sat down as Emma rushed over to embrace her. "You see, my dear, God has not abandoned you in your time of need. Christopher is here," Emma assured.

Mr. Foster cautioned that they knew not whether Christopher had been successful in finding Grace.

"You are right. We must wait upon Christopher's news," replied Anthony.

"I shall go directly to Carr's Island to inquire after him," said Mr. Foster, "Christopher is unaware of the urgency owing to the events that have taken place whilst he has been away."

"And I shall make my way over to his place to see if he stopped there," replied Anthony. "He is sure to be curious regarding the progress of Mr. Carr's men on his house."

"Jane and I shall call on the Bleasdells," replied Emma. "He would certainly call there after so many months away. Regardless, they should be informed of the arrival of the ship from England."

Chapter 29

Waiting for Christopher/Decision to Conceal a Secret

Elizabeth and Madeline were overjoyed by the news of the arrival of the ship from England. "It must be the ship on which Christopher journeyed," insisted Madeline. "There is not likely to be another for many months. And what of Mr. Carr? Has anyone seen him?"

"No one has mentioned seeing him," replied Elizabeth, but I shall be very much surprised if Christopher has not come to call by nightfall," insisted Elizabeth, in a reassuring tone. "As for Mr. Carr, after such a long journey, he may have remained in Ipswich for a few days; for that matter, Christopher may have as well."

As she had intended, Elizabeth's words served to calm everyone. Jane and Madeline decided to take Henry out for a walk while Emma inquired after Elizabeth regarding the baby. Elizabeth admitted to having some discomfort of late but nothing to point toward an imminent delivery.

"Elizabeth, you must be off your feet as much as you can manage until the baby arrives. You shall need your strength for the birth," insisted Emma.

"You are right, of course, but it is most difficult with everything that there is to do. Madeline and Henry do their best to relieve me; however, there are certain things that I alone can manage," said Elizabeth. "Emma, perhaps all of that terrible business over your skill as a midwife will come to an end once Jarret is found out."

"You may be right. If Christopher has, indeed, acquired proof of Jarret's deception, I may again have the respect of the town regarding my abilities as a midwife. Jarret certainly was successful at maligning my reputation amongst many of the members of the town."

"Emma, I am concerned that when the baby comes, if Jane is assisting, it may be too much for her."

"Not to worry. We have discussed such matters and Jane insists that it will bring her great joy to hold your little one," replied Emma.

"She continues to amaze me that one so young could be so strong," smiled Elizabeth.

Madeline, Jane, and Henry made their way down to the river, as Henry wished to skip stones. In as much as he was extremely proud of his stone-skipping skills, he liked showing off a bit whenever he found an opportunity.

"Madeline, it has been a truly long time since we last skipped stones together," said Henry.

"You are right, Henry. It has been too long. It seems that now that you are all grown up, you have been much too busy for skipping stones with good old Madeline," she said, winking at Jane.

"Oh, go on," replied Henry, with a giggle.

Madeline, Jane, and Henry stayed down by the water for a few hours before returning to the house. Everyone's hopes of finding Christopher had been dashed now that it was getting along toward nightfall.

Following his efforts to find Christopher, Anthony made his way to the Bleasdell's along with Mr. Foster. "Mr. Carr and Christopher must have remained in Ipswich. Tomorrow I shall speak with Susanna North regarding the shallop and any news she might have with regard to its passengers. Someone in town must have been on the voyage from England. If I meet with success at finding someone, I shall inquire after Christopher and Mr. Carr," insisted Anthony.

***

The following day, Anthony went by the store to speak with Susanna. "Susanna, I was informed by Mr. Foster that a ship had arrived from England."

"Indeed," replied Susanna. "It disembarked in Ipswich whereupon some of the passengers procured a shallop to convey them to Salisbury."

"Would you happen to know where I might find any of the passengers?" inquired Anthony.

"Well, Mr. Winsley and George Martin are over at the ordinary awaiting the town's approval of Mr. Winsley's land grant," replied Susanna.

"I am much obliged," said Anthony.

Anthony went directly over to the ordinary whereupon he located the passengers Susanna had mentioned that had recently arrived from England.

"I am Anthony Hall. It is nice to make your acquaintance. I must inquire after some of your fellow passengers. Would you happen to know the whereabouts of Mr. Carr and Christopher Osgood?"

"They remained in Ipswich for the marriage of Mr. Carr," replied Mr. Winsley.

"You said marriage, did you not?" inquired Anthony, with a look of astonishment.

"Indeed. You see, Mr. Carr became acquainted with a lady by the name of Elizabeth aboard the ship. To everyone's surprise, they decided to be married, without delay, in Ipswich, as her family is presently residing there."

"This is without a doubt happy news," replied Anthony. "I shall take my leave now, as there are people I must inform of the whereabouts of the two gentlemen."

"Good day to you," replied George Martin.

Anthony made haste to the Foster's home to speak with them. Emma and Jane were out working in the garden when they heard Anthony calling to them.

"Anthony, we are out here in the garden," replied Emma, peering over some of the taller plants to be seen by Anthony.

"It is good that I have found you," said Anthony, well out of breath. "I have news. Christopher is in Ipswich, at present, for the marriage of Mr. Carr."

"Mr. Carr is to be married?" replied Emma, with a smile. "Mr. Foster shall be surprised by the happy news. When is Christopher to return?"

"If I have understood correctly, his return should be imminent, as Mr. Carr was to be married right away, and Christopher would not have delayed in coming to Salisbury once it was over," replied Anthony. "So, not to worry, as we have ample time remaining until the meeting."

Mr. Foster came home as Anthony was explaining the situation to Emma and Jane; after which, Anthony and Mr. Foster set off for the Bleasdell's home to speak with Mr. Bleasdell.

Madeline and Henry were sitting out in the yard, churning butter, as Anthony and Mr. Foster arrived.

"Good day, Madeline, and to you, Henry. We have news of Christopher," said Anthony.

"Let us go in. I shall fetch Mr. Bleasdell and return to the house momentarily," replied Madeline anxiously.

Madeline located Mr. Bleasdell around the back side of the house. Upon hearing of Anthony's news, Mr. Bleasdell quickly accompanied Madeline into the house.

"Good day, Anthony, Mr. Foster," said Mr. Bleasdell. "Tell us what you have heard."

Anthony explained everything that he had learned from Mr. Winsley and George Martin; after which, everyone in the room seemed to, simultaneously, breathe a sigh of relief.

"We have, as yet, to find out what Christopher ascertained while in England," cautioned Mr. Foster. "Though, if anything could have been discovered, regarding Jarret's wife, Christopher would have found it; of that I am sure."

Everyone concurred with Mr. Foster's analysis of the situation. Mr. Foster, Mr. Bleasdell, and Anthony thought it best to obtain Reverend Worcester's advice regarding the upcoming meeting. The dilemma in which they found themselves was whether to disclose anything that Christopher might have learned prior to the meeting, or to wait and reveal all on the day of the meeting.

"If Christopher has found Grace, and brought back the necessary proof, it is my opinion that we should wait to reveal all at the meeting and not before," advised Reverend Worcester. "I am concerned that Jarret is much too clever and with a little foreknowledge could set everything that we intend to do, on its ear."

Everyone was in agreement, for they knew that there was wisdom in Reverend Worcester's words. Following their meeting with Reverend Worcester, they each set off for their respective homes with a peace that everything would turn out all right in the end.

Chapter 30

Christopher Brings Good News/Unspoken Feelings

Upon the arrival of the shallop to Salisbury, as promised, Christopher accompanied Rebecca to town where she found someone to direct her to Mr. Bailey's homestead. After sending her on her way, Christopher set off to see what had been accomplished at his homestead while he was away.

While Anthony was in town to speak with Reverend Worcester he caught sight of Christopher strolling down the road. "Christopher, how good it is to see you!" exclaimed Anthony joyously. "We have all been anxious to see you since we learned that a ship had arrived in Ipswich."

"Yes . . . well, I delayed leaving there until after the marriage of Mr. Carr," replied Christopher.

"We were pleasantly surprised by the news of Mr. Carr," Anthony responded. "But what of Grace? Were you successful at locating her?"

"There is so much to tell. Will you accompany me to my homestead? I am anxious to see the progress that has been made whilst I have been away. Moreover, I do not wish to be overheard, as the news from England is just as we had believed it to be."

"Christopher, so much has happened while you have been gone. But first, your news."

Once Anthony had accompanied Christopher to his property, Christopher informed him of everything that had taken place in England. After hearing Christopher's news, Anthony informed him of everything that had taken place in Salisbury during his absence.

"May I see the document that you have obtained?" inquired Anthony.

Christopher then showed Anthony the affidavit in which the whole truth concerning Jarret and his abandonment of Grace was disclosed. Moreover, it contained various signatures from esteemed gentlemen of Norwich.

"Anthony, there is further news from England," said Christopher, with a downcast expression.

"Judging by your expression, it must be of a most unpleasant nature."

"It is indeed. England may soon be at war," replied Christopher. "Furthermore, it is sure to have a great effect even here."

"The rumors of a war in England have already made their way here," replied Anthony. "We have heard tell of further disputes between Parliament and the king."

"It is essential that the board of selectmen address the matter as soon as possible," insisted Christopher. "Come what may, it is imperative that we are prepared."

"Once the rumors began, some have said they are prepared to return to England to fight against the king, if necessary," divulged Anthony.

"That is not surprising," replied Christopher. "Well, as there is nothing we can do about it for the moment, let us discuss the forthcoming meeting."

"Yes, the meeting. Despite all that has taken place to malign the character of Jane, it is my opinion that the document you have in your possession, shall surely save her from a compulsory marriage to Jarret," declared Anthony, relieved.

Still mulling over everything concerning Jane, Christopher said, "The poor woman, having to suffer at the hand of Jarret following the tragic loss of her husband. It is simply inconceivable to what lengths Jarret will go to get what he wants. The sooner we put an end to all of this, the better for Jane."

Given Jarret's latest offenses, Christopher was all the more convinced that God had allowed him success so that he might prevent Jarret from disrupting the lives of the members of this newly founded town any longer.

"I agree," replied Anthony, with all gratitude for his friend's efforts. "However, Christopher, there is more that I have not as yet disclosed, for it is distressing even to think of it. You see, Jane was with child up until a confrontation with Jarret in town one day; after which, she lost the child. Not many have been made aware of this, as it would surely have been fodder for the gossipmongers had it become known throughout the town."

"How terrible! I can certainly understand withholding such news considering what had been alleged," Christopher responded solemnly.

"Who knows of Grace and our plan to get the proof of her existence?" inquired Christopher.

"The Bleasdells, the Fosters, and Reverend Worcester," replied Anthony. "It became necessary to inform the aforementioned, as it was not certain that your return would be in time for the meeting. I also thought it best to give Jane hope at a time when she was beginning to sink deep into despair regarding her future."

"You did what was right, by my estimation, as it was by no means certain that I should have been successful. The truth regarding Jarret needed to be made known, at the very least, to those who were being most affected by his troublesome behavior," replied Christopher.

"Let us talk about something else for a while. Whenever I think on all that Jarret has done to Jane, it only serves to intensify my anger. If I do not keep my wits about me, I may just decide to throttle him now and not wait for the meeting. So, tell me more about Mr. Carr's marriage," said Anthony, attempting to calm himself with more uplifting conversation.

"Yes, that is a more joyful topic," replied Christopher. "Mr. Carr met his bride, Elizabeth, on our voyage. As they wished to be quickly wed, they were married the day after our arrival to Ipswich. As I have already stated, that is the reason for my delay in returning to Salisbury. Though I was eager to come directly, I thought it best to remain and see him married."

"I met some gentlemen with whom you are acquainted, Mr. Winsley and George Martin," said Anthony. "They were with you, were they not, on the ship over from England?"

"They were," replied Christopher. "Now I understand. It was they who informed you of the marriage of Mr. Carr and Elizabeth."

"Yes, I sought them out upon hearing of the arrival of a couple of gentlemen from England and you were nowhere to be found. Many of us were becoming concerned regarding your whereabouts," replied Anthony.

"To be sure, what with the meeting approaching. It is curious, but we have been so absorbed by our conversation that I have not, as yet, had a look around at my homestead. I envisioned it many times while I was away. It seems that the men have nearly completed the work."

"Yes, and proficiently so," replied Anthony.

"It was good of Mr. Carr to allow his men to come here and work," remarked Christopher.

"He was happy to have you accompany him on such a long journey. He simply wished to reward you in some way," remarked Anthony.

"I was in hopes that it might be completed upon my return. Seeing that it nearly is, I believe I shall speak with Maddie," said Christopher.

Comprehending Christopher's meaning, Anthony gleefully inquired, "Did you say that you are going to speak to Maddie?"

"Yes, I am determined that I shall not allow any more time to pass without making my feelings known to Maddie," replied Christopher.

"I have suspected that your feelings were such for some time," replied Anthony. "I too am to be wed, for I have asked Jane to marry me once this business with Jarret is behind us."

"I wish you equal felicity in marriage," said Christopher, looking very pleased. "That is, of course, if Maddie shall have me. However, let us keep what I have said between us until such time as I have spoken to Maddie."

"To be sure. I shall not breathe a word to anyone."

"Anthony, how is Maddie?" inquired Christopher.

"Madeline has become a good friend to Jane these many months that you have been away. They are regularly together along with Bridget Dudly."

"Have you been, recently, in the company of the Bleasdells?" inquired Christopher.

"Certainly," replied Anthony. "Mr. Bleasdell has been assisting in this entire matter with Jane.

"And how is Elizabeth faring?" inquired Christopher.

"Tolerably well," replied Anthony. "I do believe, however, that her time is getting close. Emma and Jane visit her on a regular basis, as they are to assist with the birth. Elizabeth is one of only a few who will allow Emma to be her midwife."

"What may I ask is the reason for this censure of Emma?" inquired Christopher stunned.

"A mother in her care had a child in which birth anomalies were found; after which, the baby survived but a short while. It is the opinion of some that Jarret is behind the censure. It was discovered that he initiated rumors that Emma was somehow the responsible party."

"Looking back over all that he has done, is it not astonishing that one man can cause so much injury to so many?" asked Christopher.

"To be sure, and just as we are lulled into complacency with regard to Jarret, he launches a new attack," replied Anthony, angrily.

"Well, no more talk of Jarret," said Christopher, wishing to change the subject. "I must make my way over to the

Bleasdell's home tomorrow, or I shall be utterly reproached by Elizabeth for not calling directly upon my arrival."

"Well, my friend, I must be off to call on the Fosters. They shall be very happy that you have finally returned with the proof that will free Jane from any further trouble with Jarret."

Anthony and Christopher said goodbye as Anthony made haste to speak with the Fosters.

Mr. Foster greeted him as he arrived and ushered him into the house.

"Good day, Emma, and, Jane," said Anthony cheerfully. "I have the best of news to share. Christopher is back with the document that we had all hoped he would secure. Contained within, is a clearly written declaration that Jarret Ormsby is married and that he has abandoned his wife, Grace, in England."

"Oh, Anthony, this is finally to be over," sighed Jane. "I am grateful beyond words to you and Christopher."

"Anthony, I do not know how we shall ever repay you for all that you have done for Jane," cried Emma. "We have all come to depend on you so."

"I am happy to be of assistance," replied Anthony. "You have all come to mean so much to me."

Anthony made his way to Carr's Island following his visit with the Fosters. Things for Jane had much improved; thus, he found himself breathing a little easier. As he sauntered along, he thought of Jane and their future together. He had scarcely allowed himself to think on such things, as the whole business with Jarret had cast such a shadow over any hope they had for a future in Salisbury. They may well have had to begin their marriage in secret, fleeing from a forced marriage. With that thought, Anthony looked up to heaven and thanked God for His mercy, asking for His blessings to be upon his union with Jane.

The Fosters conversed for hours after Anthony had gone. It was as if a dark cloud had been lifted and the sun had begun to shine once again. They spoke about happy days gone by and the much happier days that were to come now that this would all be put behind them. Jane felt that for the first time since Anthony had revealed his feelings for her, she could conceive of a life together with him.

***

The next day, Christopher rose early to call on the Bleasdells. He had been restless for most of the night with thoughts of Maddie. He wondered how she would receive him after so many months away. The closer he got to his destination, the more his heart began to race. *What shall I say to her?* he wondered as he attempted to formulate the words he would employ in expressing his feelings to Maddie.

Emma was standing in the doorway to the Bleasdell's house letting in some fresh air to cool Elizabeth as Christopher arrived. "Good day to you, Christopher," said Emma gleefully. "We are so happy that you have returned safely. You must know how indebted we all are to you for your efforts on behalf of Jane."

"It is good to be home," replied Christopher. "Concerning Jane, I am happy to oblige. Anthony apprised me of all she has been through. To have this added injury at the hands of Jarret . . . well, I am just happy that it shall soon be over."

"I must be on my way, so I shall let you get to your visit with Elizabeth," said Emma.

Elizabeth welcomed Christopher warmly as he made his way over to sit down beside her. "Christopher, we are so happy that you have returned safely. You have been continually in our thoughts and prayers. Emma and I were just now conversing with regard to your success in discovering the truth as to Jarret's forsaking of his poor wife."

"I was all too happy to report that I had been successful at finding Grace. The town of Norwich was very willing to assist me in obtaining a signed affidavit in which the details of Jarret's abandonment of his wife have been clearly stated."

"You have been to your home, have you not?" inquired Elizabeth.

"Indeed I have," replied Christopher.

"And were you not pleasantly surprised by what you found?" inquired Elizabeth.

"To be sure," replied Christopher.

"Mr. Bleasdell has been by there many times overseeing and assessing the progress," informed Elizabeth.

"That was good of him. I was in hopes of seeing Maddie and Henry. Are they to return, soon?" inquired Christopher.

"Oh my, yes," replied Elizabeth. "In fact, you may see them now if you like. They are just out in the garden."

"Thank you. I believe that I shall go directly," replied Christopher. "Good day to you, Elizabeth. It is good to see you looking so well."

Christopher hastened out the door. With his heart racing, he approached the garden. Henry spotted him as he was drawing close and yelled out his name. Upon hearing Henry yelling Christopher's name, Madeline fought to regain her composure so as not to appear anxious.

"Well now, who is this young gentleman?" inquired Christopher, with a chuckle.

"It is me, Henry. Do you not recognize me?" he replied, with a quizzical expression.

"This could not be, Henry Bleasdell," replied Christopher. "You are much too grown up to be little Henry."

Madeline smiled at Christopher as he bantered back and forth with Henry. "Christopher, it is good to see you. Have you been in to see Elizabeth?"

"Yes, and she is looking very well. She directed me to where I might find you and Henry. Maddie, it has been so long since I have had the pleasure of seeing you. How are you?"

"Just fine, and you? Are you well?"

"I am," replied Christopher. "I had intended to see you before I set off for England; however, you had already left for Ipswich."

"I, too, wished to see you before I departed," replied Maddie, nervously. "But we had to leave so quickly there was not the time to say goodbye."

"Christopher, tell me about England and the voyage," said Henry.

"I shall, Henry, but another time, all right?" asked Christopher, wishing to be alone with Maddie.

Just then, however, Mr. Bleasdell returned. Seeing Christopher in the garden, he made haste to greet him. "Christopher, how good it is to see you. We have been eager for your safe return."

"It is equally good to see you, Mr. Bleasdell," replied Christopher. "It seems that I have returned at a most opportune time, what with the meeting in a few days."

"Indeed you have," replied Mr. Bleasdell. "And from what Emma has conveyed to us, you have made some people very relieved by what you have learned whilst you were away."

"What has he learned?" inquired Henry, as he had not been privy to any of the happenings in town.

"Henry, I shall tell you all about it later," replied Christopher. "But for now I wish to speak with Maddie and Mr. Bleasdell. Mr. Bleasdell, there is another bit of pleasant news to share," Christopher said with a smile. "John Bailey's sister, Rebecca, has come to Salisbury. I conveyed her to town; at which point, one of the men accompanied her to her brother's homestead. I should like to have been there when he first set eyes on her, for he was not aware that she was coming at this time."

"That is good news to be sure," replied Mr. Bleasdell, with a smile. "He has been exceedingly lonely. Elizabeth shall be delighted to hear that Rebecca has come and will likely wish to pay them a visit."

Gazing up at Christopher, Madeline remained quiet for a moment. She could scarcely believe that he was actually standing there right in front of her after so many long months away.

Madeline and Christopher soon realized that they could not speak freely with Henry and Mr. Bleasdell there; thus, they would have to wait for another time when they might be alone to talk.

Chapter 31

Jane and Jarret Summoned to Appear/The Selectmen Reprimanded

It was a Thursday evening; the day of the meeting of the selectmen had arrived. Jarret Ormsby and Jane Dickson had been summoned to appear before the assembly. There was a gathering outside the meetinghouse anxiously awaiting the decision that was to come, regarding the compulsory marriage between Jarret and Jane.

Jarret Ormsby sat smugly at the front of the meeting hall in anticipation of Jane's arrival. He was of the opinion that the board would vote in his favor. Most of the selectmen were unaware that it had been his intention all along to force their hand in this matter.

Jane finally arrived with Mr. Foster and Emma at her side escorting her to the front of the hall; at which point, they sat down in the row behind her. Mr. Carr had arrived in town the day before the meeting and had been informed of the proceedings. After having been so many months away, he reestablished his position as moderator prior to the commencement of the meeting.

Mr. Carr called the meeting to order, requesting that those involved be seated in the front. Anthony and Christopher rose from their seats and made their way to the front. Much to Jarret's dismay, they sat down on either side of Jane blocking his view of her, just as the meeting was about to begin.

Mr. Carr began, "The board of selectmen have been called together to address the accusations that have been levied against Jane Dickson." Pausing he added, "And Jarret Ormsby. Would those through whom the accusations have been made, kindly step forward?"

A couple of the women came forward, claiming to have witnessed inappropriate behavior between Jarret and Jane. They further stated that Jarret had taken them into his confidence, admitting to have committed fornication with Jane Dickson. They then made it apparent to the board that in their opinion, Jarret had been beguiled by Jane, who, by their estimation, was a woman of ill repute. They further explained that they believed his intentions to be admirable, as he wished to do what was required and marry Jane Dickson.

Mr. Carr subsequently addressed Jarret regarding the accusations. Jarret had all of the appearance of a humble man seeking absolution by means of a marriage to what seemed to some to be a wicked woman.

"Then, it is your desire to marry Jane Dickson that you might resolve this matter in accordance with the ordinances of the town," stated Mr. Carr.

"Yes. That is my desire," replied Jarret, with his head low attempting to look like a lamb being led to the slaughter.

Mr. Carr determined not to allow Jane to be subjected to any questioning; thus, he stated, "Anthony Hall shall now address the assembly prior to hearing from Jane Dickson."

It was at this point that Jarret became suspicious, as he wondered what reason they might have for hearing from Anthony Hall. *He could not possibly know of Grace*, he reasoned, *as it has been many years since I was in England. Regardless, he has no evidence that she exists.*

"Anthony, when did you first become acquainted with Jarret Ormsby?" inquired Mr. Carr.

"My earliest acquaintance with Jarret Ormsby took place in Norwich, England, from whence we both came," replied Anthony. Jarret then blurted out, "It is a lie!"

Mr. Carr followed the outburst with a warning to Jarret that he would be escorted out and held secure until the meeting had concluded if he, again, made any such outbursts.

"Anthony, have you anything else to share regarding Jarret Ormsby from your prior acquaintance with him?" inquired Mr. Carr.

"I have," replied Anthony. "Only this; that he is presently married to a lovely young lady by the name of Grace Ormsby."

The meeting hall was all a buzz following Anthony's declaration. Unaware that Christopher was in possession of the affidavit he had obtained in Norwich, Jarret attempted, once again, to call out that what Anthony stated was a lie. Mr. Carr overlooked his second outburst, as he had no desire to have Jarret escorted out before witnessing his reaction to the affidavit.

"Thank you, Anthony Hall. If it pleases the assembly, we shall now hear from Christopher Osgood," stated Mr. Carr.

"Christopher, have you anything to add regarding Jarret Ormsby and the wife he purportedly has left behind in England?" inquired Mr. Carr.

"I have," replied Christopher. "Many of you are aware that I have only just returned from England. I had occasion, while in England, to travel to Norwich."

Jarret's eyes widened as he came to the realization that Christopher must have met with Grace, though, he thought to himself, *He cannot prove any of this. It shall be his word against mine.*

Christopher went on to say, "I had the pleasure of making the acquaintance of the young lady, Grace Ormsby. Furthermore, what Anthony has said is, indeed, true. Jarret did abandon a wife in England many years ago when he made his way across the ocean. She believed that he would send for her; however, her hopes were in vain as she never heard from him again."

"What proof have you of this," insisted Jarret. "Your dislike for me has motivated you to defend a lie!"

"You ask, what proof have I. Only this, the signed affidavit by the abandoned wife, her family members, as well as the leading officials of the town of Norwich," he said, holding up the affidavit.

Anthony reached over to squeeze Jane's hand, then smiled and said, "It is almost over now."

The board of selectmen requested that Christopher present the affidavit for inspection, to which he happily complied. Mr. Carr called the meeting to order, as the room was once again filled with chatter. Within moments, the board unanimously agreed to drop the whole matter, requesting that Jarret remain in his seat following the meeting.

Mr. Carr addressed the members regarding the reputation of Jane Dickson. "It is my hope that the members of this board shall make inquiries regarding the false and malevolent statements made against the character of Jane Dickson. Many of you need to, first, look to your own homes to find those who have aided Jarret in his deception."

The selectmen glanced sheepishly at each other, for it seemed that they had, once again, allowed rumors to harm the reputation of another of the members of their town. Once everything had settled a bit, and most had left, some of the board members moved forward to speak with Jarret. The room had cleared enough that they became aware that Jarret's seat was now empty. One of the members questioned the others regarding the request for Jarret to remain. It was then confirmed that the request had been made but that it now appeared Jarret had not complied. Mr. Carr, then, spoke with the others about removing to Jarret's house to determine his whereabouts. As it had been a repeated offense of making false accusations, on the part of Jarret, the board wished to discipline him for his actions.

Anthony grasped Christopher by the shoulders thanking him for his courage. Jane embraced Emma as the two ladies sank back into their seats. Elizabeth, now that the meeting was over, came in to the hall with Madeline. They had been anxiously waiting outside, with Henry, for news. Upon seeing the faces of everyone inside, they were relieved to see that all had gone well. They, too, sat down with the others, thankful that it was all over. Christopher, glancing back to where Maddie was seated, gave her a smile and a nod, which warmed her heart immensely.

Mr. Bleasdell finally came to where Elizabeth was seated to inquire after her comfort. Not wanting to draw attention to herself, Elizabeth explained quietly that her labor had begun.

Chapter 32

A Blessing for the Bleasdells/A Private Audience/ Mr. Bailey's Comfort

The Bleasdell homestead was bustling with anticipation for the arrival of the newest Bleasdell. Each of the participants in this blessed event had hoped to be tucked into their beds after so wearisome a night. However, this was not to be the case, as the child seemed most eager to make its entrance.

Emma and Jane were in the house assisting Elizabeth as the others anxiously waited outside. It was nearly morning and there was not a hint of any noise resembling that of a little baby. Henry grew more and more impatient as the hours passed. Observing Henry's restlessness, Christopher offered to take him for a walk, to which he responded most excitedly in the affirmative. Mr. Bleasdell was most grateful to Christopher, as he wished to remain close to the house.

Maddie glanced up at Christopher, as he was getting ready to go. He smiled at her vowing to return in a while.

"If the baby should come, send Anthony to fetch us," said Christopher.

"Yes, of course, he shall come straight away," replied Maddie.

Christopher and Henry set off in the direction of the river. Henry was delighted, for he desired to demonstrate his skill at skipping stones.

"Shall we skip stones across the top of the water?" inquired Henry enthusiastically.

"I have never been very good at getting them to skip very far," said Christopher.

"I shall demonstrate it for you exactly as Maddie taught me," replied Henry.

"Oh, this is a talent you acquired from Maddie," replied Christopher, with a chuckle. "I might have known."

Christopher thought this an opportune time to extol the virtues of God in creation, with a particular emphasis on the new life that was about to be born. Henry had many questions, to which Christopher happily responded.

Having this time with Henry reminded Christopher of his dream of teaching the scriptures to children here in the new land. He came to the realization, there with Henry, perhaps teaching opportunities had been there for him all along. All that was required was time—time to skip stones, go for walks or any number of other things, and a willingness to listen and respond. He also thought about little Zachary and how he would have been very much as Henry is now.

Back at the house, Emma remarked, "Elizabeth, it is good to know that you have remained confident in my abilities in spite of the rumors."

Elizabeth smiled and said, "Emma, I should not wish for anyone other than you to be here with me. Oh, and Jane of course."

Elizabeth's labor progressed until, finally, the sound of a baby's cry filled the air. Once the baby was born, Jane's entire focus shifted to the child as Emma bestowed her attentions on Elizabeth. The mother and daughter made a great team as they fulfilled their duties to the mother and child.

Mr. Bleasdell and Madeline glanced joyfully at each other and back to the door in anticipation of Jane beckoning for them to come in.

Mr. Foster approached just as Anthony was about to set off to find Henry and Christopher to inform them of the arrival of the baby.

"Mr. Foster, the baby has come!" exclaimed Madeline.

"That is good news, indeed," replied Mr. Foster.

"Good day, Mr. Foster," said Anthony. "I am off to fetch Christopher and Henry."

"Yes, no doubt Henry shall be overjoyed," replied Mr. Foster. "Mr. Bleasdell, what a happy occasion this is."

"Indeed, though I had not thought it possible after so long a time between Henry and the arrival of this little one," replied Mr. Bleasdell.

At last, the door opened, and Jane quietly motioned them in to see the new baby. Mr. Bleasdell observed that Elizabeth, though quite at ease now, was visibly exhausted.

"You have a beautiful daughter," said Elizabeth. "Come and see your little Mary."

With tears streaming down his cheeks, Mr. Bleasdell drew near to Elizabeth and his new little daughter. "God has been good to grant us another child," he cried, as he took the baby in his arms.

Anthony finally caught up with Henry and Christopher to give them the good news. "The baby has come."

Excitedly, Henry and Christopher returned with Anthony to the house; at which point, Henry was overjoyed to see his new baby sister. "What shall we call her?" he inquired.

"Her name is Mary," replied Elizabeth.

After a short visit with Elizabeth and Mary, Henry and Christopher joined the others outside to give the mother and baby a rest. Madeline and Jane fell back together onto the ground, giggling incessantly out of sheer exhaustion.

Aware that Mr. Foster had stayed in town to inquire after the whereabouts of Jarret, Mr. Bleasdell asked, "What has become of Jarret?"

"It appears that he has thrown some of his possessions together and made a hasty escape," replied Mr. Foster. "I cannot say that I am unhappy to see him go; however, in so doing, he has avoided the consequences of his actions."

A while later, to relieve Mr. Bleasdell of some of the chores, Anthony and Christopher worked around the Bleasdell homestead for a few hours. However, when Jane was finally ready to go home, Anthony took leave of his work to accompany her. In spite of the fact that they had been up all night and most of the day, they found themselves to be full of enthusiasm with regard to the new birth as well as their future plans to marry.

"I cannot believe that I am finally rid of Jarret," said Jane, with a sigh.

"Yes and Mr. Foster informed me that he has run off rather than face the punishment for his actions. So we may never see him again," said Anthony, with delight.

"What a turnabout for us. It is Jarret who has felt the need to escape," giggled Jane.

Back at the Bleasdell's, Christopher and Maddie talked for a while regarding all that had happened. Though Christopher longed to tell her how he felt, he was aware that this was not a good time, as she was utterly exhausted. Maddie hoped, as well, to have their feelings out in the open, but she also realized that it would have to keep for now.

"Maddie, I must take my leave, as we are much in need of rest. However, I wish to have an audience with you tomorrow," said Christopher, while taking her by the hand.

Maddie's heart began to pound so loudly she was fearful that Christopher might hear.

As Christopher turned to leave, she was so overcome by emotion, the only thing she could do in the way of a response was to smile and nod. After he had gone, she hurried into the house hoping to rest fast that tomorrow would soon come.

The following morning, Emma came to call on Elizabeth and Mary. As Madeline opened the door, she discreetly handed Madeline the quilt to present to Elizabeth.

"Elizabeth, how are you today?"

"Very well, Emma," she replied. "God has truly blessed us, has He not?"

"Indeed He has," replied Emma. "Madeline, what have you to do today?"

"I believe that I shall stick by Elizabeth and Mary, as they are certain to have need of me," replied Madeline.

"Do you not have something you wished to present to Elizabeth for Mary?" inquired Emma with a smile.

"Indeed," replied Madeline as she brought the quilt out from behind her back. "Elizabeth, this is a quilt that I, and many helpers, have made for you."

"Oh, Madeline, it is beautiful, but when did you have the time to make such a wonderful gift?" inquired Elizabeth, as she continued to admire Madeline's handy work.

"Most of my visits to the Foster's home were spent working on the quilt. Jane and Bridget assisted; otherwise, I could not have accomplished it."

"Thank you so much, my dear. I shall treasure it always," said Elizabeth, with a tear in her eye.

"I see that Jane did not accompany you today," said Madeline, still smiling at Elizabeth's reaction to her gift.

"No, indeed, for she and Anthony shall be meeting with Reverend Worcester to post their banns, as required," replied Emma. "You know they must post them for three consecutive weeks. And as they wish to be soon married, they desired to do it as quickly as possible."

"We are so very happy for them," replied Elizabeth.

Just then, a knock came at the door. Madeline opened it and found Christopher standing there. Her heart felt as if it skipped a beat as she welcomed him inside. Elizabeth and Emma greeted Christopher warmly as Madeline offered him a seat.

Christopher visited a while before announcing that he wished to speak with Maddie alone, suggesting they go for a walk, to which Maddie readily complied.

Elizabeth and Emma happily speculated on the purpose for which Christopher required a private audience with Madeline. They were joyful at the prospect of another well-suited marriage.

"In the scriptures, Isaiah speaks of God healing the brokenhearted and bringing beauty from ashes, referring to Israel's deliverance and rebuilding. It is my belief that we are seeing God doing that very thing for Jane, Madeline, and Christopher, just as He did for me some years ago," said Emma, with joy.

"Indeed, after the loss of two of my little ones, to look upon Mary is to know that what you have said is true," replied Elizabeth. "He truly does bring beauty from ashes."

Just as Emma was getting ready to go, someone knocked at the door. Emma opened it to Mr. Bailey and his sister, Rebecca. Elizabeth called to them to come in and be seated. She was delighted that they had come for a visit.

"Mr. Bailey, you have come just in time to greet our little Mary. She has only been with us a day," said Elizabeth smiling.

Mr. Bailey was not aware before coming that Elizabeth had only just received Mary into the world. "Mary, what a wonderful name," he said, scooping her up in his arms.

"She is lovely," said Rebecca, with a smile.

"Rebecca, I was overjoyed to hear of your coming," said Elizabeth. "What a surprise you must have been to Mr. Bailey."

"Indeed she was," laughed Mr. Bailey. "John Jr. and I were astonished when we opened the door and found Rebecca standing there."

"We met Mr. Bailey on our journey over from England," explained Elizabeth to Rebecca.

"Yes, he told me of the passengers that traveled with him that now reside in Salisbury," replied Rebecca. "Moreover, he has informed me of your kindness to him, for which I am eternally grateful."

"Oh now, we have not done so very much," replied Elizabeth, a little embarrassed by the compliment, for she had long felt they had not done nearly enough for the dear man.

"You and Mr. Bleasdell stood by me in Ipswich when others did not," replied Mr. Bailey. "Furthermore, had it not been for Mr. Bleasdell's assistance, I should not have been able to remove to Salisbury."

"Mr. Bleasdell has been desirous to make your acquaintance, Rebecca," said Elizabeth.

"I too, have been anxious to meet all of you," replied Rebecca.

"You had occasion, I am told, to meet Christopher on your journey over from England," remarked Elizabeth.

"Yes, and we traveled on the shallop together from Ipswich, which is where I first learned of his connection to John," replied Rebecca.

"And how was your voyage from England?" inquired Elizabeth.

"We had an easy journey compared to what you and John encountered on your voyage, what with the shipwreck and loss of lives," replied Rebecca. "It is not a wonder that he could not, again, attempt a journey back to England."

"Mr. Bailey, no one could blame you," encouraged Elizabeth. "I, too, am happy to remain on dry ground."

Mr. Bailey smiled at Elizabeth, grateful for her understanding.

Mr. Bleasdell returned home to find Mr. Bailey and Rebecca visiting with Elizabeth. "Well, Mr. Bailey, good day to you and this must be Rebecca," said Mr. Bleasdell with a broad smile.

"Mr. Bleasdell, it is nice to make your acquaintance," replied Rebecca.

"We have come at a happy time for your family, Mr. Bleasdell," said Mr. Bailey. "I have an idea that Mary is a most welcome addition to your home."

"Indeed, Mary has been an unexpected blessing for which we are most grateful," replied Mr. Bleasdell. "With so many years between Henry's birth and her arrival, we had thought we should never, again, hold another of our own children."

"Yes, I too have received an unexpected blessing," said Mr. Bailey, with a smile directed at Rebecca.

"Well, we must be off. Elizabeth and Mary are in need of rest," said Rebecca.

"It was delightful to have met you, Rebecca. Come again and very soon," said Elizabeth.

"We shall," replied Mr. Bailey.

Mr. Bleasdell accompanied Mr. Bailey and his sister part of the way down the road. Upon returning to the house, he remarked to Elizabeth, "Mr. Bailey and his sister appear to get on very well together."

To which Elizabeth replied, "Yes, and what a good and kind sort Rebecca seems to be. Do you not think that Mr. Bailey appears much improved now that Rebecca has come?"

"I agree. His countenance was full of joy rather than the despair that was so evident before," replied Mr. Bleasdell. "God has not answered our prayers and petitions, regarding Mr. Bailey, in the way we may have expected, but He has brought about what was needed in order to bring him comfort."

Chapter 33

The Proposal/The Publishing of Banns/Expressions of Gratitude

Maddie anxiously strolled alongside of Christopher as they made their way down the road. She could scarcely believe this day had finally come. Before long, they found themselves down by the river; at which time, Christopher gently took hold of her arm guiding her over to a large rock to be seated. Settling down beside her, he placed her hand in his and began to reveal all that had been on his heart.

"Maddie, I must explain why I sought a private audience with you."

"Very well," replied Maddie, with great anticipation.

"Allow me to begin at the point when I first came to the realization that I had acquired intense feelings for you. It was on the day that you and the Bleasdells removed to Colechester. I remember rushing into town only to learn that you had already departed from Ipswich. Then and there, a deep sense of loss swept over me leaving me in utter despair. I knew that it was solely connected to the thought of not seeing you again. I could no longer deny the feelings I had for you, as they were now most evident. That day was one of the most wretched of my life."

Maddie listened intently, remembering that day and how she too had felt an overwhelming feeling of sadness.

Christopher continued, "However, that evening I felt a tremendous sense of guilt as my mind hearkened back to Oliver and his sacrifice. His illness and death were a direct result of his having spent many hours with the children who were ill aboard the ship, one of whom was my son. At that moment, it seemed terribly wrong for me to seek happiness with his widow. Therefore, I determined not to allow such sentiment to enter my mind ever again. I knew that had I not brushed my feelings aside I should have made haste to follow after you."

Maddie's eyes filled with tears as Christopher spoke. She never knew that he had felt this way. She was beginning to understand why he, at times, seemed so distant. As Christopher continued, she endeavored to keep her composure.

"However, when the opportunity presented itself to come to Salisbury, my heart raced at the thought of seeing you again. I realized that though I had attempted to stifle my feelings, they had only grown in intensity. It was then that I began earnestly seeking God's will as to whether or not to come. After a while, I started to believe that He did, indeed, desire for me to take leave of Ipswich and come to Salisbury. Once I had made the decision to come, I knew that I must be forthcoming with regard to my feelings for you."

At that point, Maddie was puzzled as to why he had not followed through with his plan of revealing his feelings.

He continued, "But when our paths crossed again out on the island, I thought I had lost you to another. So, once again, I decided to remain silent regarding my true feelings. You can never understand the degree of relief that came when I learned that Jarret had not secured your affections."

At that point, Maddie began to speak; however, Christopher placed his hand gently on her lips to prevent her.

"Maddie, if you will permit me, I should like to conclude before you respond," to which she gave an assenting nod. Thus he continued, "Maddie, I so longed to see you before I left for

England. However, that was not to be, as you were off to Ipswich before it could take place. You will never know the distress I felt when I learned that you had gone. To be away for nearly a year without having first told you the level to which I have come to admire and cherish you seemed an intolerable situation. I thought that, having missed the opportunity, I might lose you to another while I was so long away. And yet, had I seen you then, I most likely would not have revealed my feelings. I now know that it took the long separation from you to show me that I did not want to be without you no matter my feelings regarding Oliver and his sacrifice."

Maddie understood fully, as she harkened back to the day she returned from Ipswich only to learn that Christopher would be away for so long a time.

"Maddie, before another day slips away, I must tell you that I love you. And if you will have me, I should like for you to do me the honor of becoming my wife."

As Christopher concluded, he fixed his eyes upon Maddie as if to interpret her thoughts as he anxiously awaited a response.

With tears of joy, Maddie replied, "Yes, yes I shall marry you. Christopher, a great deal of what you have said resonates with what my own feelings have been, as I too have denied my feelings out of loyalty for Oliver. We shall always hold a special place in our hearts for Oliver and Hannah, there is no denying that; however, God in His mercy has allowed us to love once again."

"You have made me so very happy," replied Christopher, with tears in his eyes.

Maddie and Christopher remained for a long time gazing out over the sparkling river. At long last, they were free to express the deep love that each had for the other. They talked for hours about everything that had happened to them from the time they embarked on their voyage from England until the present. They spoke about the hopes and dreams they had for the future—Christopher, with his desire to teach children, and Maddie eager to be by his side.

All at once, they realized the others would be concerned for them, as it was growing quite dark. Reluctantly they began making their way back home, neither wanting the evening to end.

Elizabeth and Mr. Bleasdell restlessly awaited Madeline's return. They were a bit concerned that she had been gone for so long, but mostly they were anxious to hear why Christopher had sought an audience with her.

"They have been gone for quite some time. Perhaps we shall soon learn that there is to be a wedding," said Elizabeth, with a smile. "What other reason might there be for their delay, considering that it is even now growing dark. They must have had a great deal to share with each other."

"Perhaps you are right," replied Mr. Bleasdell. "Their affection for one another has long been known to us; that they should finally express it brings me much happiness."

Just then, Madeline and Christopher entered the room eager to give a report of what had taken place between them.

"My dear child, you look as if you have some wonderful secret to disclose," giggled Elizabeth.

"Indeed, for Christopher has asked me to marry him," replied Madeline, with joy.

"We have been expecting this happy event for some time," said Mr. Bleasdell.

"It was foolish for us to deny our affection for each other for so long. We each had a misguided belief that we were, in some way, disrespecting Oliver and Hannah by caring for another," replied Christopher.

"We could not have hoped for a better partner for either of you," said Elizabeth excitedly.

"Well, I must be off," said Christopher, as he let go of Maddie's hand. "I shall be back tomorrow, for there are plans to be made."

Maddie walked him to the door and watched after him until he was out of sight. The house was so full of exhilaration that it was difficult to think about retiring for the night. Madeline could not contain her joy, as she yearned for tomorrow to come to share her news with Bridget and Jane.

***

The following day, Anthony unexpectedly met up with Christopher as he was on his way to see Madeline. "Good day," said Anthony. "I had not expected to find you in town today. I had been informed by some of the men that you were to be out on the island."

"Yes, that was my intention; however, that has altogether changed. Have you not heard the news?" inquired Christopher joyfully. "Naturally, you could not have, as it was decided only yesterday."

"No, but judging by your expression I believe I can guess. You must have spoken with Madeline," replied Anthony.

"Indeed, and she has consented to my proposal," announced Christopher.

"Well, that is excellent news," replied Anthony.

"Goodbye, Anthony. No time to talk, for I am expected at the Bleasdell homestead," said Christopher, smiling as he turned to leave.

"Off with you. I should not want to keep you from Madeline," chuckled Anthony.

Anthony and Christopher each hurried off to their future brides to arrange wedding plans.

Chapter 34

Happy Endings

Madeline began her day much as usual, assisting Elizabeth with the daily chores. However, she worked with so much haste, it alerted Elizabeth to the fact that she preferred to be finished as quickly as possible.

"Madeline, I believe that you have long desired to be off to see Jane and Bridget," said Elizabeth grinning.

"I am rather anxious to give them my happy news," replied Madeline.

"I daresay that you have done more than your fair share of the chores. Go on and see your friends. Furthermore, Emma shall be coming today. She will assist me in whatever else there is to be done."

"Yes, I am aware that she is coming," replied Madeline, "but I had not planned to go before she arrived."

"I shall be quite all right, so off with you now," insisted Elizabeth.

"No, I must not leave you before Emma arrives," insisted Madeline. "And I am expecting Christopher to come calling at some point in the day."

"Henry is just outside if I have need of him," said Elizabeth. "If Christopher arrives before you return, I am sure that he would be more than happy to wait."

At Elizabeth's continued insistence, Madeline finally relented and was off to call on Jane and Bridget.

Not long after Madeline had left, Christopher arrived at the Bleasdell's home. Seeing that Maddie was not there, he inquired after the whereabouts of Mr. Bleasdell.

"Christopher, Mr. Bleasdell is outside somewhere. He has only just returned from town," replied Elizabeth.

"Thank you. I shall return in a while."

Finding Mr. Bleasdell out behind the house, Christopher seized the opportunity to speak with him regarding the situation in England. "Mr. Bleasdell, I had been hoping for a private moment to speak with you. Are you aware of the situation in England?"

"I have heard the many rumors floating about concerning a possible war between Parliament and the Crown," replied Mr. Bleasdell. "Were they speaking of war in England whilst you were there?"

"To be sure, though many dared not speak of it for fear of addressing someone with a contrary opinion to their own. In fact, Mr. Carr and I felt very much the same. We spoke only in private concerning the situation."

"Yes, it may be dangerous, particularly in England, to have an opposing viewpoint to that of the Crown," replied Mr. Bleasdell. "I am afraid it shall tear England apart if a war does come, as the people will be divided in their loyalties."

"Mr. Bleasdell, one of the king's emissaries was aboard the ship on which we traveled. We heard rumors that his mission shall be to impede any support for Parliament amongst the colonies."

"It seems that war is truly inevitable if the king is already seeking to suppress any uprising," warned Mr. Bleasdell.

"It is my belief that the board of selectmen ought to be informed regarding the king's emissary. What is your opinion?" inquired Christopher.

"We should not make it known to the entire board, as there are those who are sympathetic to the Crown amongst them," replied Mr. Bleasdell.

"Perhaps we might speak individually with those known to be supporters of Parliament," replied Christopher.

"Agreed," replied Mr. Bleasdell. "However, there are other things to attend to at present. We must not allow ourselves to be carried away by all of this business. We shall do what we can and leave the rest in the Almighty's hands."

"Indeed, for if I am to be soon married, I must see to the publishing of the banns," replied Christopher, with delight.

With that, Christopher returned to the house to wait for Maddie.

***

Finding Jane at home with Emma, Madeline informed them of her engagement to Christopher. Though not at all surprised, they were overjoyed by the news.

"Madeline, let us go directly to call on Bridget before Anthony is to arrive," insisted Jane. "As there are two of us with news of this kind, she shall be surprised."

"No doubt, for so much has happened in so short a time," laughed Madeline.

Upon their arrival to Bridget's, Jane and Madeline were welcomed warmly and whisked inside. Once they were seated and tea was presented, Bridget insisted on hearing more of the meeting concerning Jane and Jarret. Though John had informed her of the outcome, she wished to learn more of the particulars.

"Bridget, we will give you a full report on the meeting; however, we each have something we wish to tell you," said Madeline, with a smile.

"I cannot fathom any news as being more important than the details of the meeting in which Jane was released from the clutches of Jarret Ormsby. However, seeing that you each have something you are eager to share, you have my full attention," replied Bridget, insisting that they fill her in on the meeting afterwards.

Madeline and Jane turned toward each other, nodded, and grinned as an indication that they wished to inform Bridget in unison.

"We are getting married," said Madeline and Jane, with a giggle.

"What! You both are getting married?" inquired Bridget astonished.

"You heard right. It is as we have said," replied Madeline. "Christopher and Anthony have proposed marriage and we have consented."

"That is extraordinary," replied Bridget, while collapsing back in her chair to lend a dramatic effect to the news. "What wonderful news. When is this all to take place?"

"Anthony and I have published our first week of banns. Once the final two weeks have passed, we shall be married," replied Jane, with great excitement.

"And you, Madeline?" inquired Bridget.

"Christopher is to come to the Bleasdell's today; at which point, we shall have further discussion with regard to such details."

"What a complete turn of events," laughed Bridget. "To think, that just a few days ago things appeared so desperate."

"Perhaps if I had placed more trust in God I should not have been so overwhelmed by worry," frowned Jane. "As evidenced by this recent ordeal, I have not, as yet, mastered a worry-free faith."

"We all are in need of that lesson, and you do better than most with everything that you have been through, Jane," replied Madeline.

"The loss of the baby was a real test of my faith as was losing Nathan; however, I am now at peace knowing that the child and Nathan are with God."

"I am not certain I would do so well as you with all that you have been through. Every time I believe that I have conquered the worry beast, another circumstance rises up to test me. Some trials I seem to pass splendidly, yet others tend to drag me down," insisted Madeline.

"That is true of me as well," replied Bridget, with a sigh.

Jane and Madeline remained a while longer with their jubilant friend before setting off for their respective homes to wait upon Christopher and Anthony.

***

The time quickly passed for the final week of the banns to conclude for each of the young couples; at which point, their marriages took place a week apart. The Fosters and the Bleasdells were in one accord in their belief that there were never two more suitable couples. Furthermore, they were confident that with young people such as these, Salisbury was sure to have a wonderful future.

Sometime later, Mr. Bleasdell and Elizabeth set off for a picnic in the direction of the shoreline. Looking out over the vast ocean, Mr. Bleasdell observed, "God brought us safely across the sea to this new land, and He gave us the freedom to follow after Him according to what He has lain down in the scriptures without the restrictions of the Church of England. He has also seen fit to bless us with another child, one that has never even been to England. It is as if she is to be a reminder that we now belong to this place, never to return from whence we came. Moreover, if we the people of this land shall keep the Lord as our God and follow wholly after Him, we shall be blessed as it says in Psalms 33:12: 'Blessed is the nation whose God is the Lord.' As fallible men and women, we are sure to make mistakes as we forge ahead. However, if we truly seek the Lord's will, I am confident that He shall guide us in making this into a venerated land."

The End

Resources

Genealogical Outline Published by the Blaisdell Family National Association.

Cartland, Henry, 1899. *Ten years at Pemaquid: Sketches of its history and its ruins.* Pemaquid.

Warren, C. Riess, 2001. *Angel Gabriel the elusive galleon.* Bristol: 1797 House.

Blaisdell Family National Association: http://www.blaisdell.org/

The Uniqueness of the Ralph Bleasdale, by R. Carter Blaisdell: http://www.blaisdell.org/

Hoyt, David W., 1897. *Vol. I, The old families of Salisbury and Amesbury, Massachusetts: With some related families of Newbury, Haverhill, Ipswich and Hampton.* Providence R.I.: Snow and Farnham.

The York Maine Historical Society

CPSIA information can be obtained at www.ICGtesting.com
Printed in the USA
BVOW070215200313

315941BV00001B/4/P